POKÉMON™ X•Y

STORY
Hidenori Kusaka

ART
Satoshi Yamamoto

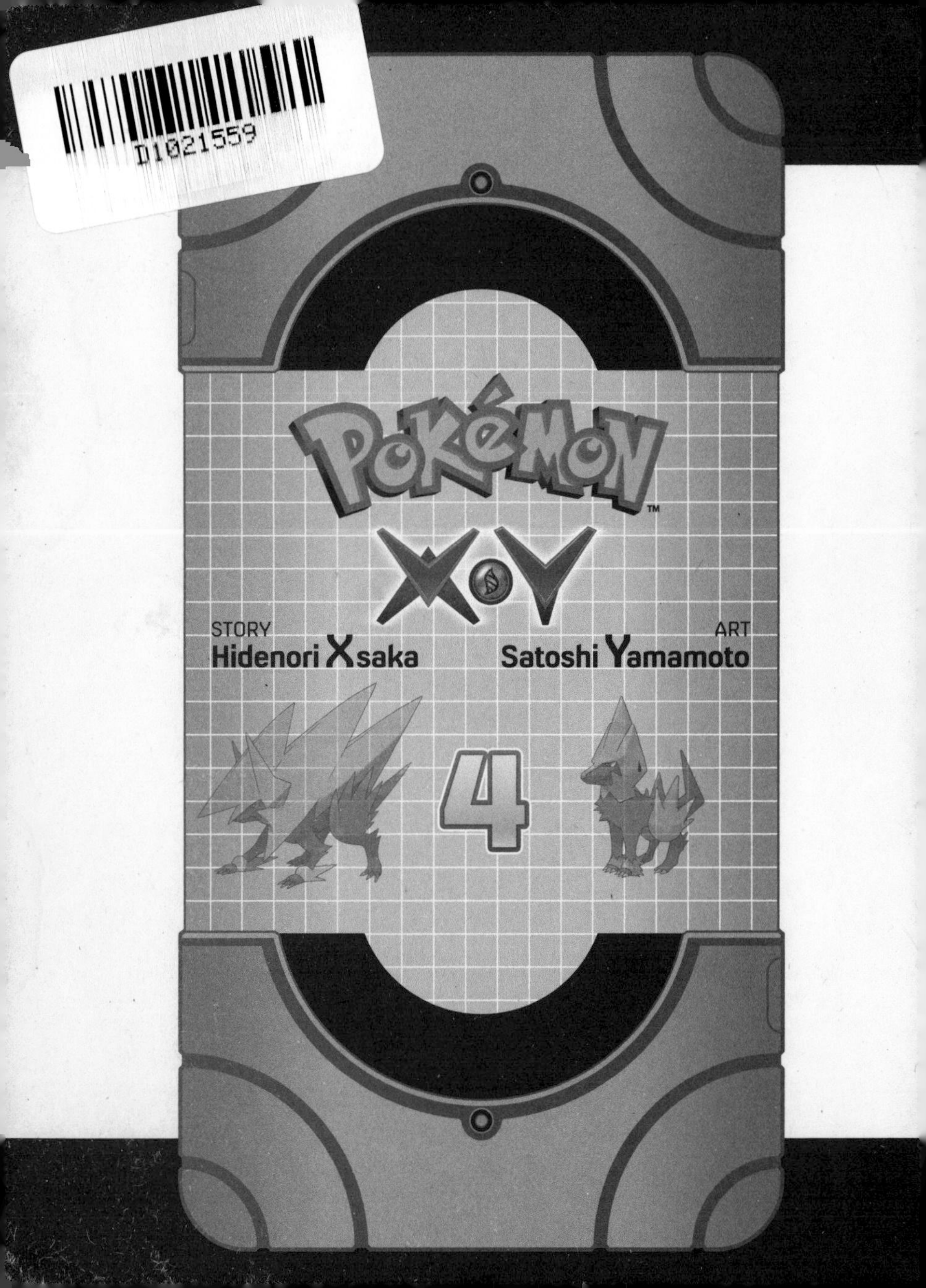

4

CHARACTERS

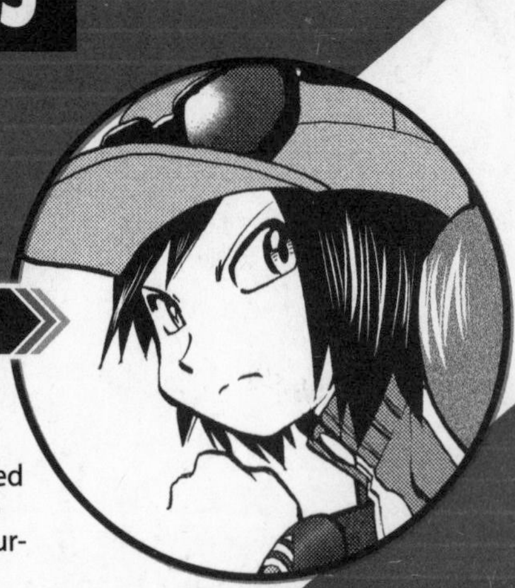

X

The main character of this chapter, and one of five close childhood friends. He was once a highly skilled Trainer who even won the Junior Pokémon Battle Tournament, but now...

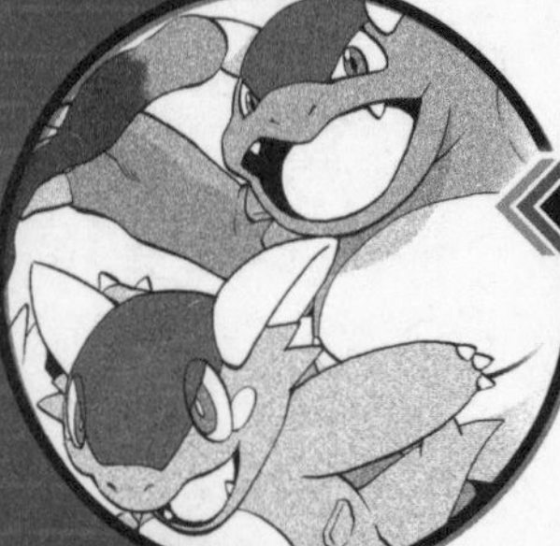

KANGA & LI'L KANGA

X's longtime Pokémon partners with whom he won the Junior Tournament.

OUR STORY THUS FAR...

In Vaniville Town in the Kalos region, X was a Pokémon Trainer child prodigy. But now he's depressed and hides in his room avoiding everyone—including his best friend Y. An attack on their hometown by Legendary Pokémon Xerneas and Yveltal, led by Team Flare, forces X outside... Now he and his closest childhood friends—Y, Trevor, Tierno and Shauna—are on the run!

Trouble arises in Santalune City when Shauna is mind-controlled by Team Flare scientist Celosia! Fortunately, X and a new ally, Shalour City Gym Leader Korinna, defeat Celosia and free Shauna. Now our friends must move on to the next town, with Team Flare in hot pursuit... Where will they end up next and what will befall them there...?

MEET THE

Y

X's best friend, a Sky Trainer trainee. Her full name is Yvonne Gabena.

TREVOR

One of the five friends. A quiet boy who hopes to become a fine Pokémon Researcher one day.

SHAUNA

One of the five friends. Her dream is to become a Furfrou Groomer. She is quick to speak her mind.

TIERNO

One of the five friends. A big boy with an even bigger hea He is currently training to be come a dancer.

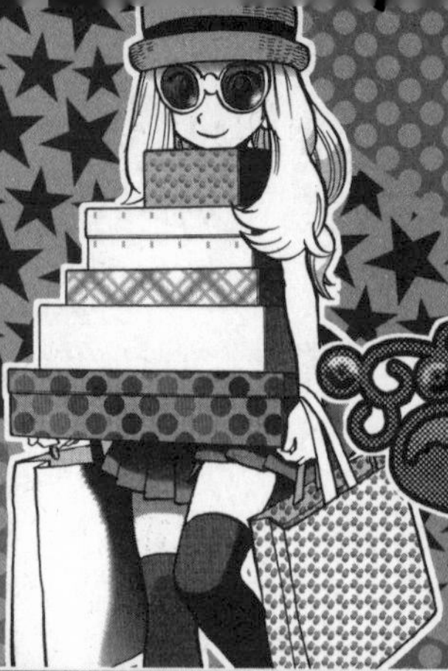

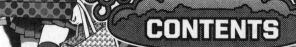

CONTENTS

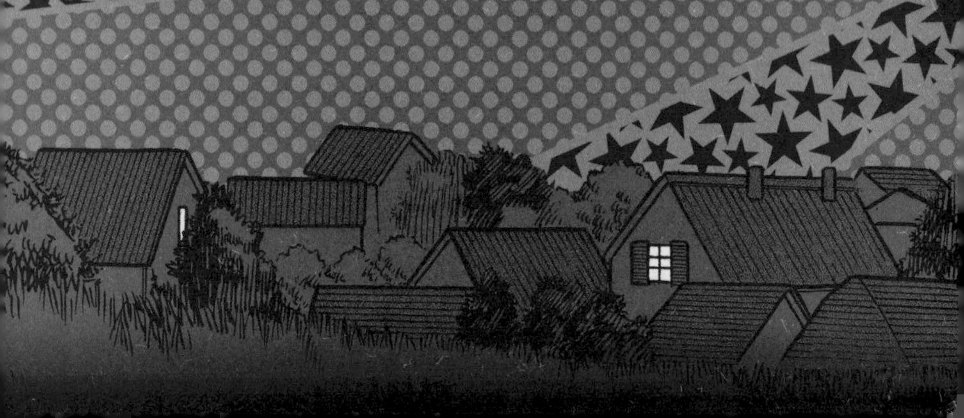

Adventure 11 Charging After Electrike

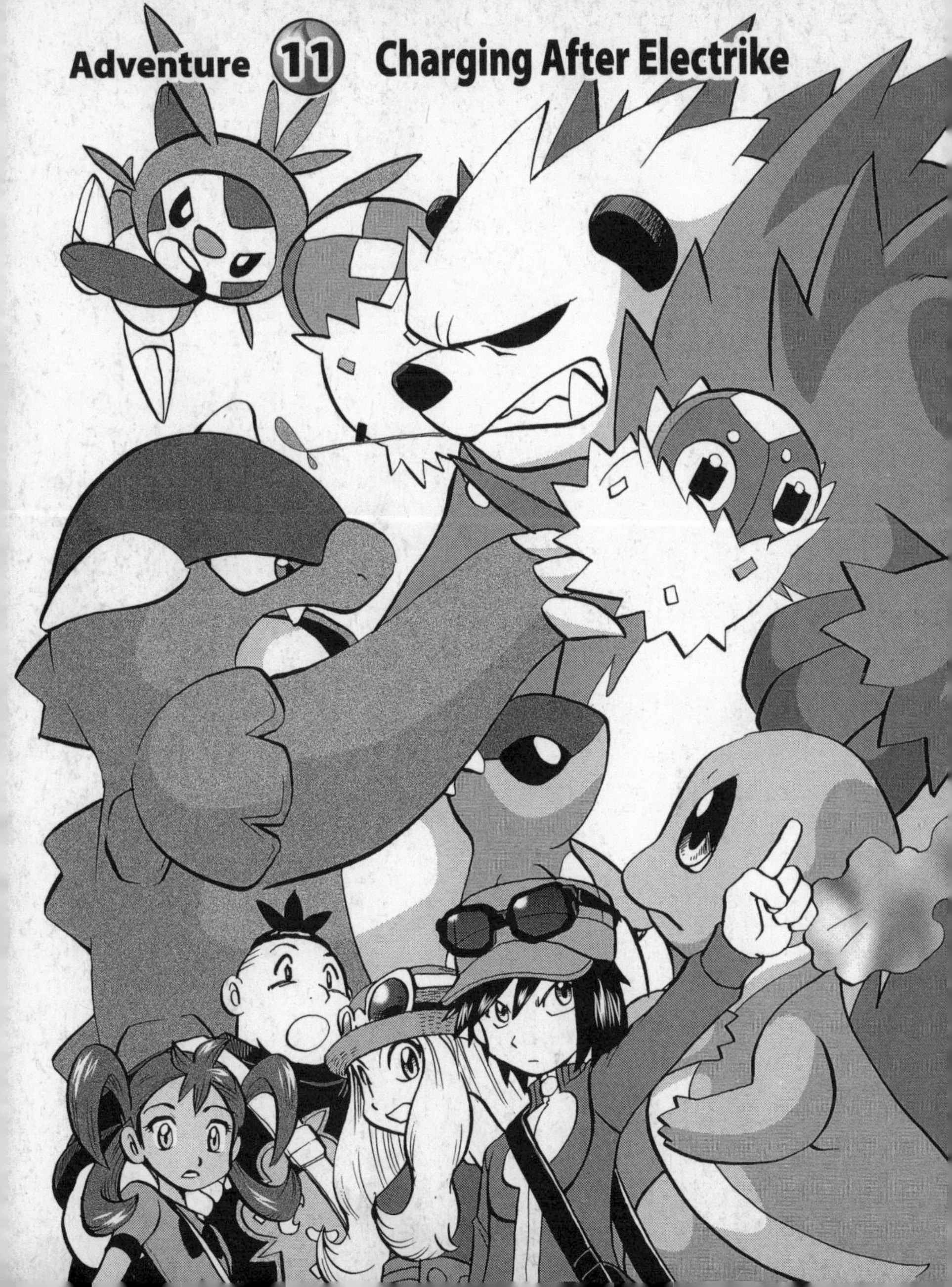

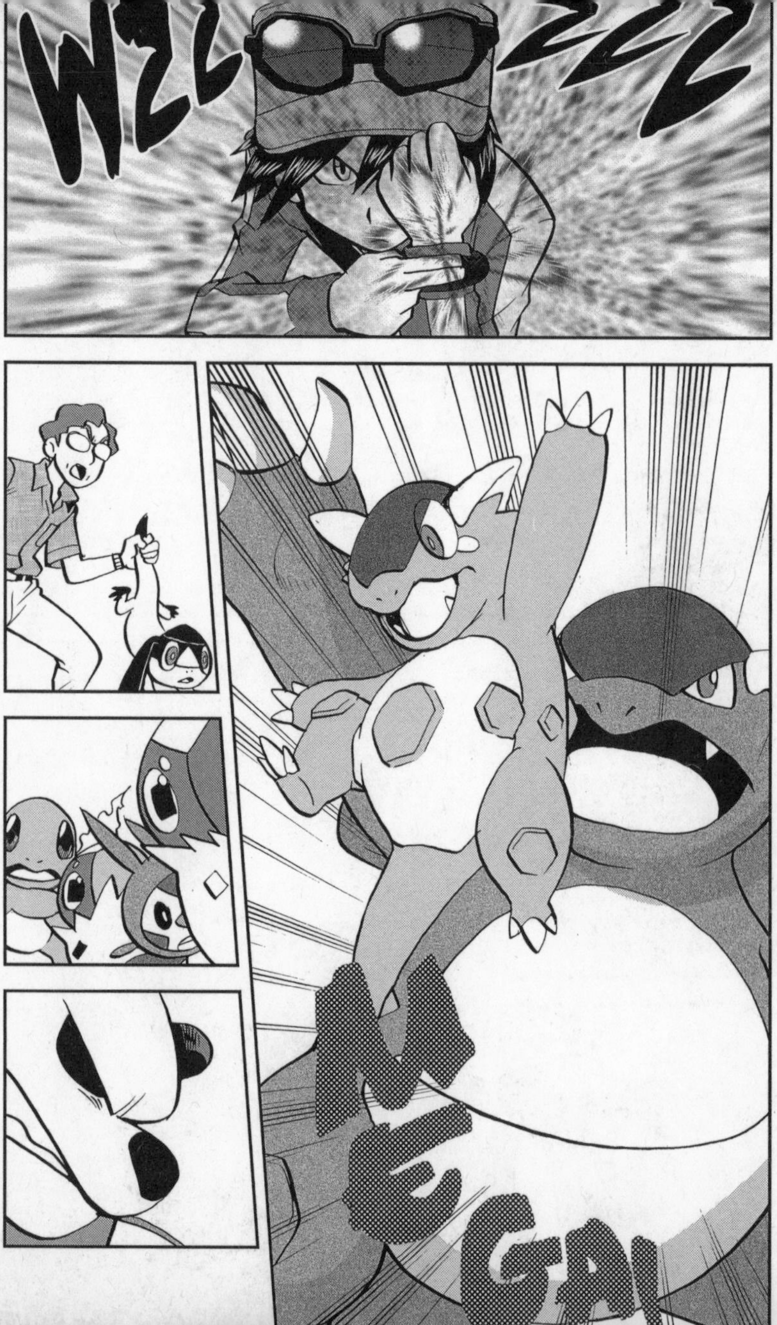
MEGA!

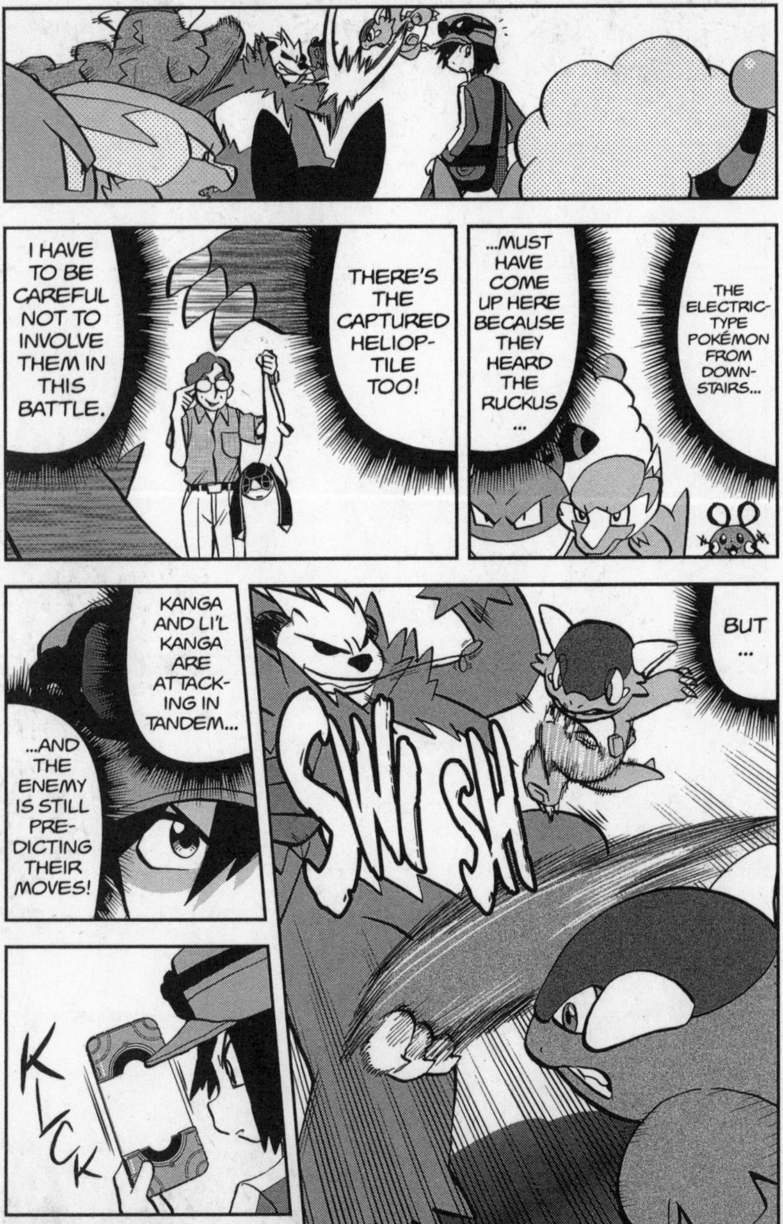
THE ELECTRIC-TYPE POKÉMON FROM DOWNSTAIRS...
...MUST HAVE COME UP HERE BECAUSE THEY HEARD THE RUCKUS...
THERE'S THE CAPTURED HELIOPTILE TOO!
I HAVE TO BE CAREFUL NOT TO INVOLVE THEM IN THIS BATTLE.
KANGA AND LI'L KANGA ARE ATTACKING IN TANDEM...
...AND THE ENEMY IS STILL PREDICTING THEIR MOVES!
BUT ...
SWISH
KLICK

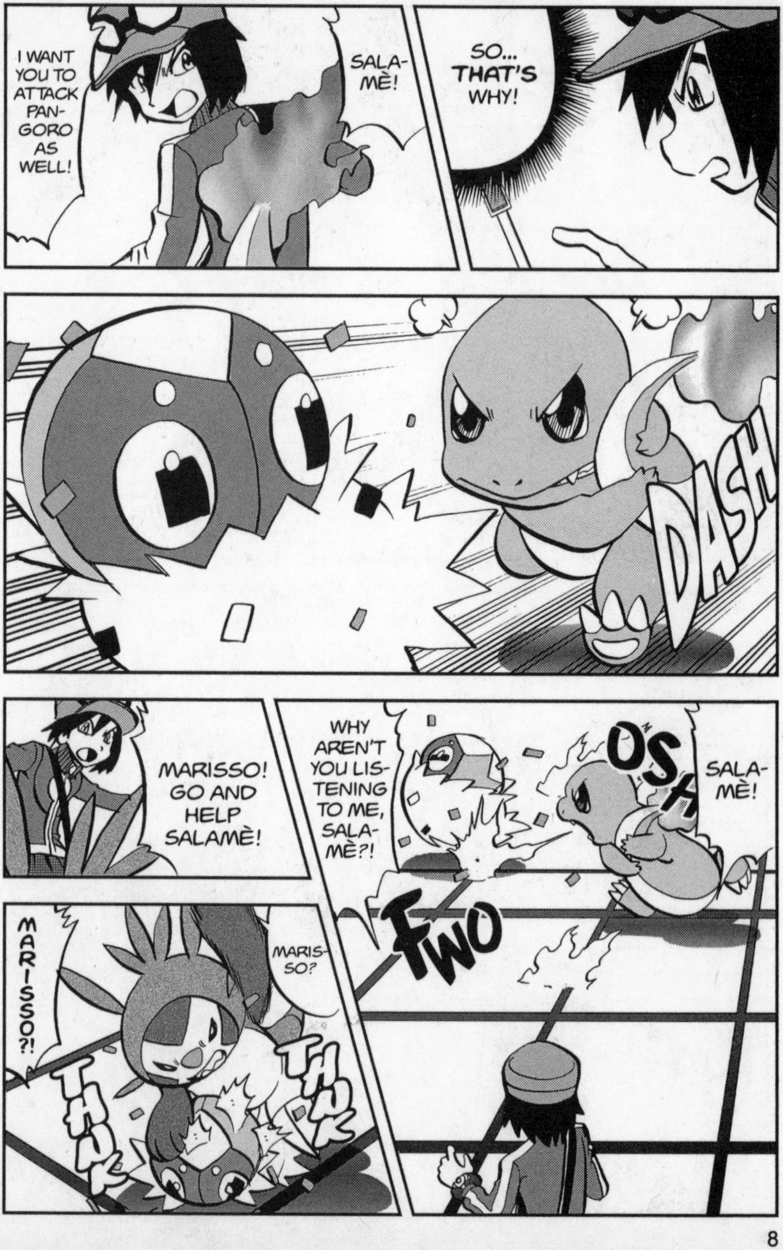
SO... THAT'S WHY!
SALA-MÈ!
I WANT YOU TO ATTACK PAN-GORO AS WELL!
DASH
SALA-MÈ!
OSH
WHY AREN'T YOU LIS-TENING TO ME, SALA-MÈ?!
MARISSO! GO AND HELP SALAMÈ!
FWO
MARIS-SO?
MARISSO?!
THOK
THOK

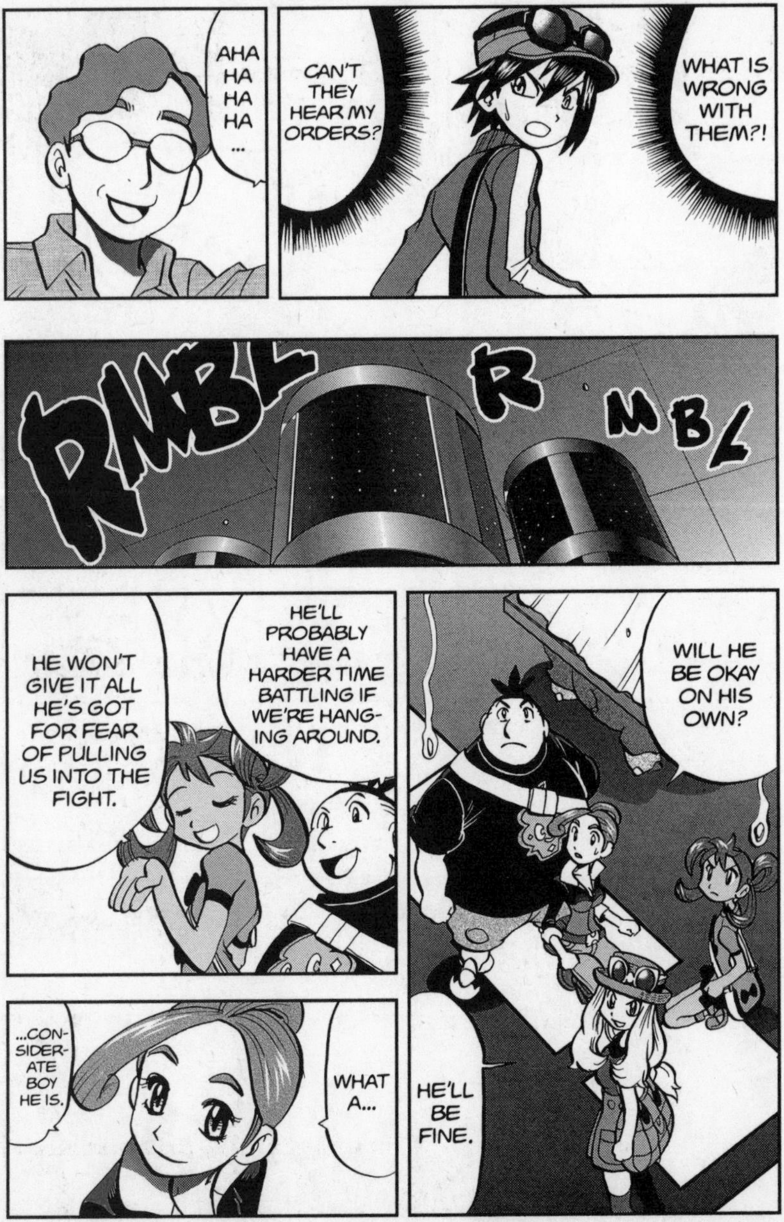
WHAT IS WRONG WITH THEM?!
CAN'T THEY HEAR MY ORDERS?
AHA HA HA HA ...
RMBL R MBL
WILL HE BE OKAY ON HIS OWN?
HE'LL BE FINE.
HE'LL PROBABLY HAVE A HARDER TIME BATTLING IF WE'RE HANGING AROUND.
HE WON'T GIVE IT ALL HE'S GOT FOR FEAR OF PULLING US INTO THE FIGHT.
WHAT A...
...CONSIDERATE BOY HE IS.

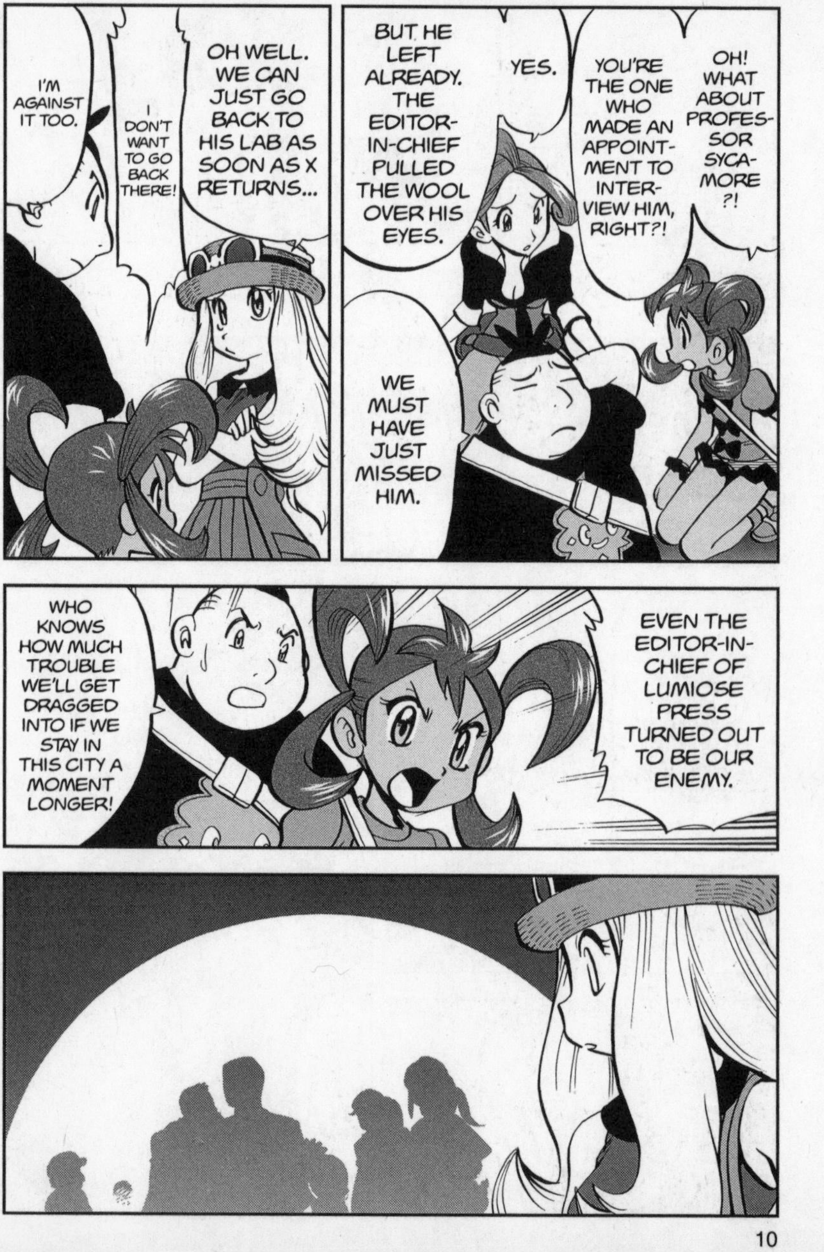
OH! WHAT ABOUT PROFESSOR SYCAMORE?!
YOU'RE THE ONE WHO MADE AN APPOINTMENT TO INTERVIEW HIM, RIGHT?!
YES.
BUT HE LEFT ALREADY. THE EDITOR-IN-CHIEF PULLED THE WOOL OVER HIS EYES.
WE MUST HAVE JUST MISSED HIM.
OH WELL. WE CAN JUST GO BACK TO HIS LAB AS SOON AS X RETURNS...
I DON'T WANT TO GO BACK THERE!
I'M AGAINST IT TOO.
EVEN THE EDITOR-IN-CHIEF OF LUMIOSE PRESS TURNED OUT TO BE OUR ENEMY.
WHO KNOWS HOW MUCH TROUBLE WE'LL GET DRAGGED INTO IF WE STAY IN THIS CITY A MOMENT LONGER!

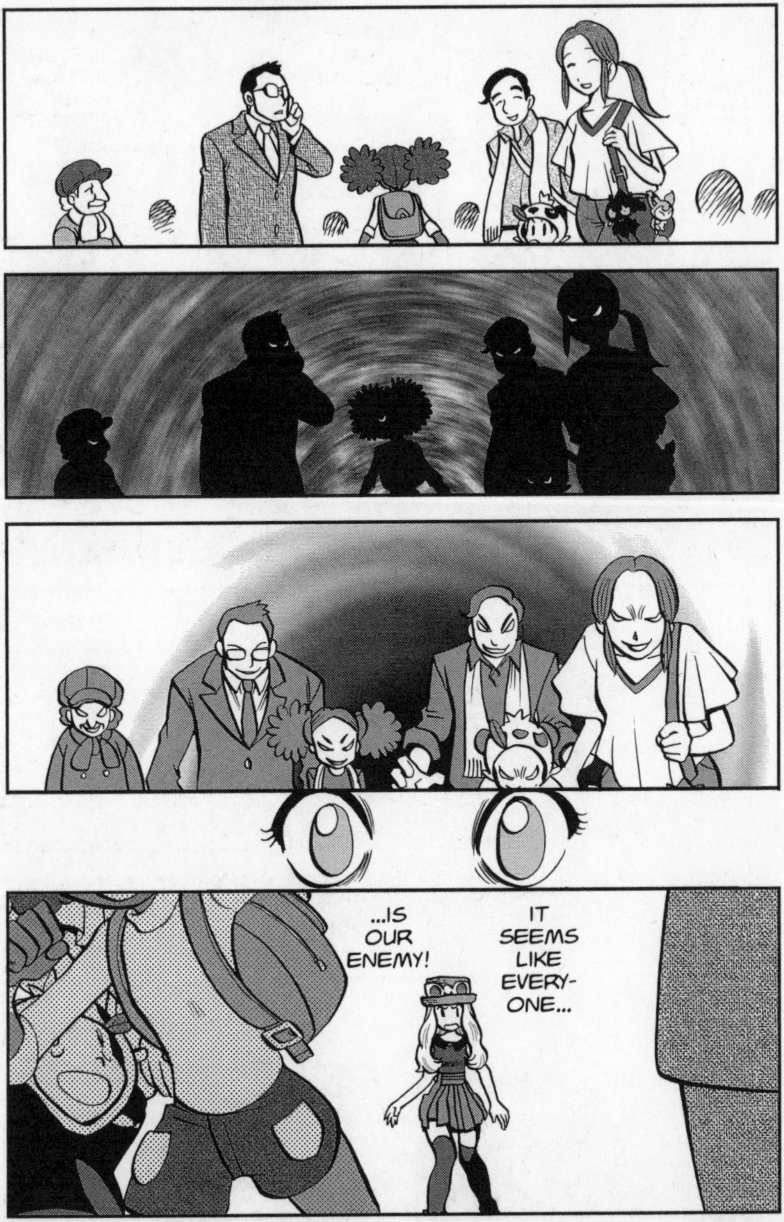
IT SEEMS LIKE EVERY-ONE...
...IS OUR ENEMY!

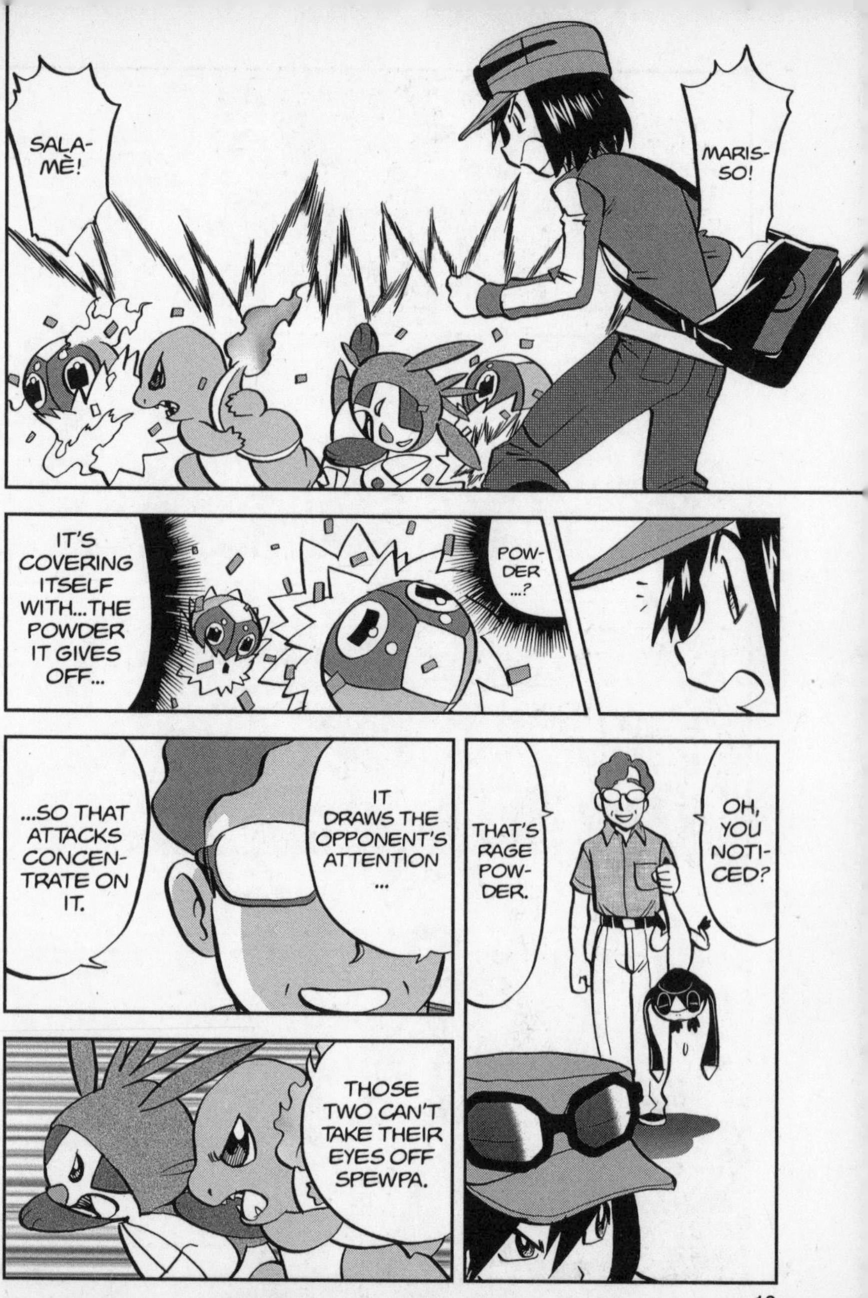
MARIS-SO!
SALA-MÈ!
POW-DER ...?
IT'S COVERING ITSELF WITH...THE POWDER IT GIVES OFF...
OH, YOU NOTI-CED?
THAT'S RAGE POW-DER.
IT DRAWS THE OPPONENT'S ATTENTION ...
...SO THAT ATTACKS CONCEN-TRATE ON IT.
THOSE TWO CAN'T TAKE THEIR EYES OFF SPEWPA.

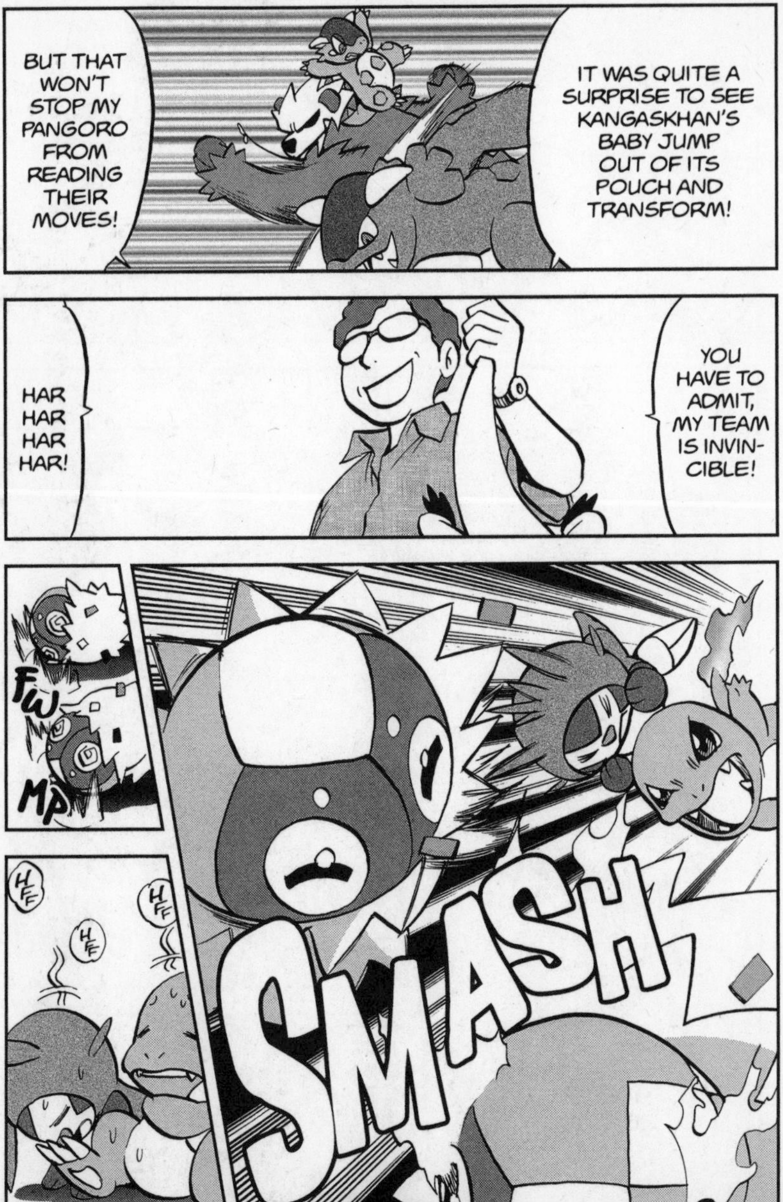
IT WAS QUITE A SURPRISE TO SEE KANGASKHAN'S BABY JUMP OUT OF ITS POUCH AND TRANSFORM!
BUT THAT WON'T STOP MY PANGORO FROM READING THEIR MOVES!
YOU HAVE TO ADMIT, MY TEAM IS INVIN-CIBLE!
HAR HAR HAR HAR!
SMASH
FWUMP
HFF
HFF
HFF

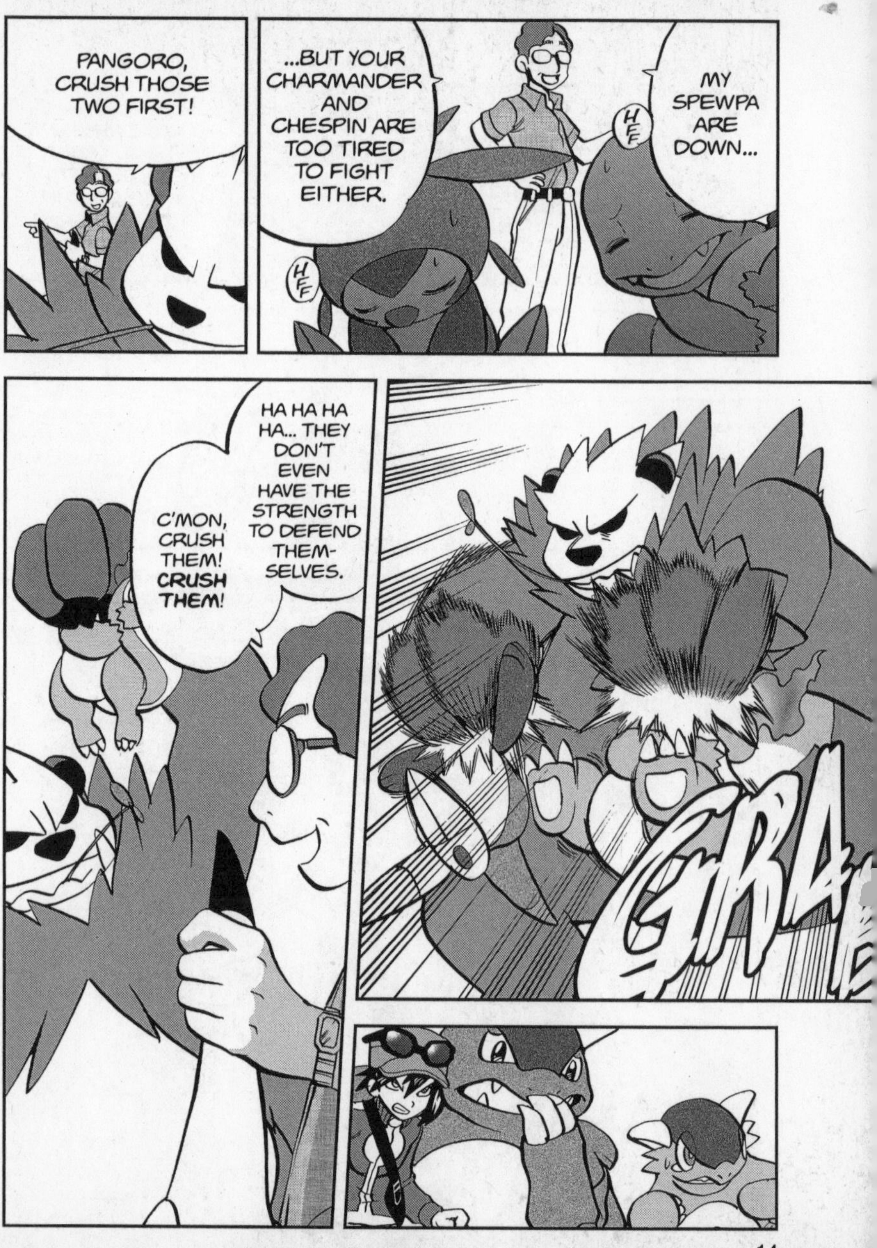
H
FF
MY SPEWPA ARE DOWN...
...BUT YOUR CHARMANDER AND CHESPIN ARE TOO TIRED TO FIGHT EITHER.
H
FF
PANGORO, CRUSH THOSE TWO FIRST!
GRA
HA HA HA HA... THEY DON'T EVEN HAVE THE STRENGTH TO DEFEND THEM-SELVES.
C'MON, CRUSH THEM! **CRUSH THEM!**

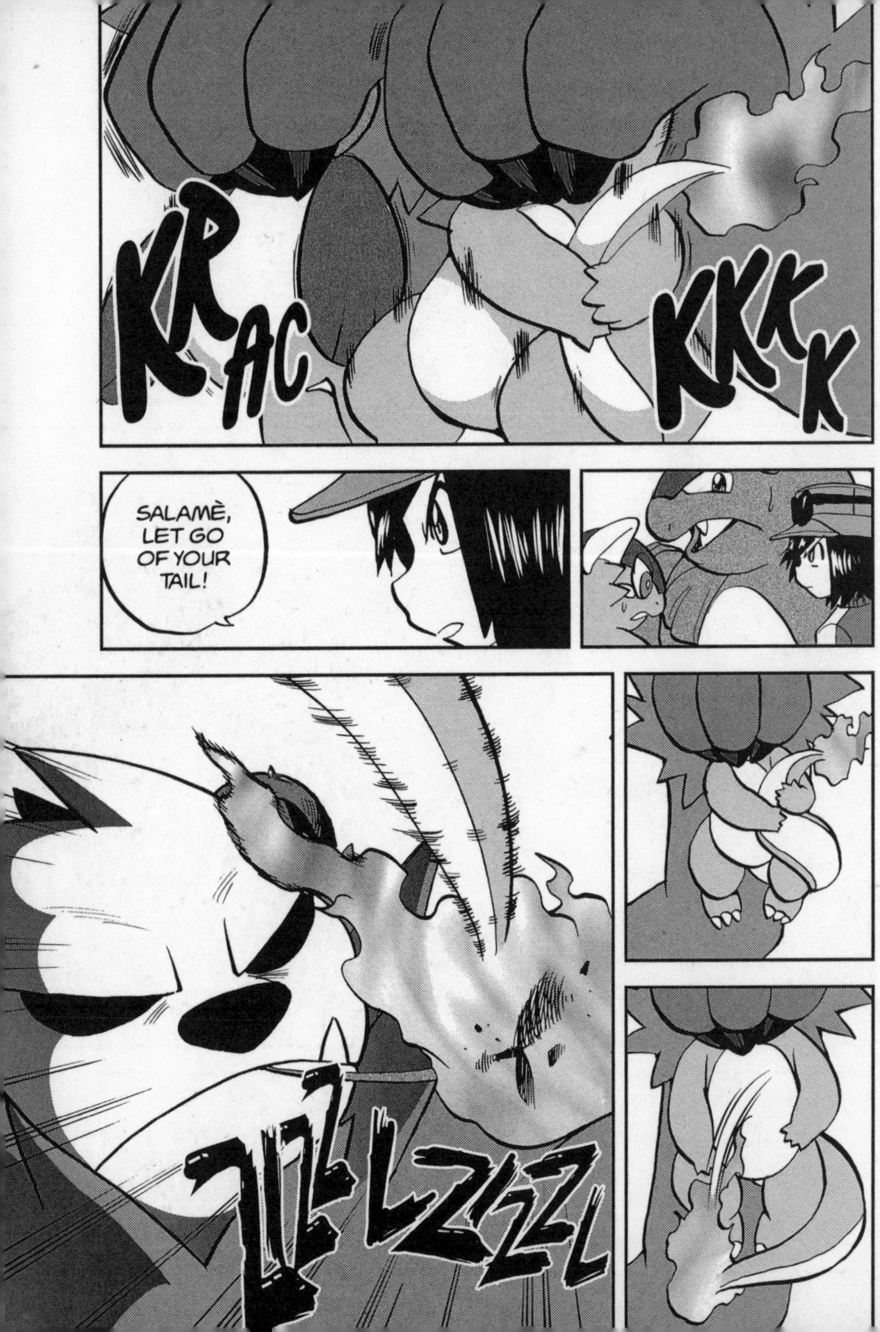
KRAC
KKKKK
SALAMÈ, LET GO OF YOUR TAIL!
ZZZZZZZZ

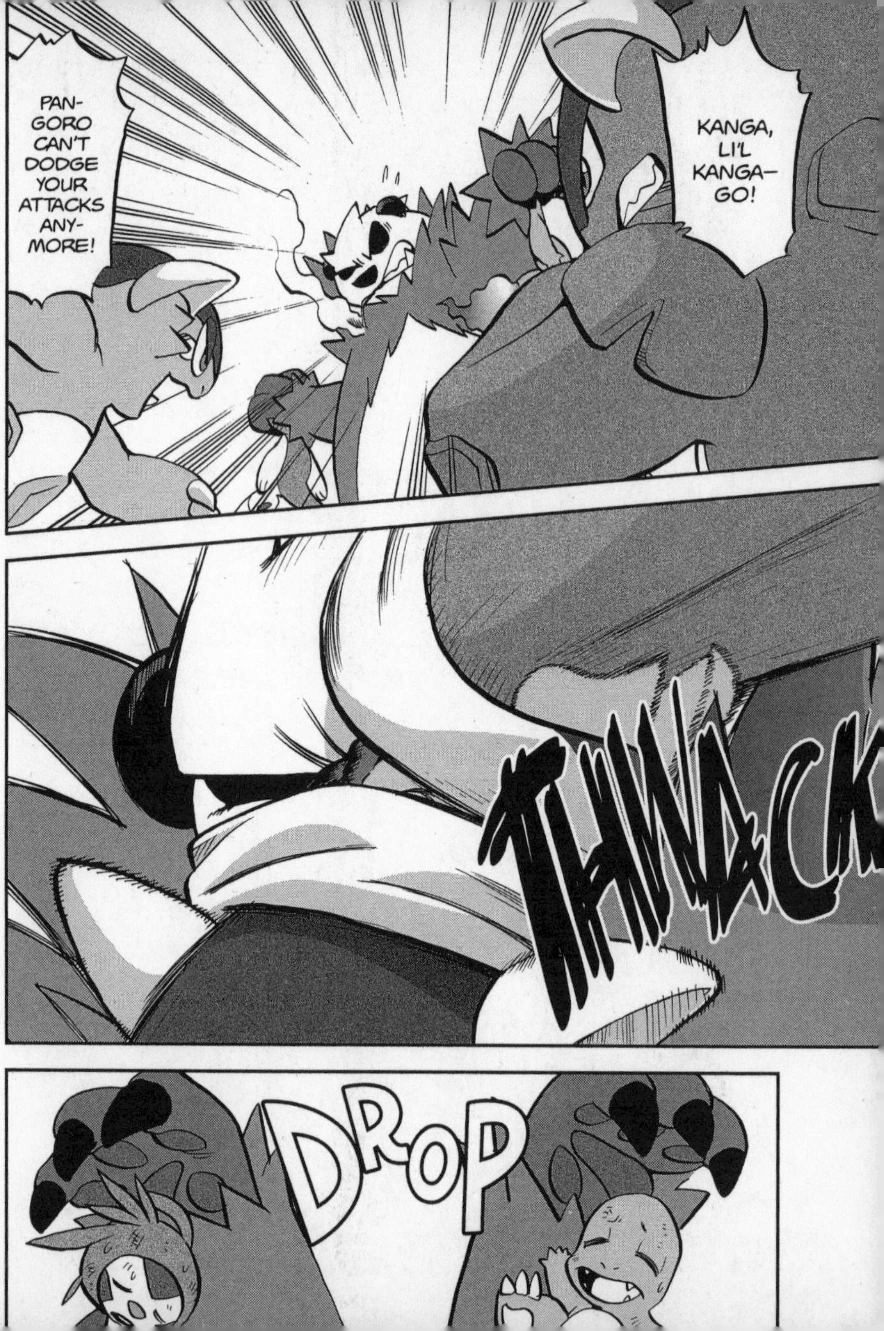
KANGA, LI'L KANGA—GO!
PAN-GORO CAN'T DODGE YOUR ATTACKS ANY-MORE!
THWACK
DROP

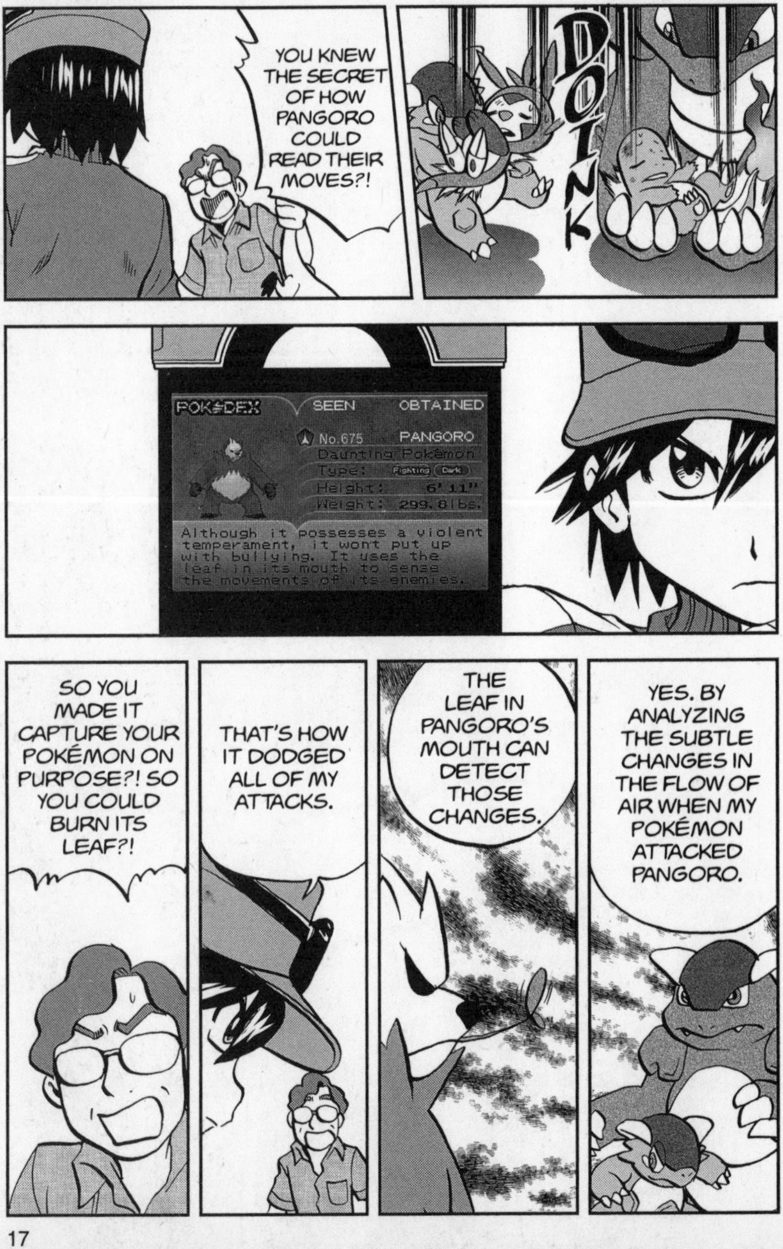
DOINK
YOU KNEW THE SECRET OF HOW PANGORO COULD READ THEIR MOVES?!
POKéDEX
SEEN
OBTAINED
No.675
PANGORO
Daunting Pokémon
Type: Fighting Dark
Height: 6' 11"
Weight: 299.8lbs.
Although it possesses a violent temperament, it won't put up with bullying. It uses the leaf in its mouth to sense the movements of its enemies.
YES. BY ANALYZING THE SUBTLE CHANGES IN THE FLOW OF AIR WHEN MY POKéMON ATTACKED PANGORO.
THE LEAF IN PANGORO'S MOUTH CAN DETECT THOSE CHANGES.
THAT'S HOW IT DODGED ALL OF MY ATTACKS.
SO YOU MADE IT CAPTURE YOUR POKéMON ON PURPOSE?! SO YOU COULD BURN ITS LEAF?!

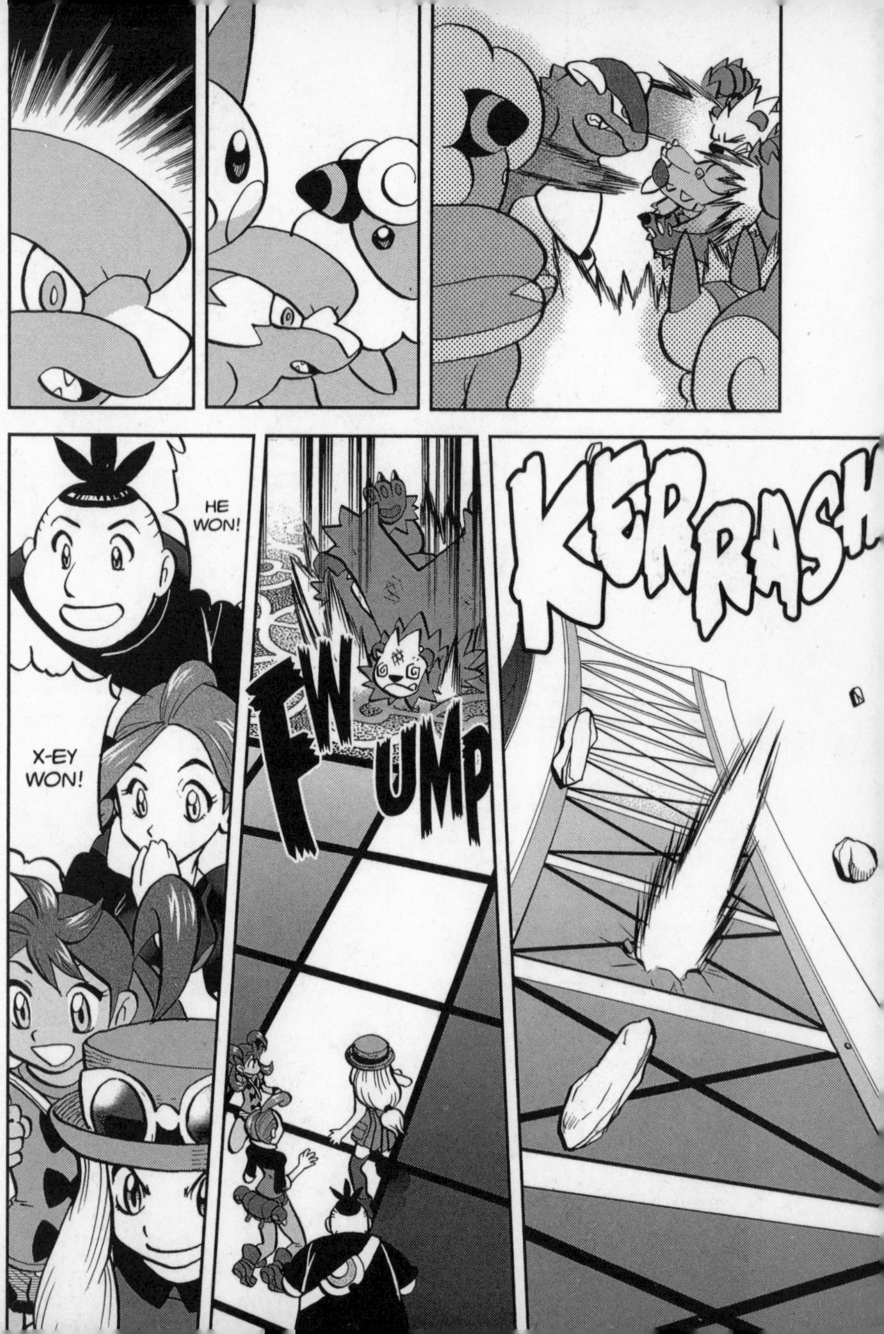
KERRASH
FWUMP
HE WON!
X-EY WON!

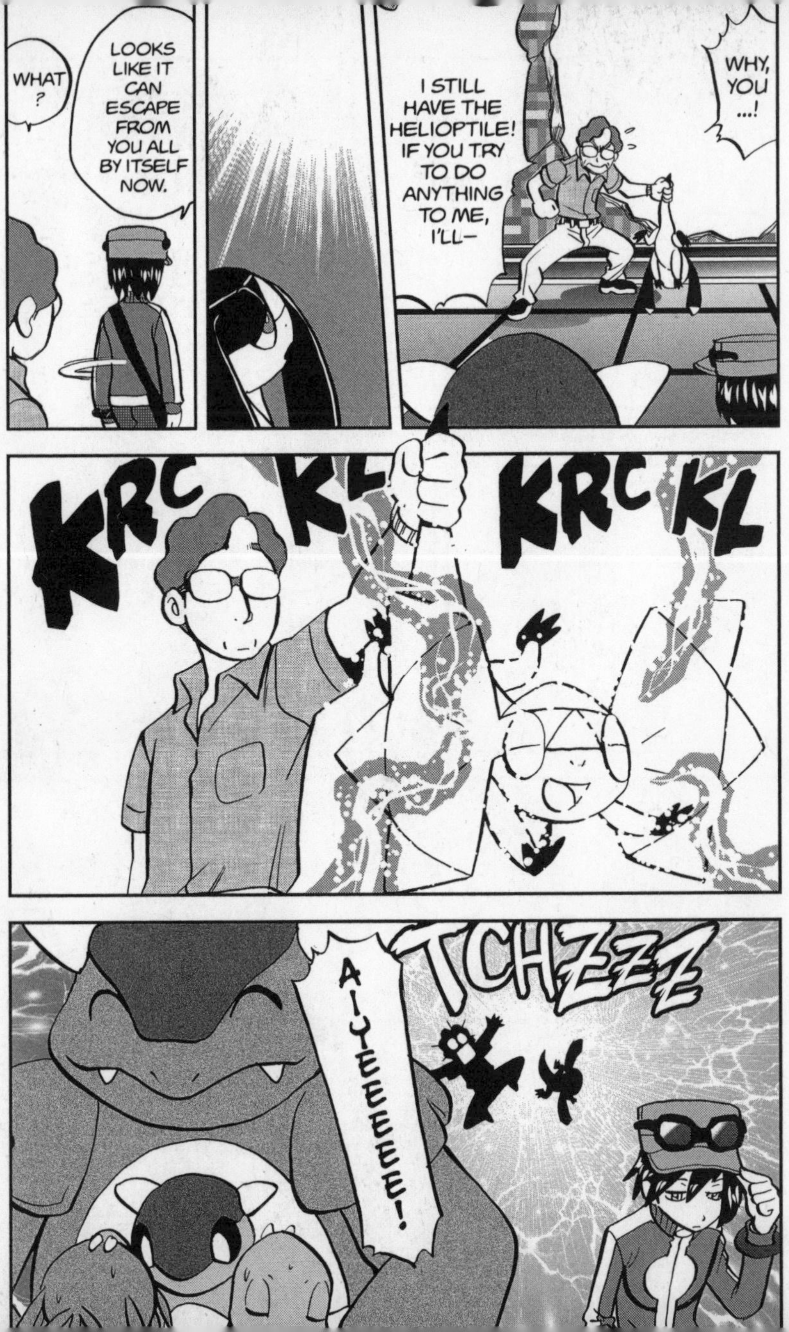
WHY, YOU ...!
I STILL HAVE THE HELIOPTILE! IF YOU TRY TO DO ANYTHING TO ME, I'LL—
LOOKS LIKE IT CAN ESCAPE FROM YOU ALL BY ITSELF NOW.
WHAT?
KRCKL KRCKL
TCHZZZ
AIYEEEEEEE!

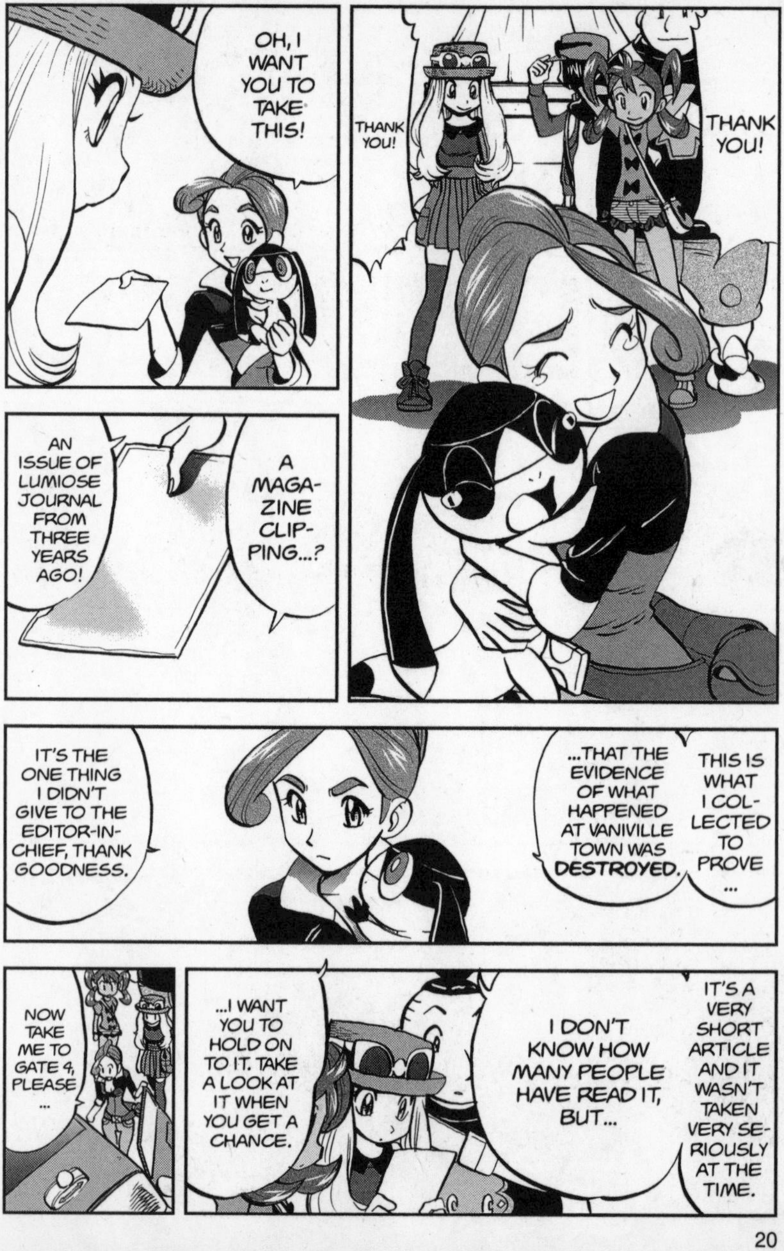
THANK YOU!
THANK YOU!
OH, I WANT YOU TO TAKE THIS!
A MAGAZINE CLIPPING...?
AN ISSUE OF LUMIOSE JOURNAL FROM THREE YEARS AGO!
THIS IS WHAT I COLLECTED TO PROVE...
...THAT THE EVIDENCE OF WHAT HAPPENED AT VANIVILLE TOWN WAS **DESTROYED.**
IT'S THE ONE THING I DIDN'T GIVE TO THE EDITOR-IN-CHIEF, THANK GOODNESS.
IT'S A VERY SHORT ARTICLE AND IT WASN'T TAKEN VERY SERIOUSLY AT THE TIME.
I DON'T KNOW HOW MANY PEOPLE HAVE READ IT, BUT...
...I WANT YOU TO HOLD ON TO IT. TAKE A LOOK AT IT WHEN YOU GET A CHANCE.
NOW TAKE ME TO GATE 4, PLEASE...

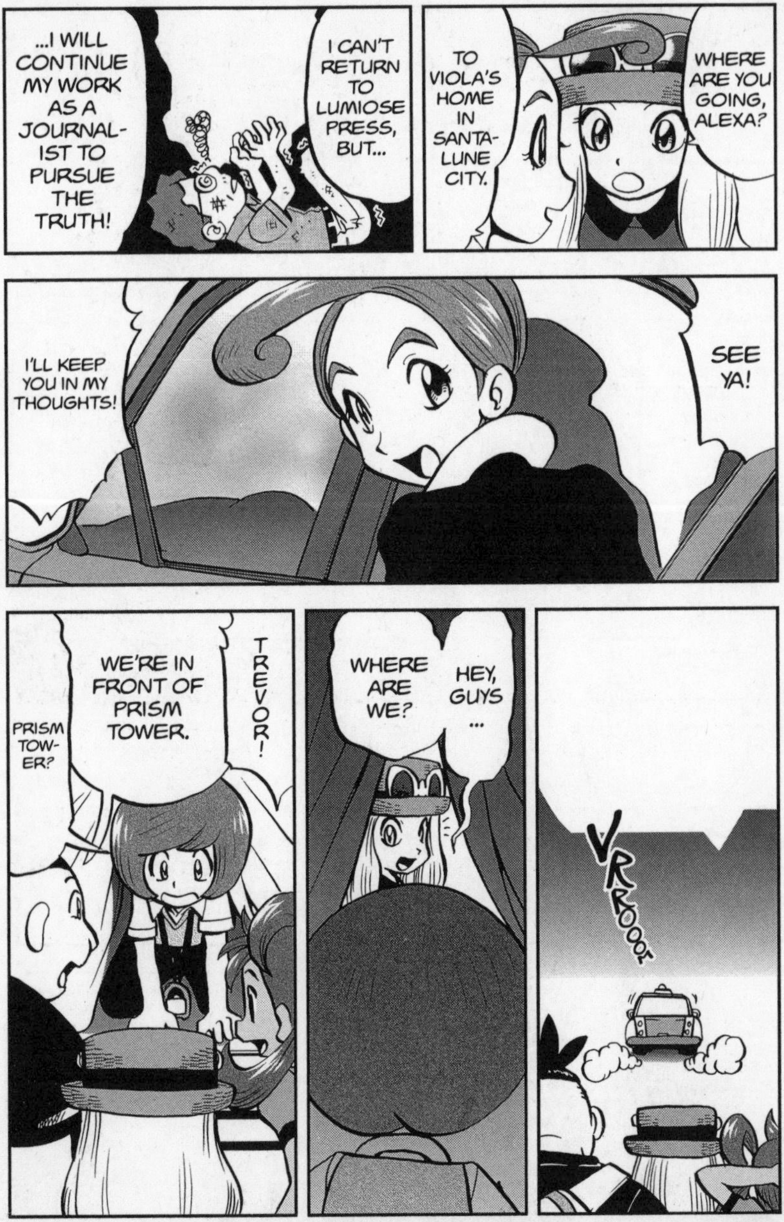
WHERE ARE YOU GOING, ALEXA?
TO VIOLA'S HOME IN SANTALUNE CITY.
I CAN'T RETURN TO LUMIOSE PRESS, BUT...
...I WILL CONTINUE MY WORK AS A JOURNALIST TO PURSUE THE TRUTH!
SEE YA!
I'LL KEEP YOU IN MY THOUGHTS!
VRROOOM
HEY, GUYS...
WHERE ARE WE?
TREVOR!
WE'RE IN FRONT OF PRISM TOWER.
PRISM TOWER?

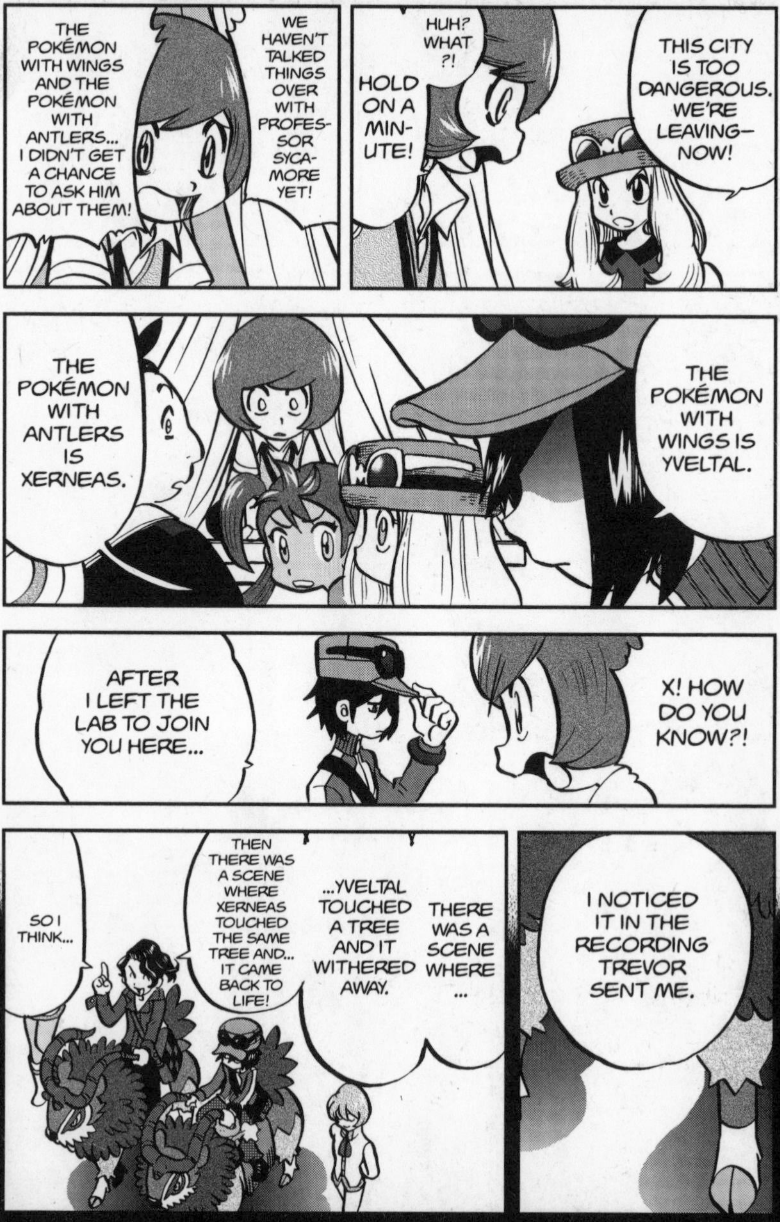
THIS CITY IS TOO DANGEROUS. WE'RE LEAVING— NOW!
HUH? WHAT?!
HOLD ON A MIN-UTE!
WE HAVEN'T TALKED THINGS OVER WITH PROFES-SOR SYCA-MORE YET!
THE POKÉMON WITH WINGS AND THE POKÉMON WITH ANTLERS... I DIDN'T GET A CHANCE TO ASK HIM ABOUT THEM!
THE POKÉMON WITH WINGS IS YVELTAL.
THE POKÉMON WITH ANTLERS IS XERNEAS.
X! HOW DO YOU KNOW?!
AFTER I LEFT THE LAB TO JOIN YOU HERE...
I NOTICED IT IN THE RECORDING TREVOR SENT ME.
THERE WAS A SCENE WHERE ...
...YVELTAL TOUCHED A TREE AND IT WITHERED AWAY.
THEN THERE WAS A SCENE WHERE XERNEAS TOUCHED THE SAME TREE AND... IT CAME BACK TO LIFE!
SO I THINK...

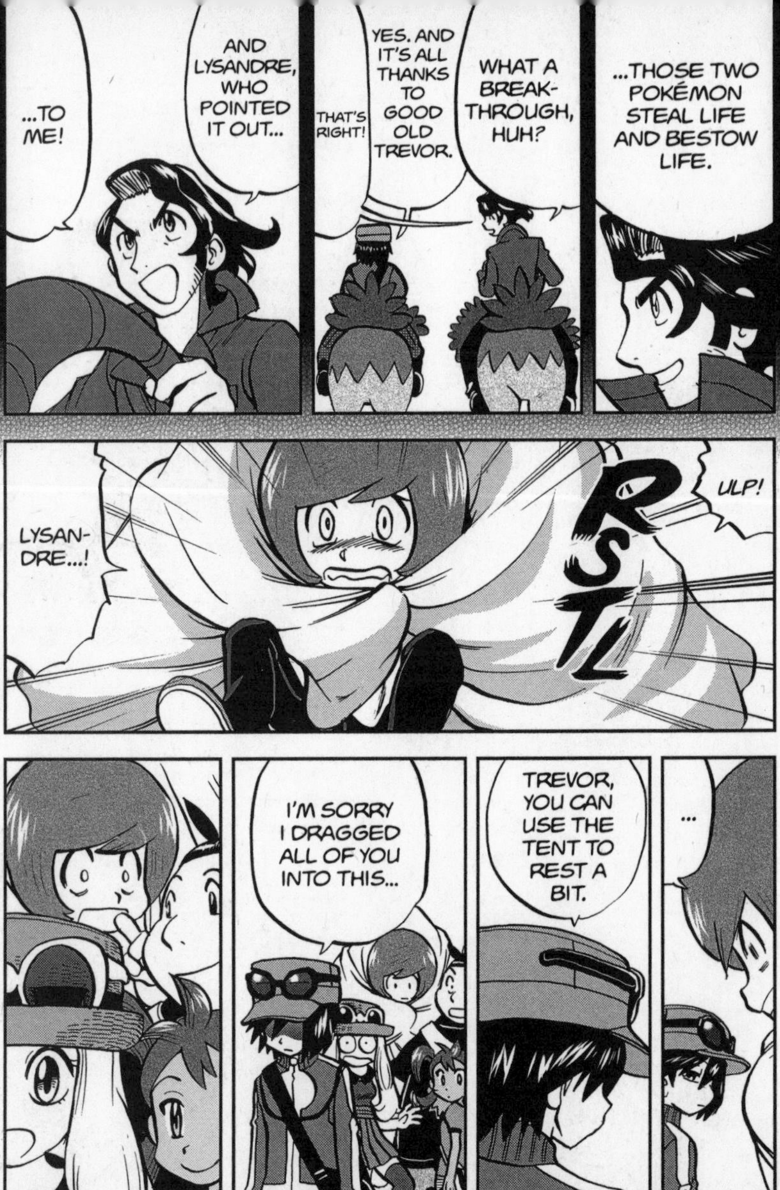
...THOSE TWO POKÉMON STEAL LIFE AND BESTOW LIFE.
WHAT A BREAK-THROUGH, HUH?
YES. AND IT'S ALL THANKS TO GOOD OLD TREVOR.
THAT'S RIGHT!
AND LYSANDRE, WHO POINTED IT OUT...
...TO ME!
ULP!
RSTL
LYSAN-DRE...!
...
TREVOR, YOU CAN USE THE TENT TO REST A BIT.
I'M SORRY I DRAGGED ALL OF YOU INTO THIS...

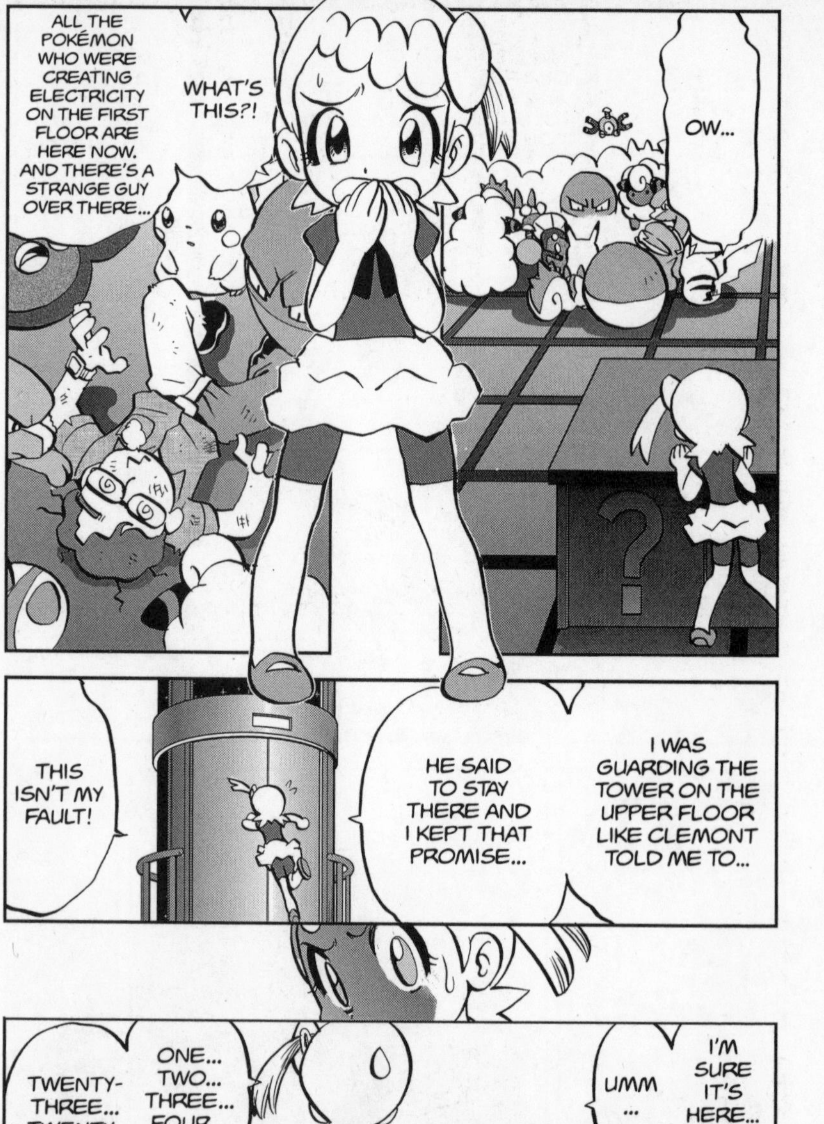
OW...
WHAT'S THIS?!
ALL THE POKÉMON WHO WERE CREATING ELECTRICITY ON THE FIRST FLOOR ARE HERE NOW. AND THERE'S A STRANGE GUY OVER THERE...
I WAS GUARDING THE TOWER ON THE UPPER FLOOR LIKE CLEMONT TOLD ME TO...
HE SAID TO STAY THERE AND I KEPT THAT PROMISE...
THIS ISN'T MY FAULT!
I'M SURE IT'S HERE... SOME-PLACE...
UMM ...
ONE... TWO... THREE... FOUR...
TWENTY-THREE... TWENTY-FOUR...

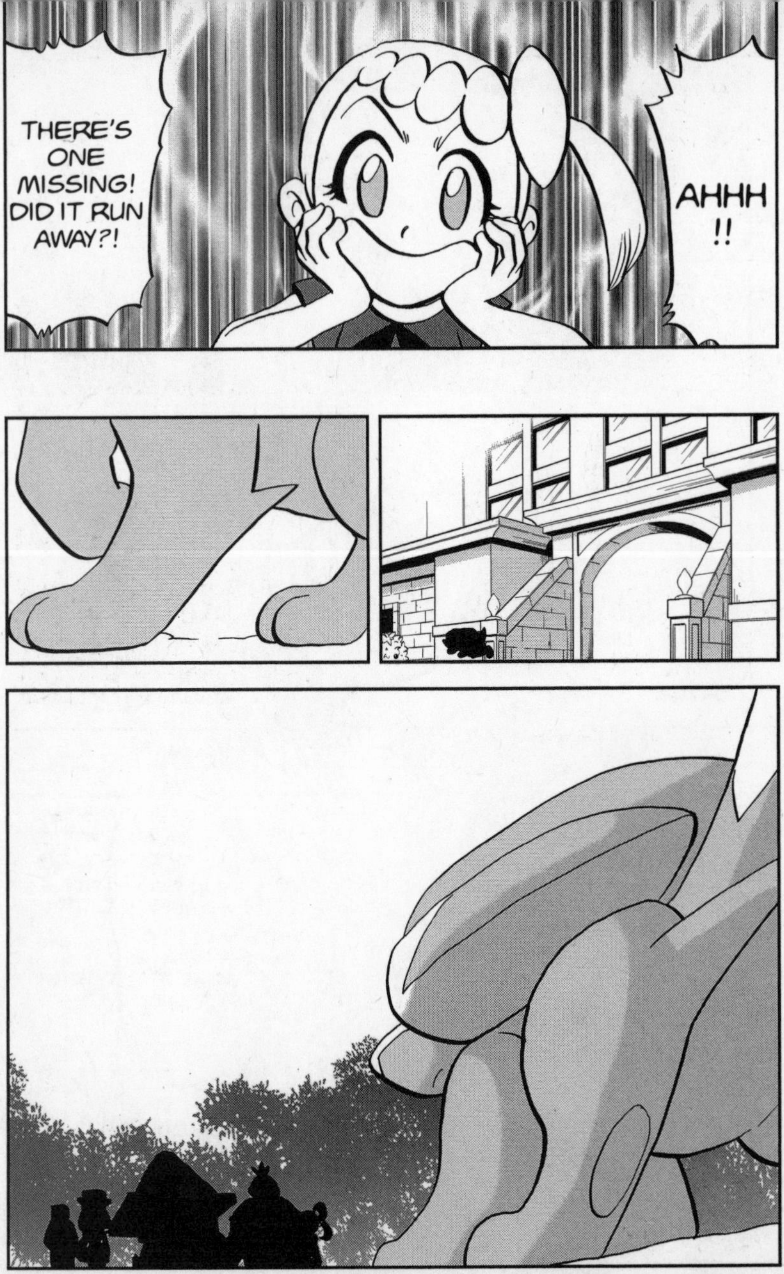
AHHH !!
THERE'S ONE MISSING! DID IT RUN AWAY?!

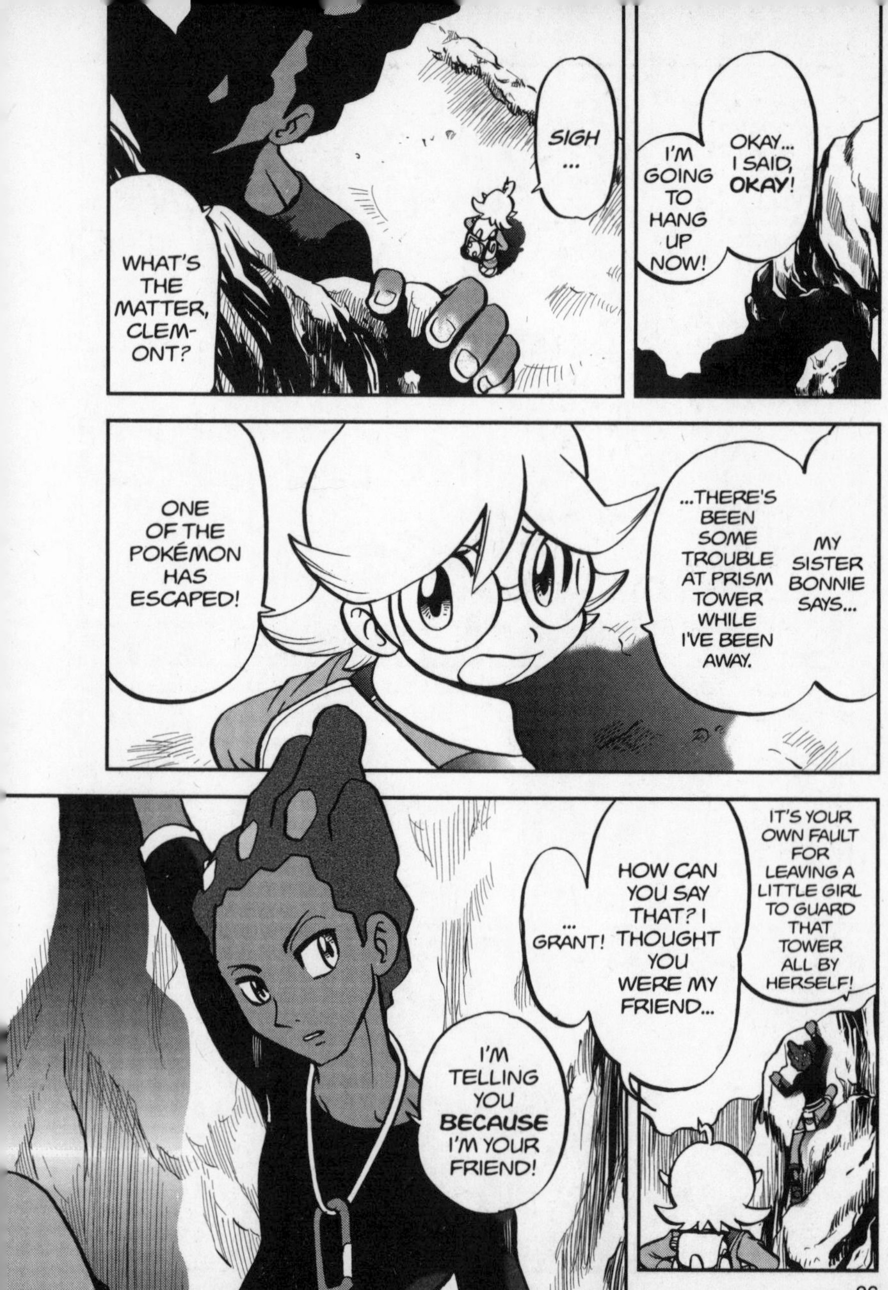
OKAY... I SAID, **OKAY**!
I'M GOING TO HANG UP NOW!
SIGH ...
WHAT'S THE MATTER, CLEM-ONT?
MY SISTER BONNIE SAYS...
...THERE'S BEEN SOME TROUBLE AT PRISM TOWER WHILE I'VE BEEN AWAY.
ONE OF THE POKÉMON HAS ESCAPED!
IT'S YOUR OWN FAULT FOR LEAVING A LITTLE GIRL TO GUARD THAT TOWER ALL BY HERSELF!
HOW CAN YOU SAY THAT? I THOUGHT YOU WERE MY FRIEND...
... GRANT!
I'M TELLING YOU **BECAUSE** I'M YOUR FRIEND!

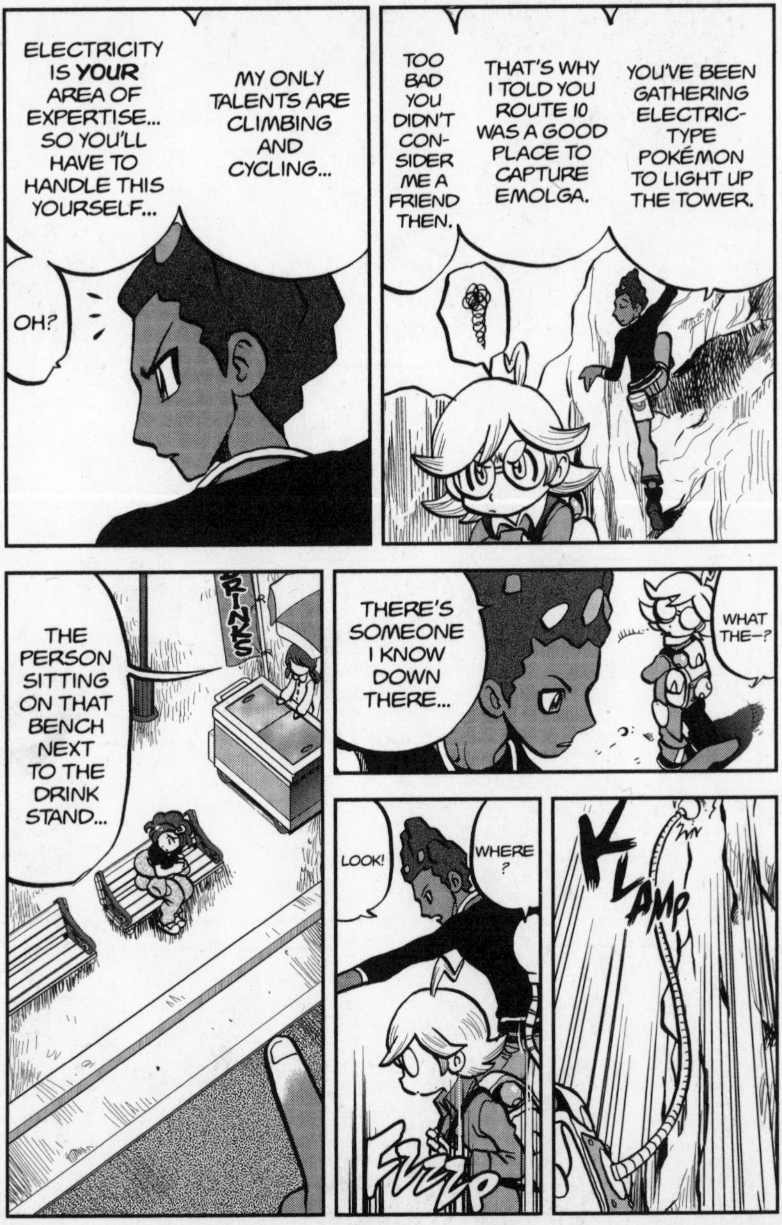
YOU'VE BEEN GATHERING ELECTRIC-TYPE POKÉMON TO LIGHT UP THE TOWER.
THAT'S WHY I TOLD YOU ROUTE 10 WAS A GOOD PLACE TO CAPTURE EMOLGA.
TOO BAD YOU DIDN'T CON-SIDER ME A FRIEND THEN.
MY ONLY TALENTS ARE CLIMBING AND CYCLING...
ELECTRICITY IS **YOUR** AREA OF EXPERTISE... SO YOU'LL HAVE TO HANDLE THIS YOURSELF...
OH?
WHAT THE—?
THERE'S SOMEONE I KNOW DOWN THERE...
KLAMP
WHERE?
LOOK!
FZZZP
THE PERSON SITTING ON THAT BENCH NEXT TO THE DRINK STAND...
DRINKS

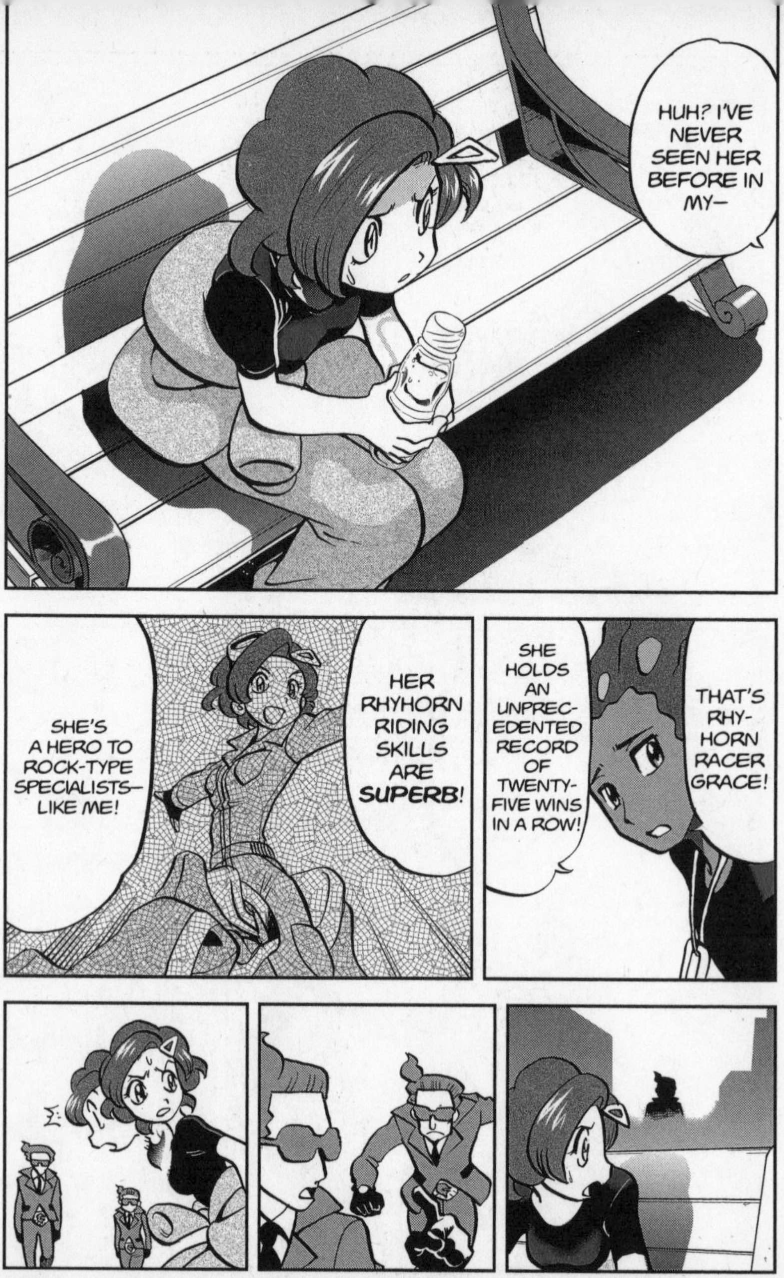
HUH? I'VE NEVER SEEN HER BEFORE IN MY—
THAT'S RHY-HORN RACER GRACE!
SHE HOLDS AN UNPREC-EDENTED RECORD OF TWENTY-FIVE WINS IN A ROW!
HER RHYHORN RIDING SKILLS ARE **SUPERB**!
SHE'S A HERO TO ROCK-TYPE SPECIALISTS—LIKE ME!

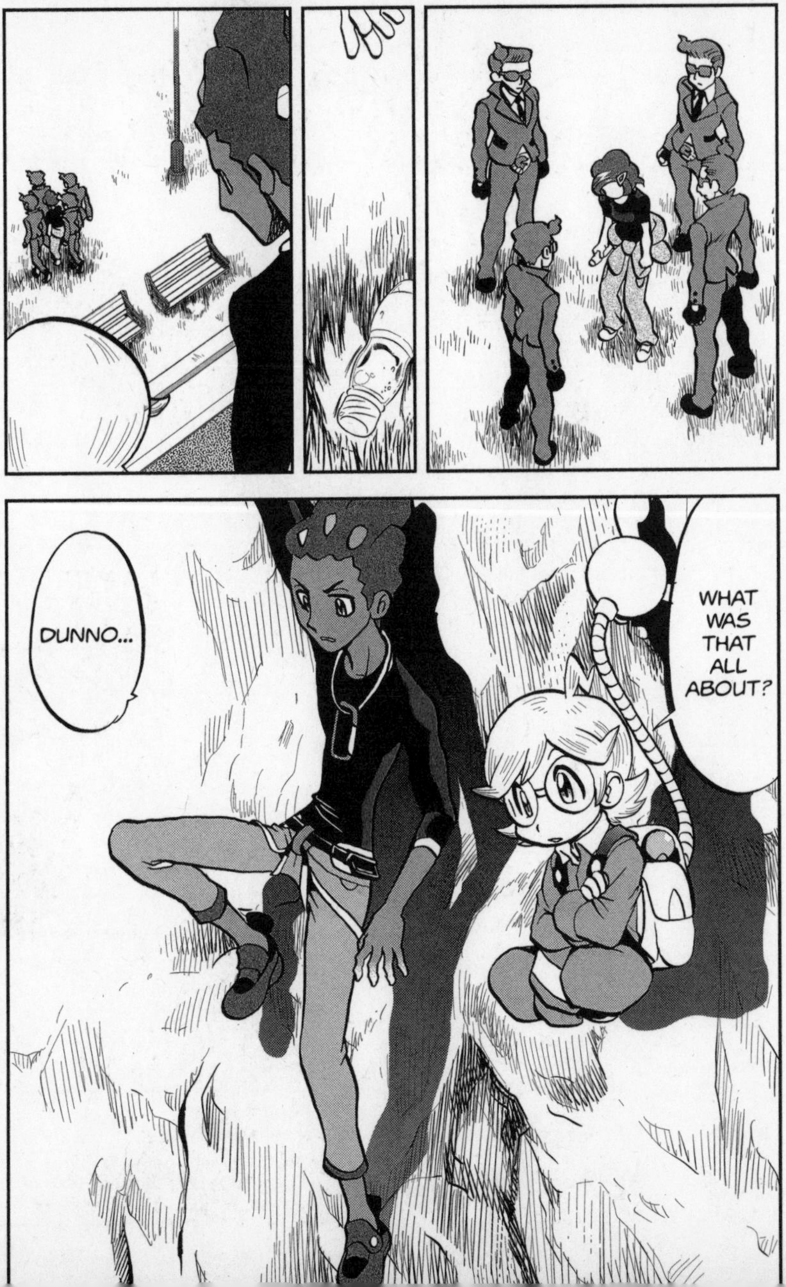
WHAT WAS THAT ALL ABOUT?
DUNNO...

⊕ **Current Location**

Lumiose City

A dazzling metropolis of art and artifice, located in the very heart of the Kalos region.

Adventure 12 Fast-Thinking Froakie

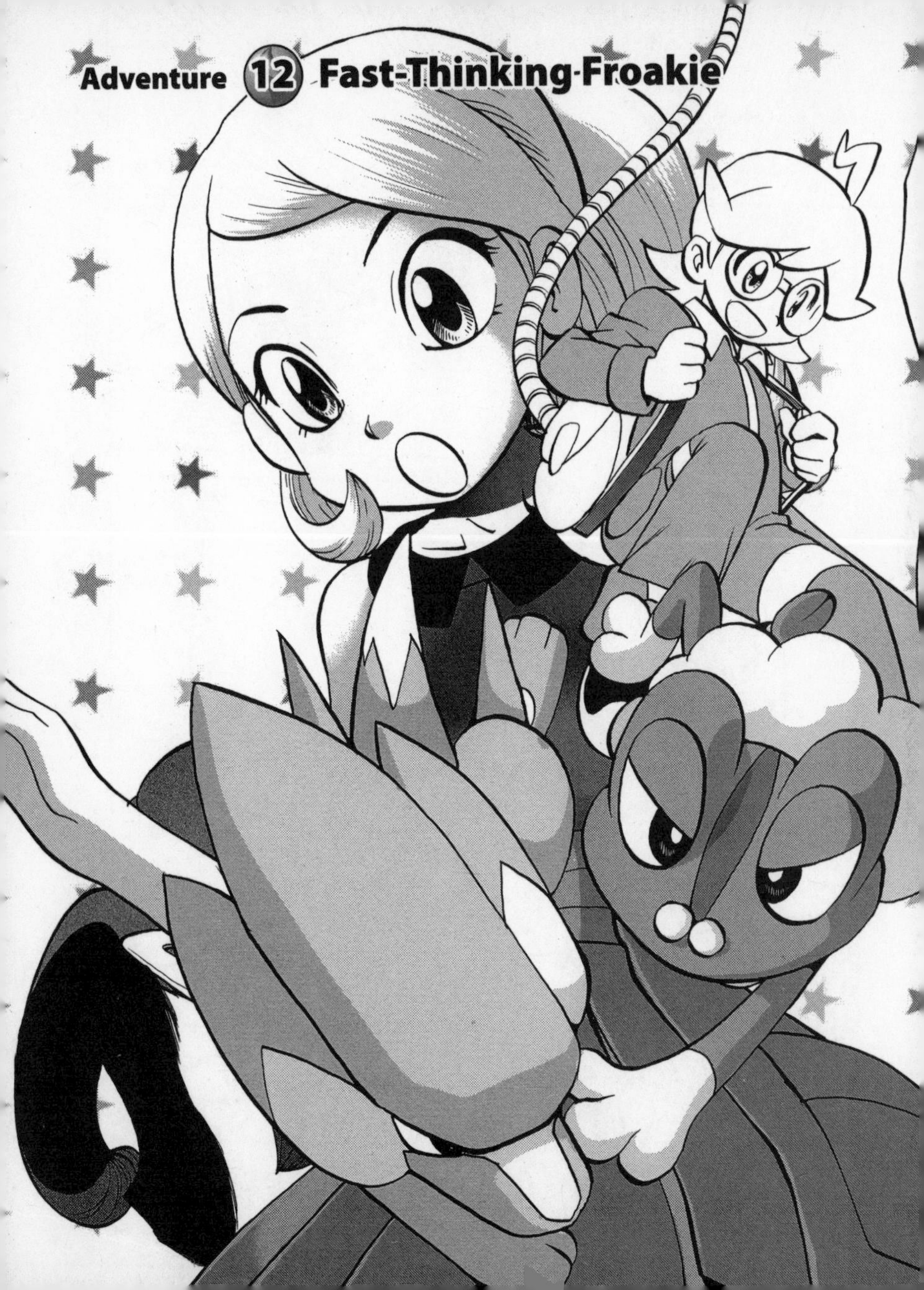

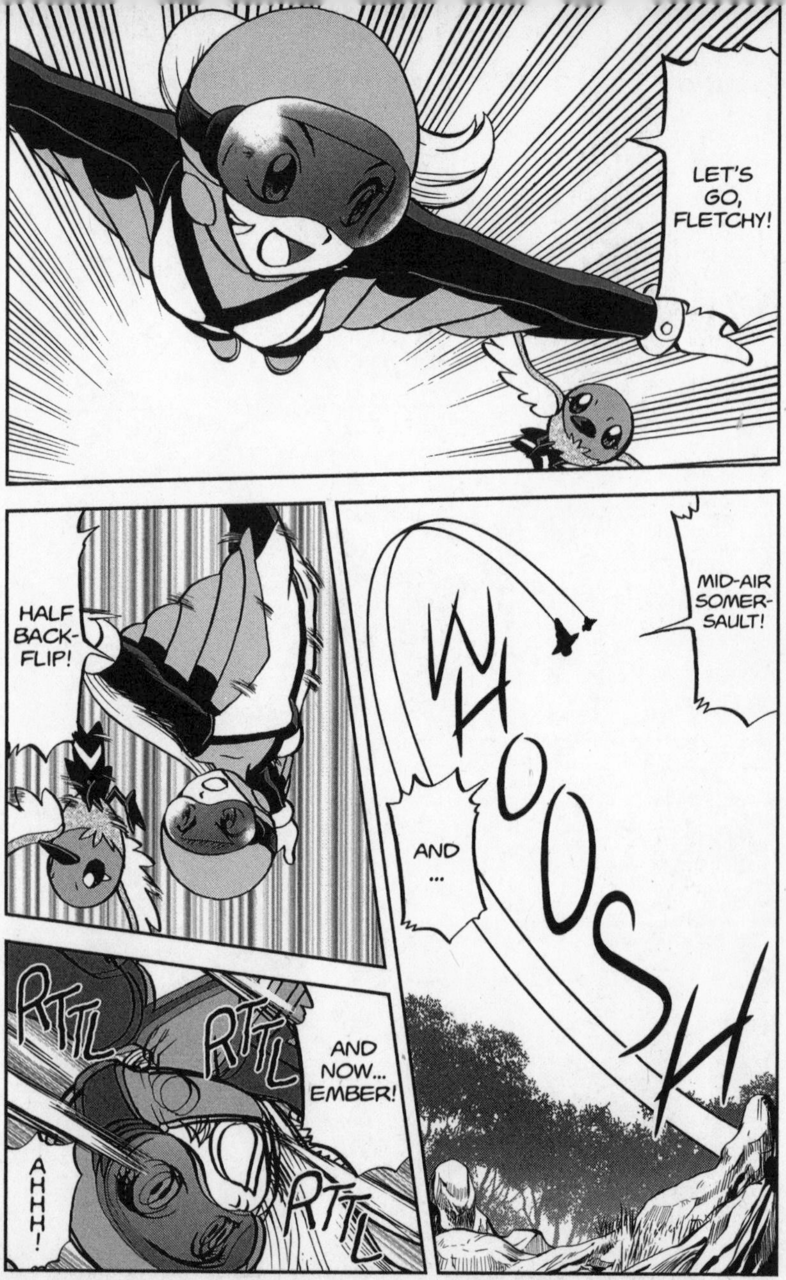
LET'S GO, FLETCHY!
MID-AIR SOMER-SAULT!
WHOOSH
AND ...
HALF BACK-FLIP!
AND NOW... EMBER!
RTTL
RTTL
RTTL
AHHH!

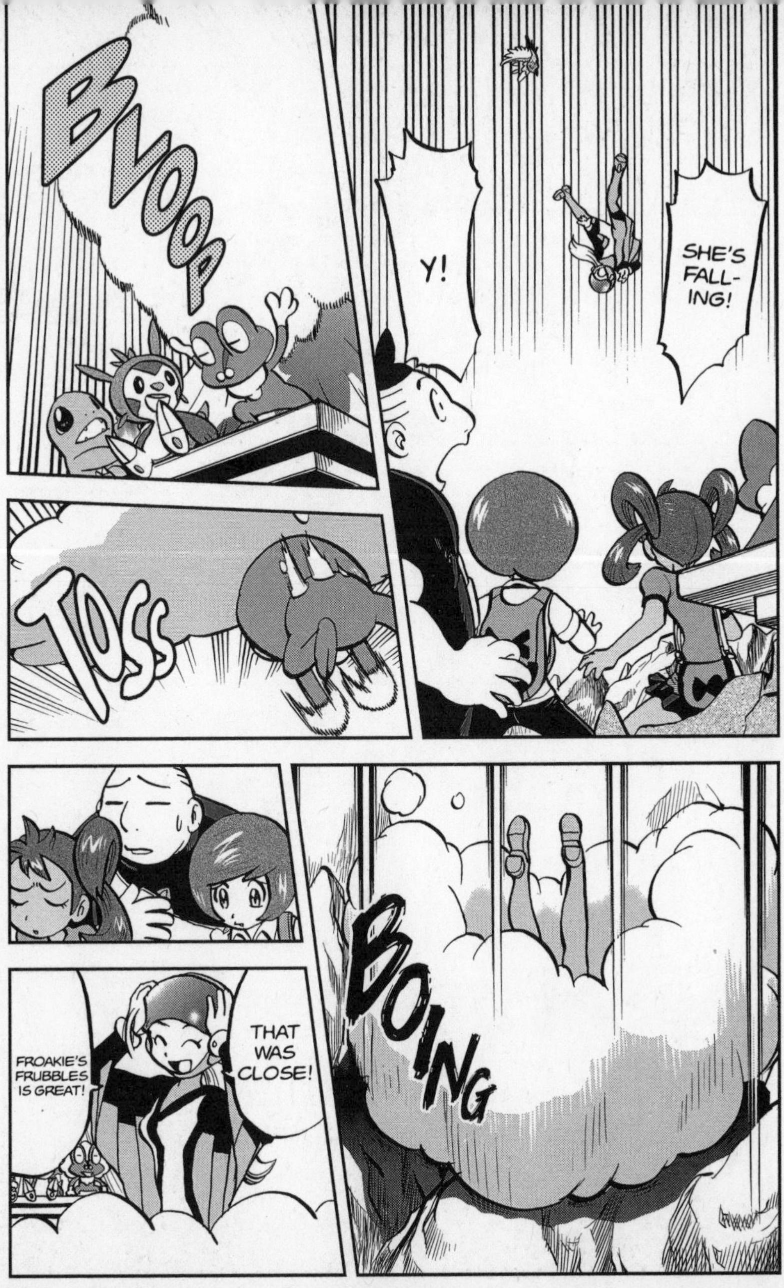
SHE'S FALL-ING!
Y!
BVOOP
TOSS
BOING
THAT WAS CLOSE!
FROAKIE'S FRUBBLES IS GREAT!

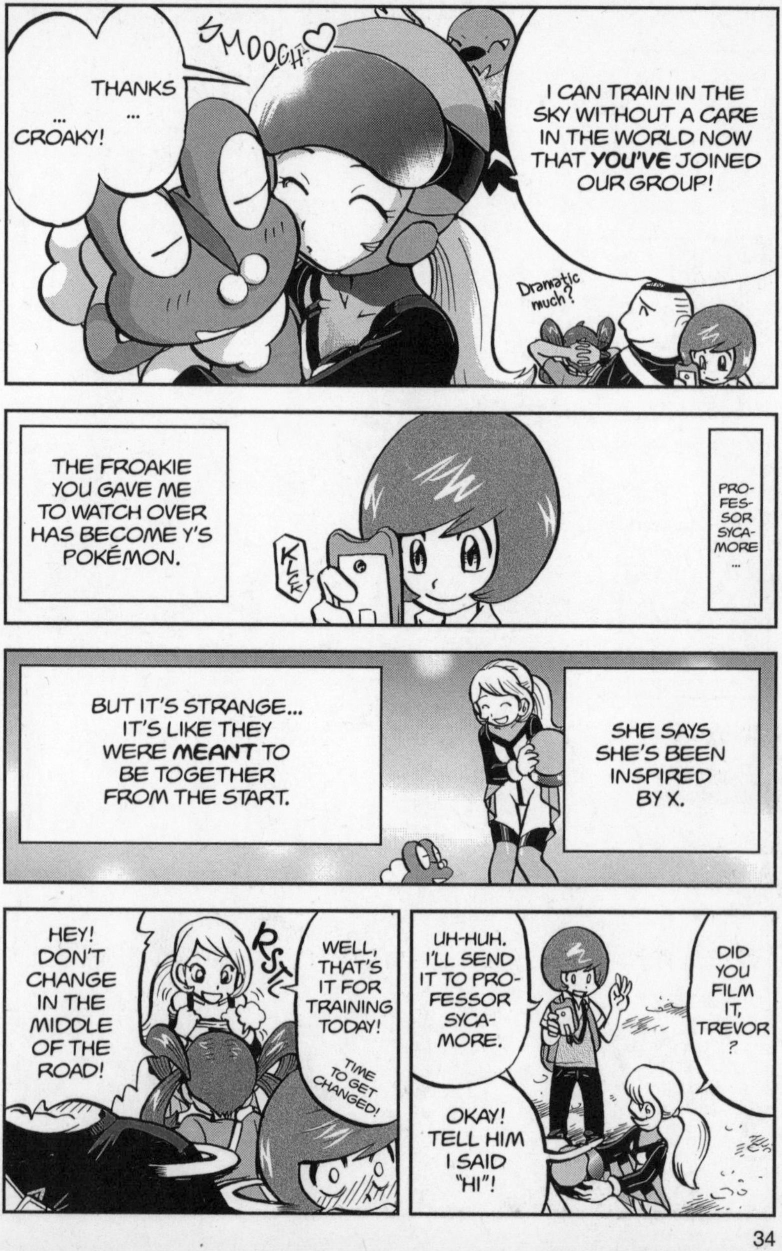
I CAN TRAIN IN THE SKY WITHOUT A CARE IN THE WORLD NOW THAT YOU'VE JOINED OUR GROUP!
SMOOCH♡
THANKS ... ... CROAKY!
Dramatic much?
PROFESSOR SYCAMORE...
THE FROAKIE YOU GAVE ME TO WATCH OVER HAS BECOME Y'S POKÉMON.
KLICK
SHE SAYS SHE'S BEEN INSPIRED BY X.
BUT IT'S STRANGE... IT'S LIKE THEY WERE MEANT TO BE TOGETHER FROM THE START.
DID YOU FILM IT, TREVOR?
UH-HUH. I'LL SEND IT TO PROFESSOR SYCAMORE.
OKAY! TELL HIM I SAID "HI"!
WELL, THAT'S IT FOR TRAINING TODAY!
RSTL
TIME TO GET CHANGED!
HEY! DON'T CHANGE IN THE MIDDLE OF THE ROAD!

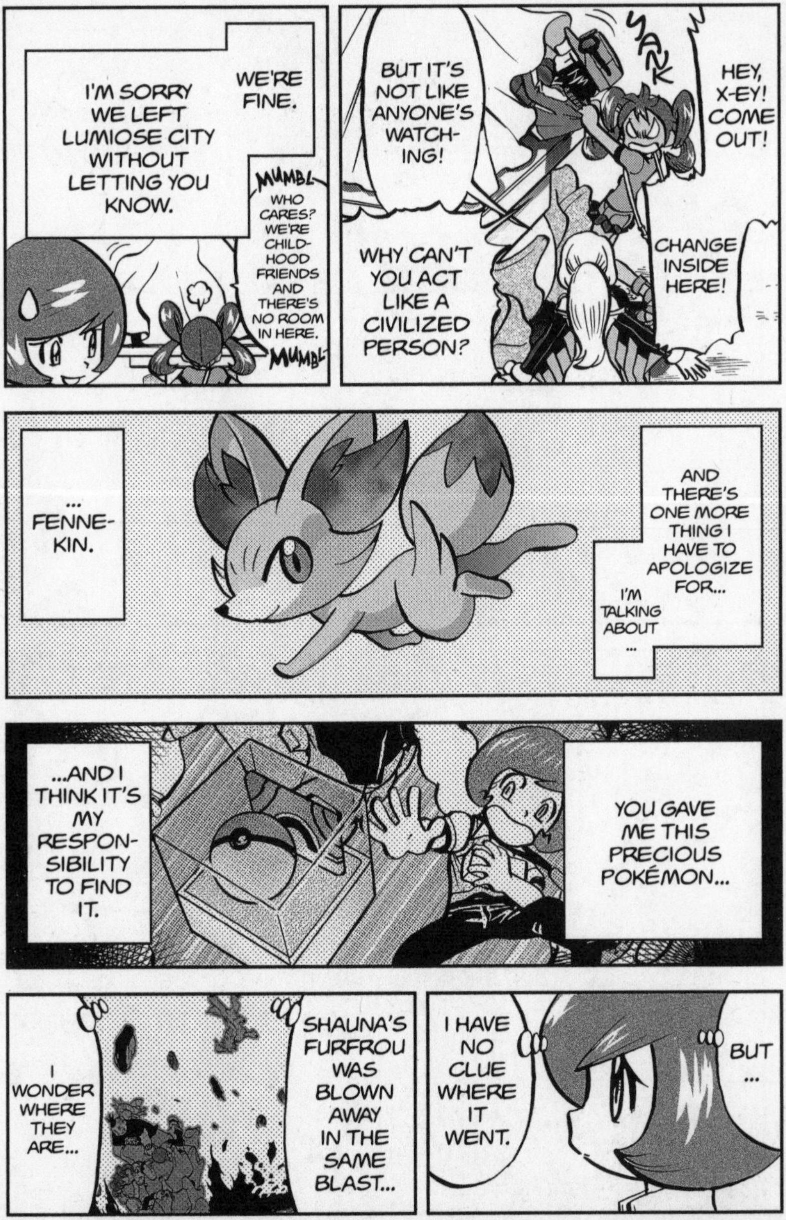
HEY, X-EY! COME OUT!
YANK
BUT IT'S NOT LIKE ANYONE'S WATCHING!
CHANGE INSIDE HERE!
WHY CAN'T YOU ACT LIKE A CIVILIZED PERSON?
WE'RE FINE.
I'M SORRY WE LEFT LUMIOSE CITY WITHOUT LETTING YOU KNOW.
MUMBL
WHO CARES? WE'RE CHILDHOOD FRIENDS AND THERE'S NO ROOM IN HERE.
MUMBL
AND THERE'S ONE MORE THING I HAVE TO APOLOGIZE FOR...
I'M TALKING ABOUT...
... FENNEKIN.
YOU GAVE ME THIS PRECIOUS POKÉMON...
...AND I THINK IT'S MY RESPONSIBILITY TO FIND IT.
BUT...
I HAVE NO CLUE WHERE IT WENT.
SHAUNA'S FURFROU WAS BLOWN AWAY IN THE SAME BLAST...
I WONDER WHERE THEY ARE...

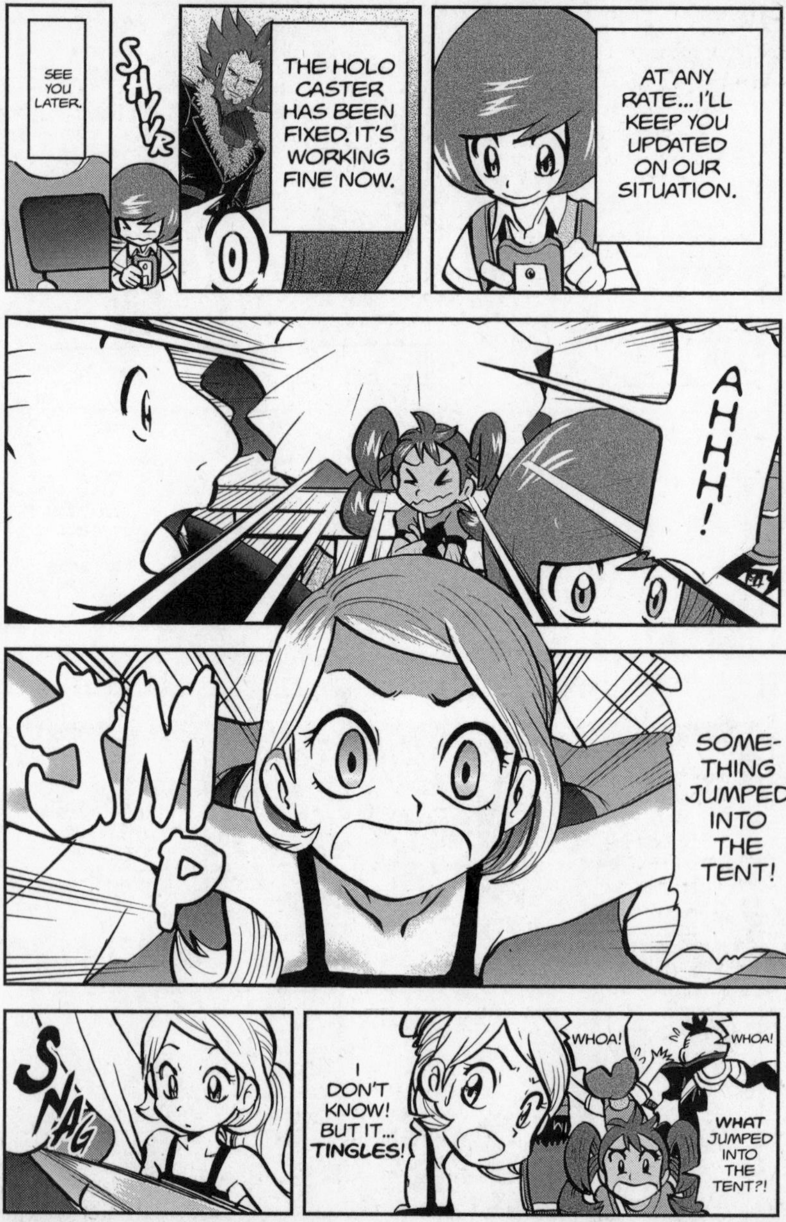
AT ANY RATE... I'LL KEEP YOU UPDATED ON OUR SITUATION.
THE HOLO CASTER HAS BEEN FIXED. IT'S WORKING FINE NOW.
SHVR
SEE YOU LATER.
AHHHH!
SOMETHING JUMPED INTO THE TENT!
JUMP
WHOA!
WHOA!
WHAT JUMPED INTO THE TENT?!
I DON'T KNOW! BUT IT... TINGLES!
SNAG

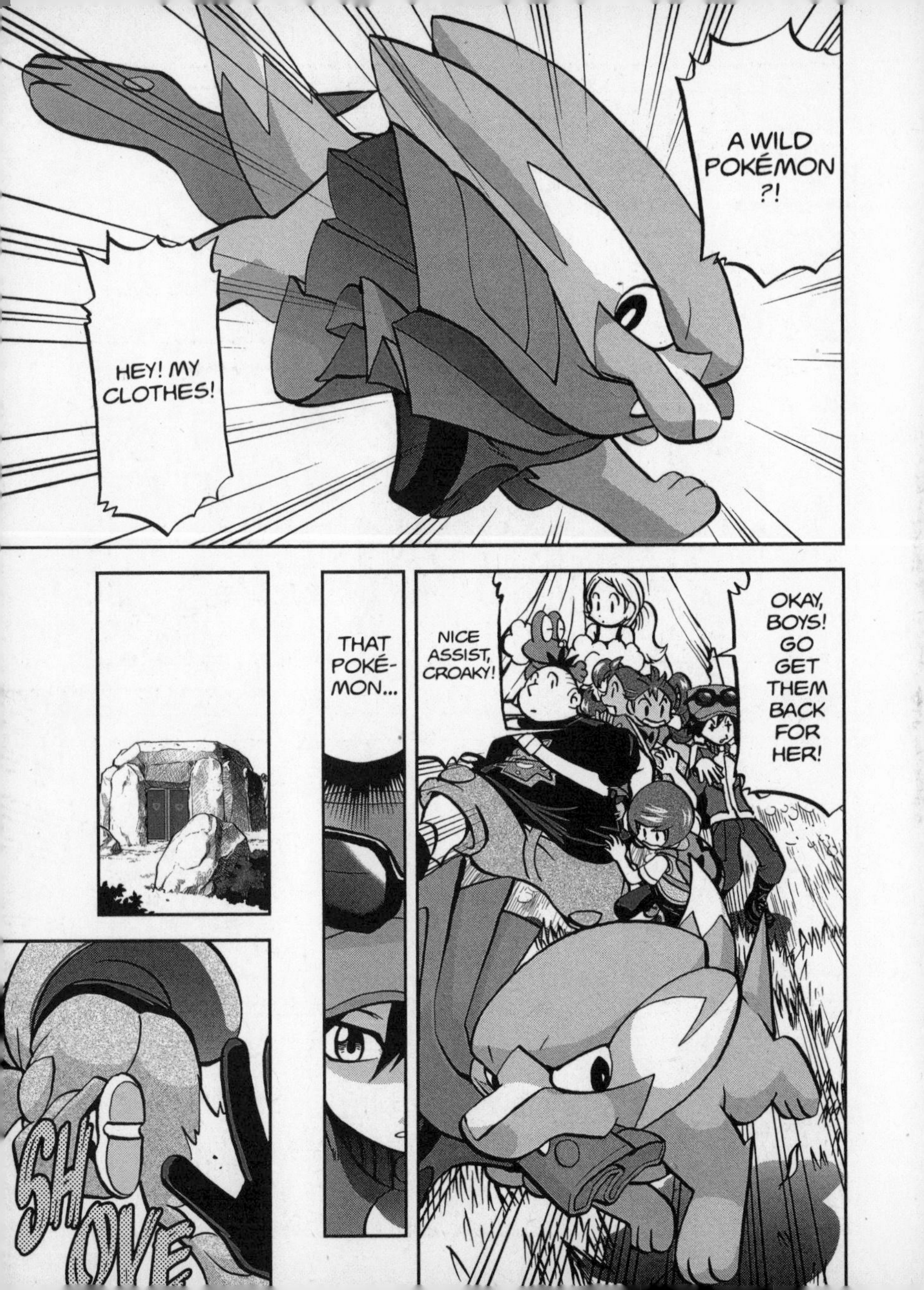
A WILD POKÉMON ?!
HEY! MY CLOTHES!
OKAY, BOYS! GO GET THEM BACK FOR HER!
NICE ASSIST, CROAKY!
THAT POKÉ-MON...
SHOVE

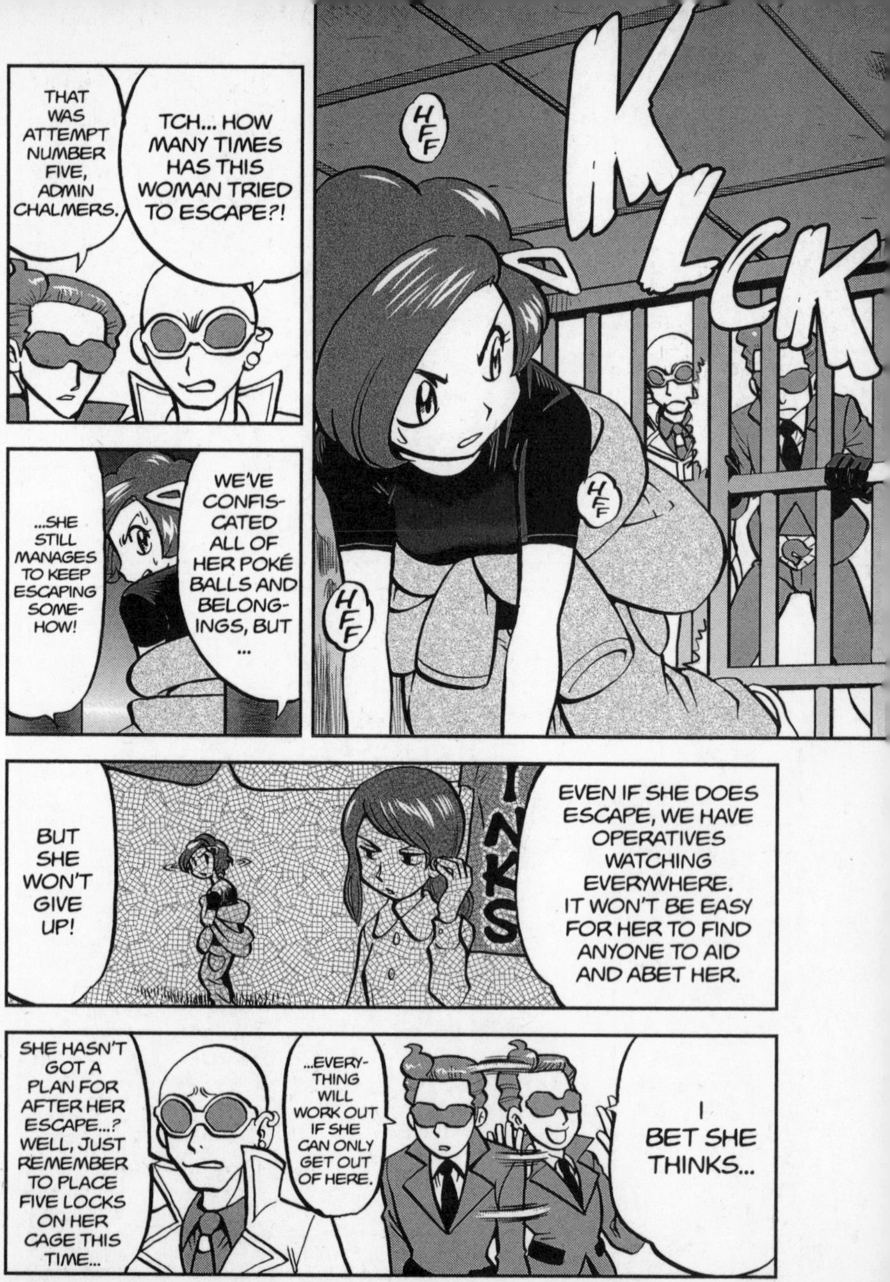
KLCK
HFF
HFF
HFF
TCH... HOW MANY TIMES HAS THIS WOMAN TRIED TO ESCAPE?!
THAT WAS ATTEMPT NUMBER FIVE, ADMIN CHALMERS.
WE'VE CONFISCATED ALL OF HER POKÉ BALLS AND BELONGINGS, BUT ...
...SHE STILL MANAGES TO KEEP ESCAPING SOMEHOW!
EVEN IF SHE DOES ESCAPE, WE HAVE OPERATIVES WATCHING EVERYWHERE. IT WON'T BE EASY FOR HER TO FIND ANYONE TO AID AND ABET HER.
BUT SHE WON'T GIVE UP!
I BET SHE THINKS...
...EVERYTHING WILL WORK OUT IF SHE CAN ONLY GET OUT OF HERE.
SHE HASN'T GOT A PLAN FOR AFTER HER ESCAPE...? WELL, JUST REMEMBER TO PLACE FIVE LOCKS ON HER CAGE THIS TIME...

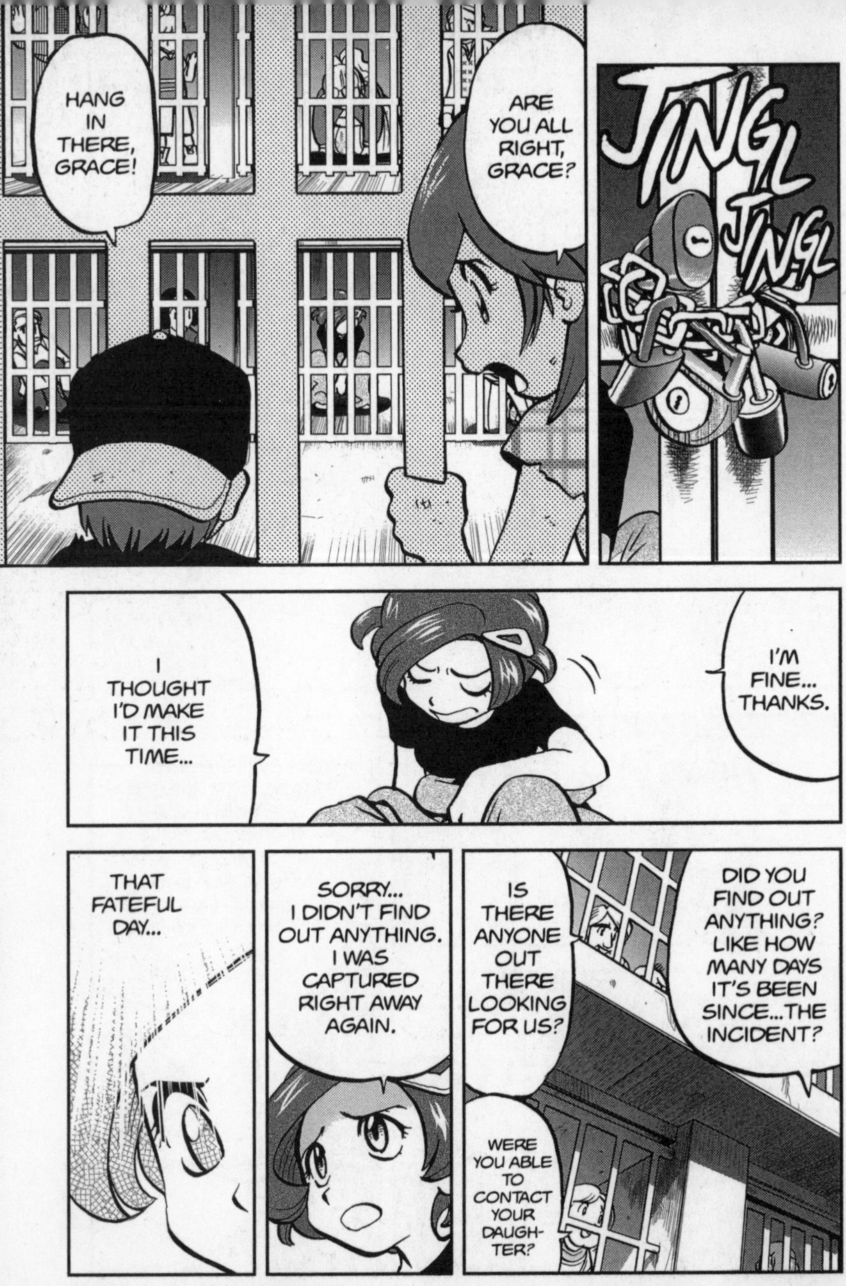
JINGL
JINGL
JINGL
ARE YOU ALL RIGHT, GRACE?
HANG IN THERE, GRACE!
I'M FINE... THANKS.
I THOUGHT I'D MAKE IT THIS TIME...
DID YOU FIND OUT ANYTHING? LIKE HOW MANY DAYS IT'S BEEN SINCE...THE INCIDENT?
IS THERE ANYONE OUT THERE LOOKING FOR US?
WERE YOU ABLE TO CONTACT YOUR DAUGH-TER?
SORRY... I DIDN'T FIND OUT ANYTHING. I WAS CAPTURED RIGHT AWAY AGAIN.
THAT FATEFUL DAY...

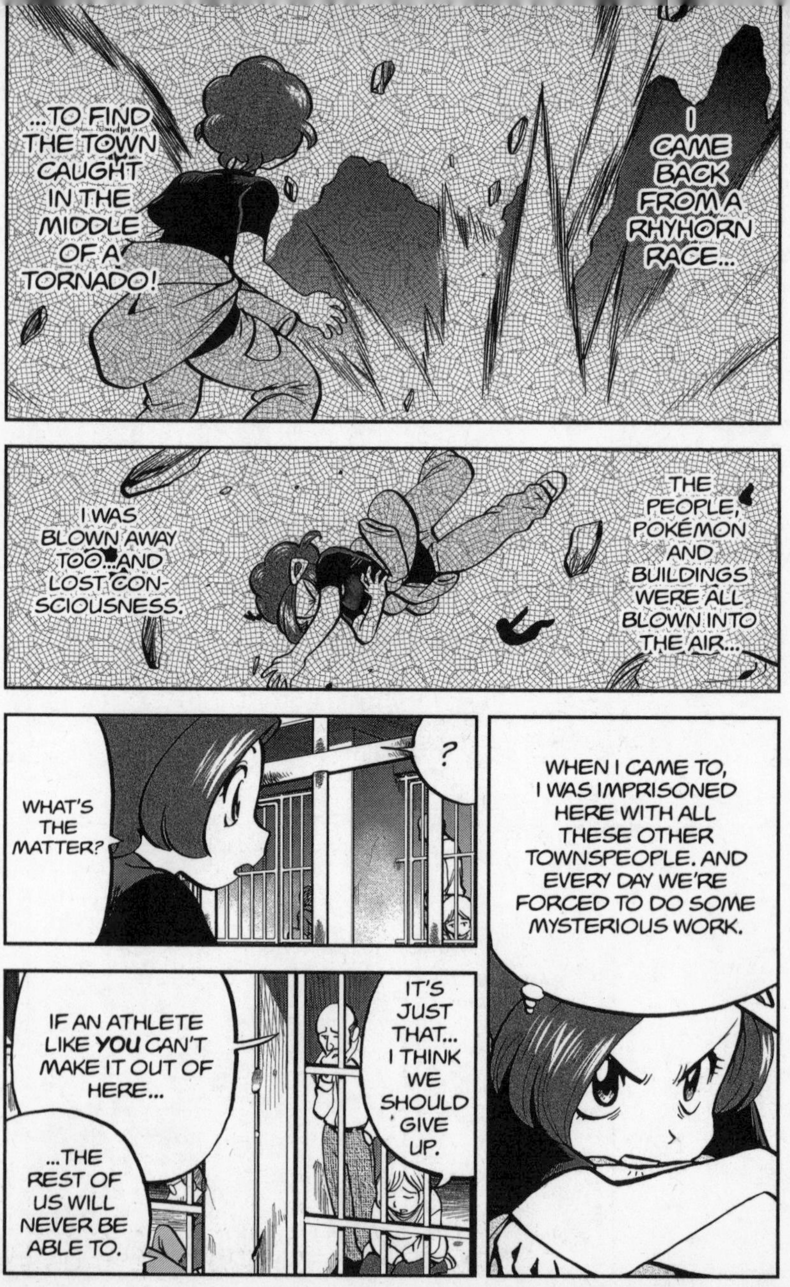
I CAME BACK FROM A RHYHORN RACE...
...TO FIND THE TOWN CAUGHT IN THE MIDDLE OF A TORNADO!
THE PEOPLE, POKÉMON AND BUILDINGS WERE ALL BLOWN INTO THE AIR...
I WAS BLOWN AWAY TOO...AND LOST CON-SCIOUSNESS.
WHEN I CAME TO, I WAS IMPRISONED HERE WITH ALL THESE OTHER TOWNSPEOPLE. AND EVERY DAY WE'RE FORCED TO DO SOME MYSTERIOUS WORK.
?
WHAT'S THE MATTER?
IT'S JUST THAT... I THINK WE SHOULD GIVE UP.
IF AN ATHLETE LIKE **YOU** CAN'T MAKE IT OUT OF HERE...
...THE REST OF US WILL NEVER BE ABLE TO.

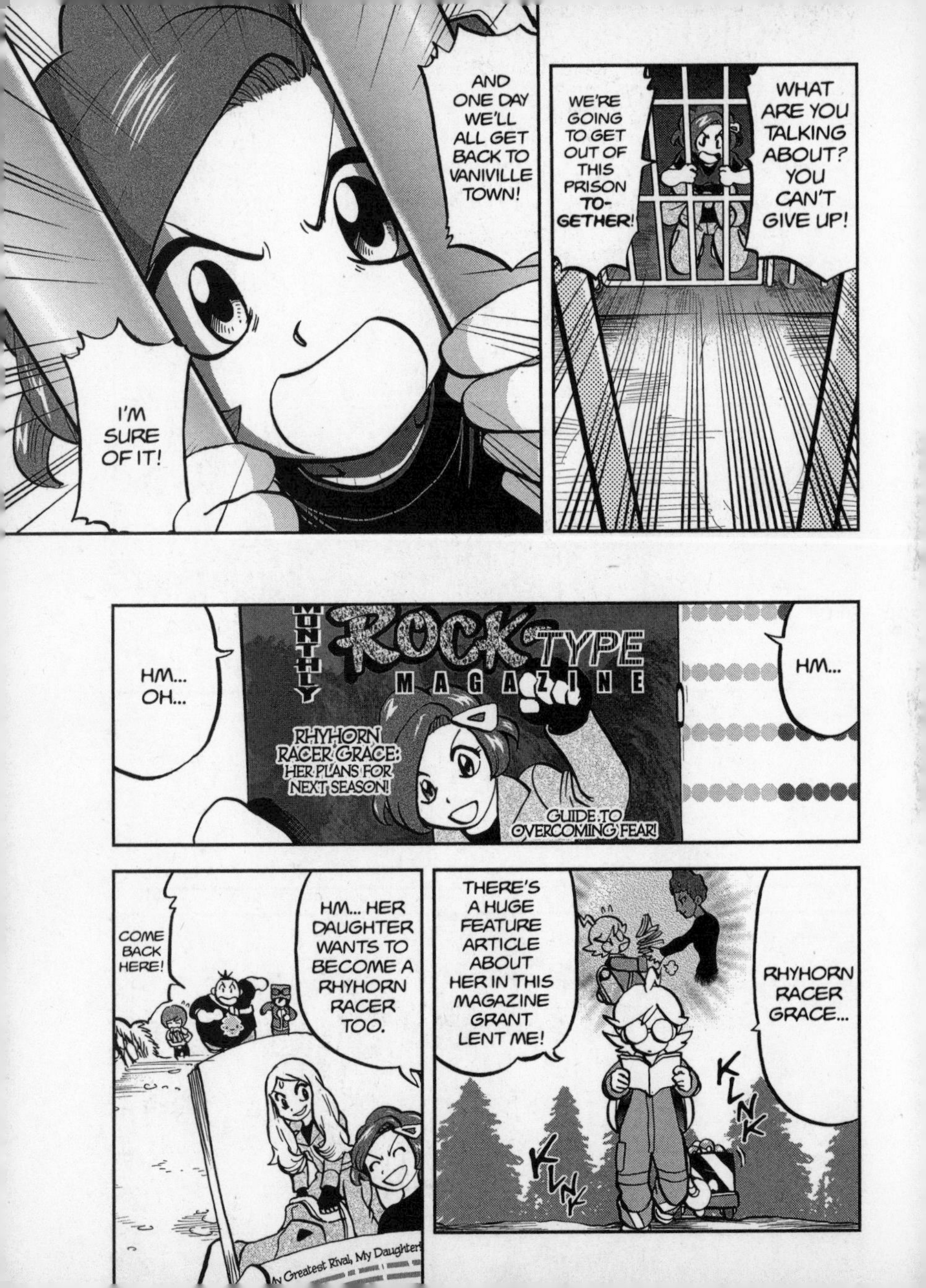
WHAT ARE YOU TALKING ABOUT? YOU CAN'T GIVE UP!
WE'RE GOING TO GET OUT OF THIS PRISON TO-GETHER!
AND ONE DAY WE'LL ALL GET BACK TO VANIVILLE TOWN!
I'M SURE OF IT!
HM...
MONTHLY ROCK-TYPE MAGAZINE
RHYHORN RACER GRACE: HER PLANS FOR NEXT SEASON!
GUIDE TO OVERCOMING FEAR!
HM... OH...
RHYHORN RACER GRACE...
KLNK
THERE'S A HUGE FEATURE ARTICLE ABOUT HER IN THIS MAGAZINE GRANT LENT ME!
KLNK
HM... HER DAUGHTER WANTS TO BECOME A RHYHORN RACER TOO.
COME BACK HERE!
My Greatest Rival, My Daughter!

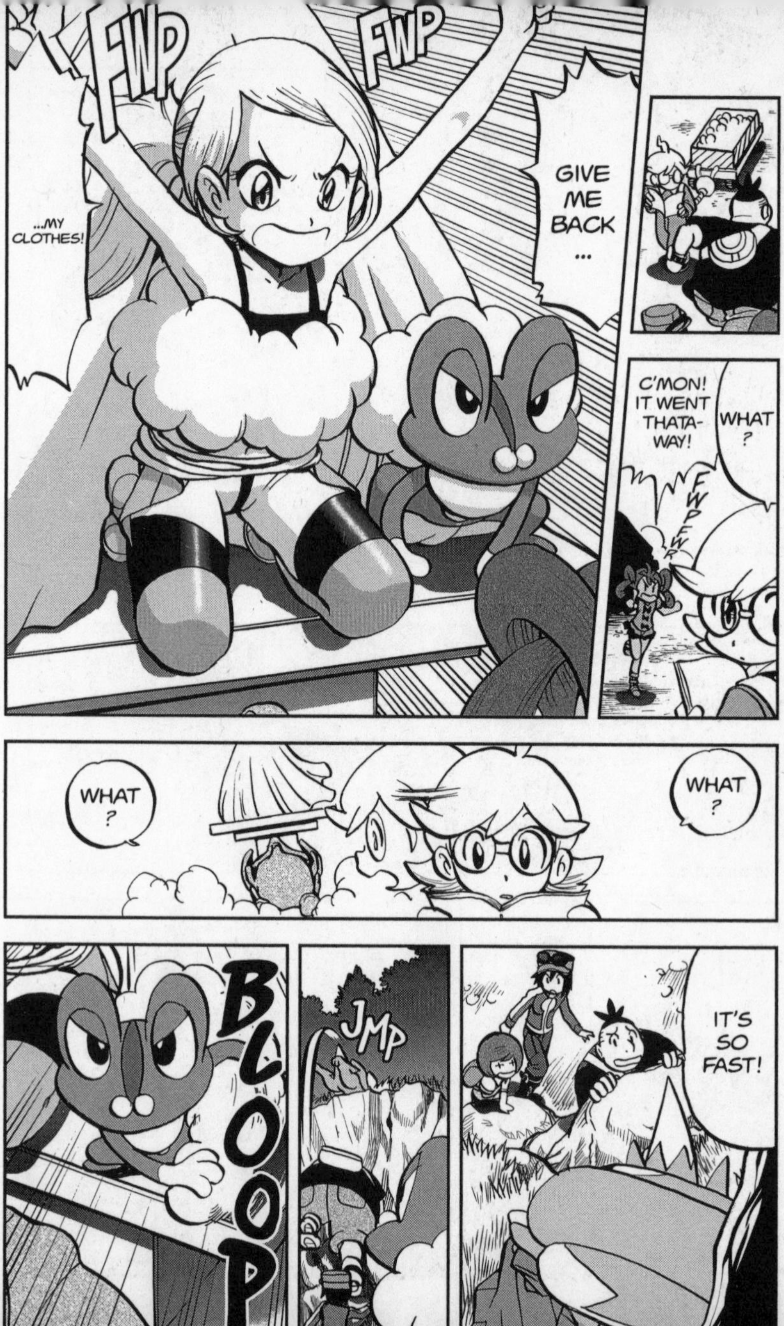
WHAT ?
C'MON! IT WENT THATA-WAY!
FWPEWR
FWP
FWP
GIVE ME BACK ...
...MY CLOTHES!
WHAT ?
WHAT ?
IT'S SO FAST!
JMP
BLOOP

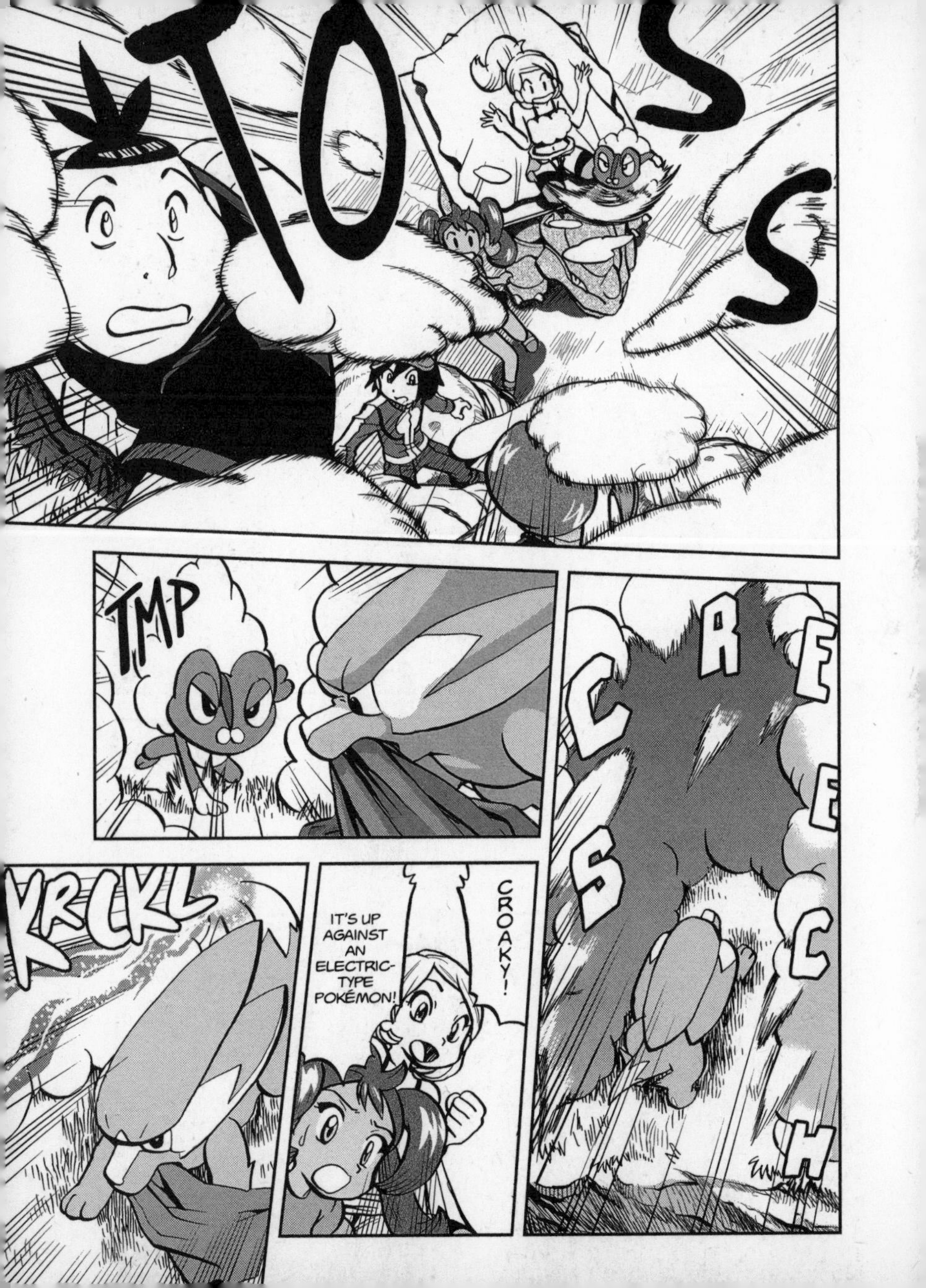
TOSS
TMP
CROAKY!
IT'S UP AGAINST AN ELECTRIC-TYPE POKÉMON!
KRCKL

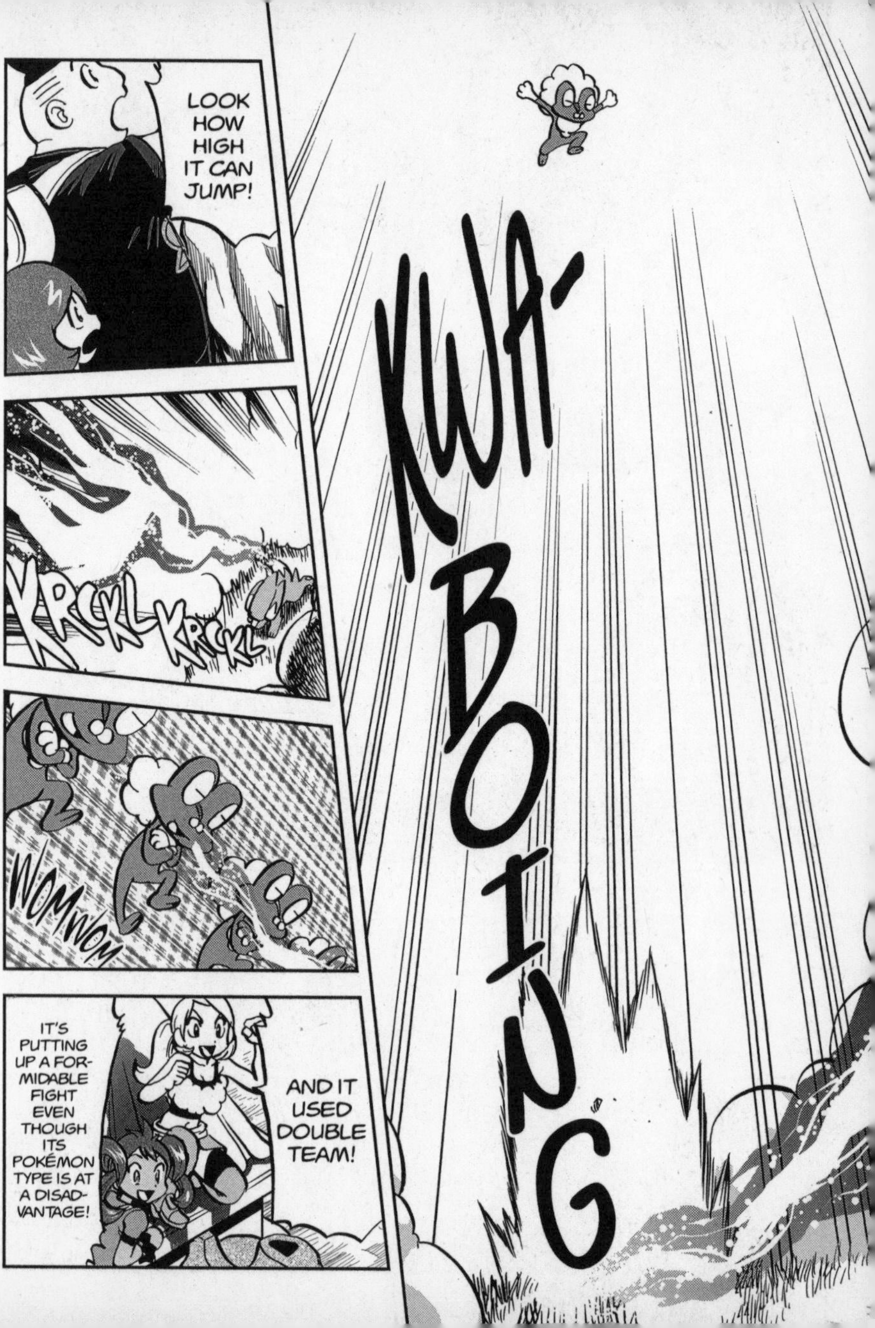
KWA-BOING
LOOK HOW HIGH IT CAN JUMP!
KRCKL KRCKL
WOMWOM
AND IT USED DOUBLE TEAM!
IT'S PUTTING UP A FOR-MIDABLE FIGHT EVEN THOUGH ITS POKÉMON TYPE IS AT A DISAD-VANTAGE!

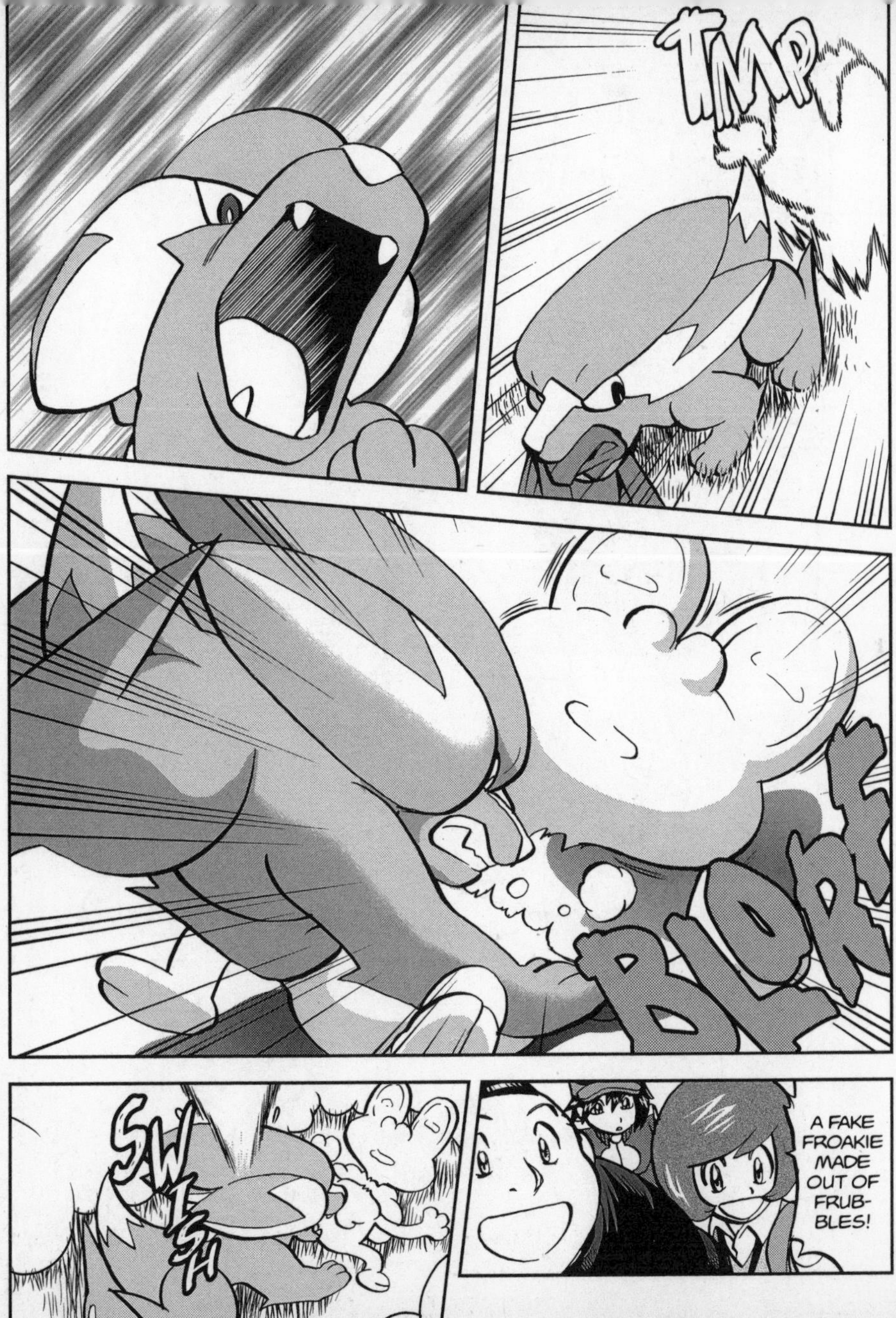
TMP
BLORF
A FAKE FROAKIE MADE OUT OF FRUB-BLES!
SWISH

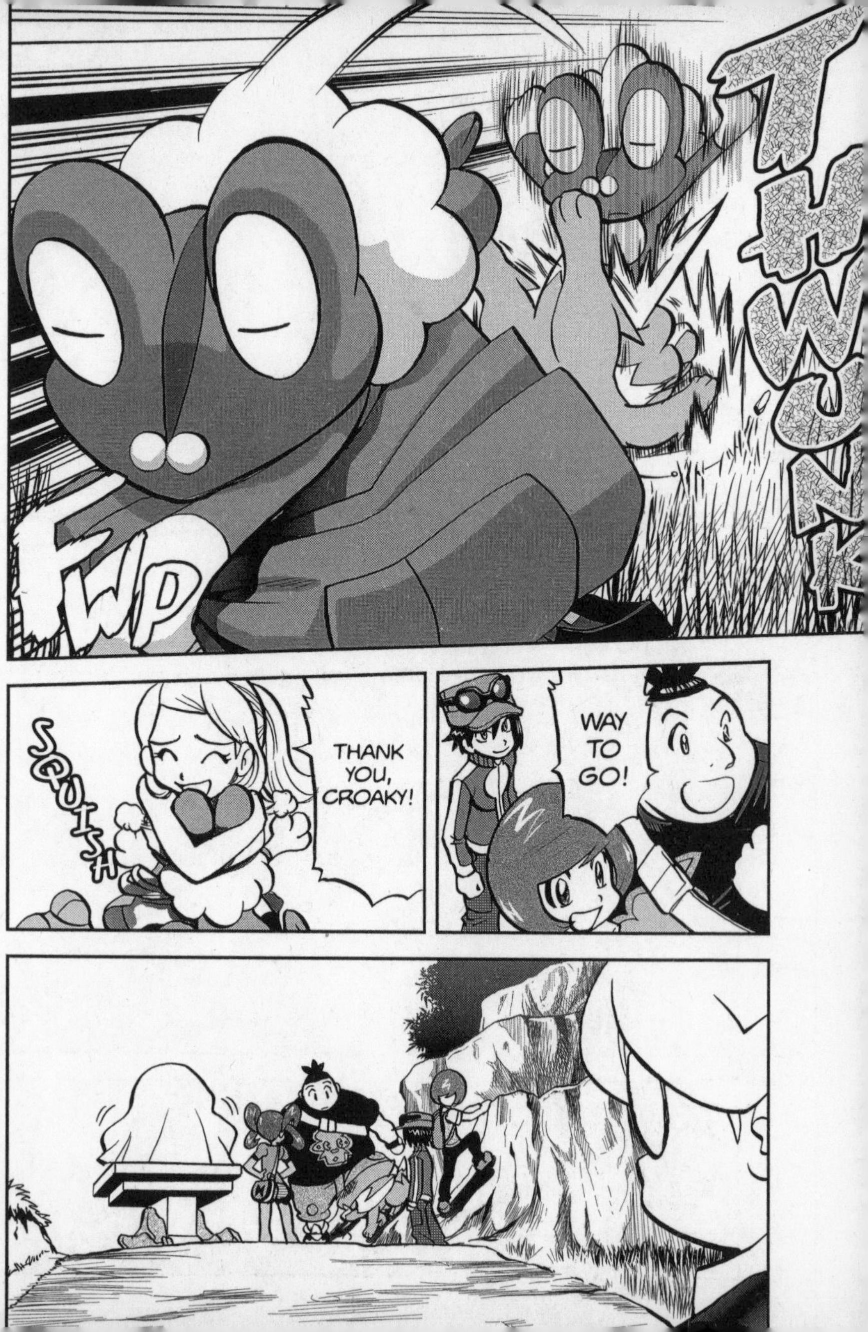
THWUNK
FWP
WAY TO GO!
THANK YOU, CROAKY!
SQUISH

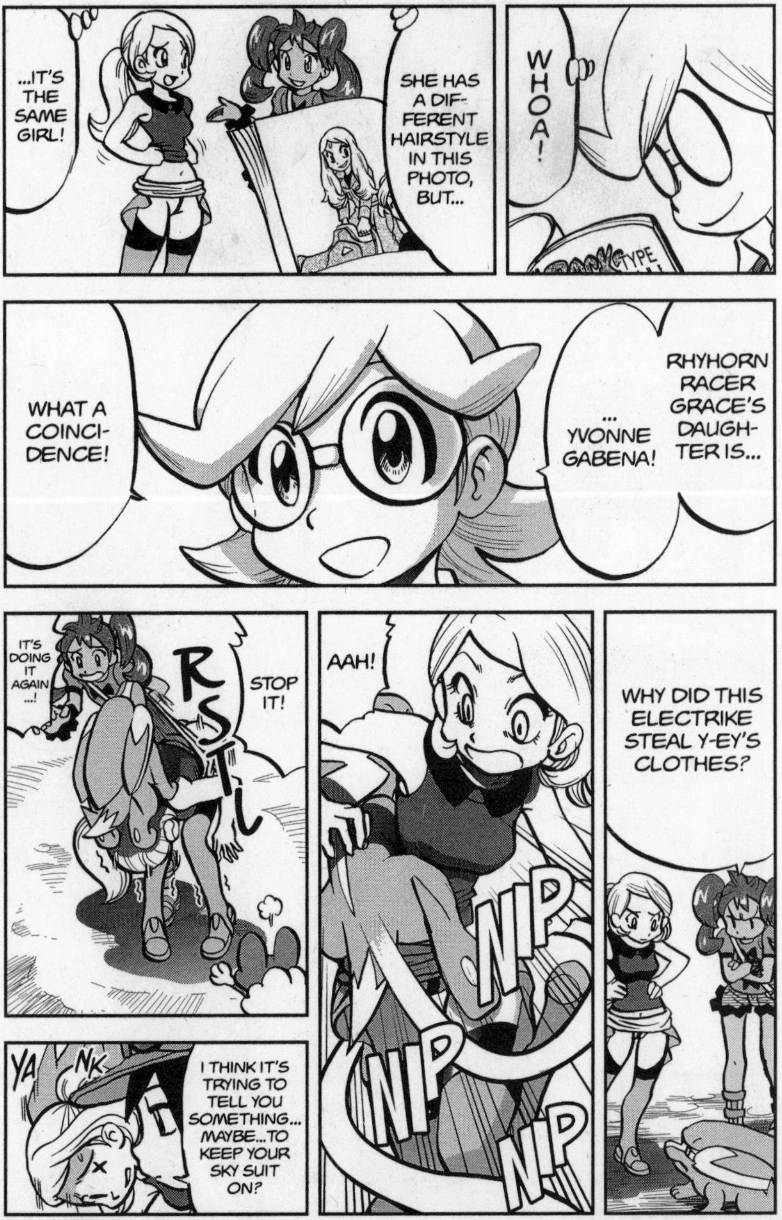
WHOA!
SHE HAS A DIFFERENT HAIRSTYLE IN THIS PHOTO, BUT...
...IT'S THE SAME GIRL!
TYPE
RHYHORN RACER GRACE'S DAUGHTER IS...
... YVONNE GABENA!
WHAT A COINCIDENCE!
WHY DID THIS ELECTRIKE STEAL Y-EY'S CLOTHES?
AAH!
NIP NIP NIP NIP
STOP IT!
RSTL
IT'S DOING IT AGAIN ...!
YANK
I THINK IT'S TRYING TO TELL YOU SOMETHING... MAYBE...TO KEEP YOUR SKY SUIT ON?

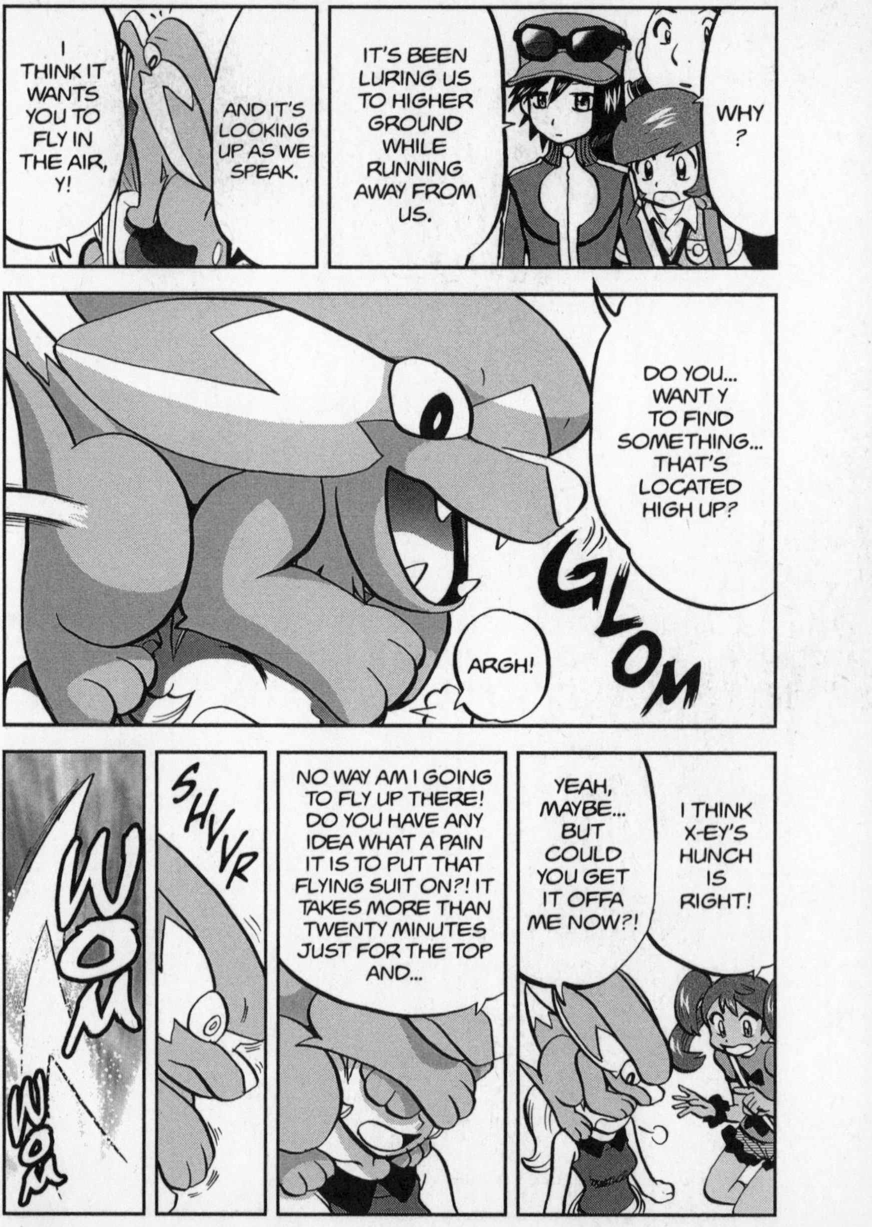

WHY?
IT'S BEEN LURING US TO HIGHER GROUND WHILE RUNNING AWAY FROM US.
AND IT'S LOOKING UP AS WE SPEAK.
I THINK IT WANTS YOU TO FLY IN THE AIR, Y!
DO YOU... WANT Y TO FIND SOMETHING... THAT'S LOCATED HIGH UP?
GLOM
ARGH!
I THINK X-EY'S HUNCH IS RIGHT!
YEAH, MAYBE... BUT COULD YOU GET IT OFFA ME NOW?!
NO WAY AM I GOING TO FLY UP THERE! DO YOU HAVE ANY IDEA WHAT A PAIN IT IS TO PUT THAT FLYING SUIT ON?! IT TAKES MORE THAN TWENTY MINUTES JUST FOR THE TOP AND...
SHVVVR
WOM
WOM

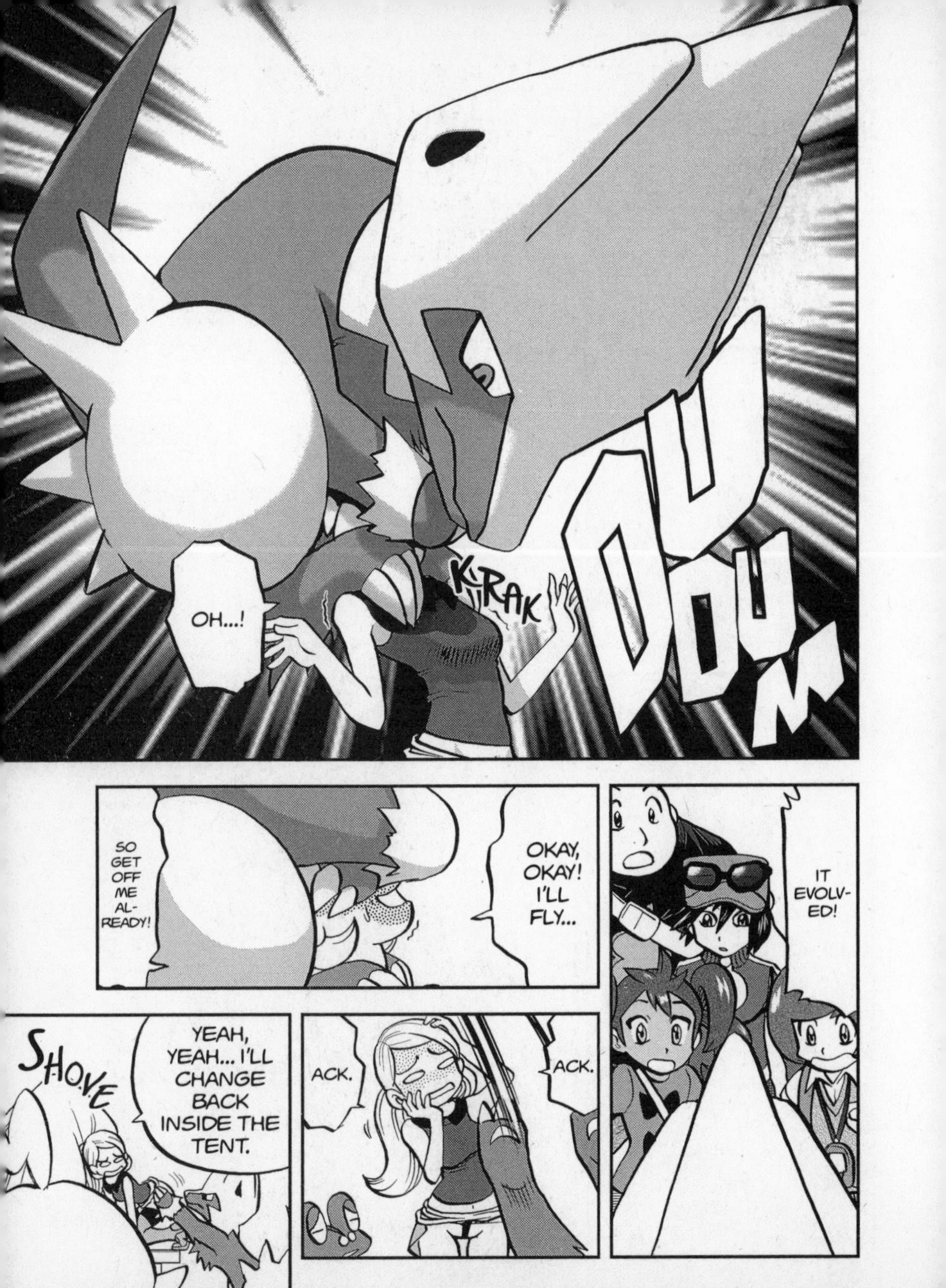
DOUM
KRAK
OH...!
IT EVOLV-ED!
OKAY, OKAY! I'LL FLY...
SO GET OFF ME AL-READY!
ACK.
ACK.
YEAH, YEAH... I'LL CHANGE BACK INSIDE THE TENT.
SHOVE

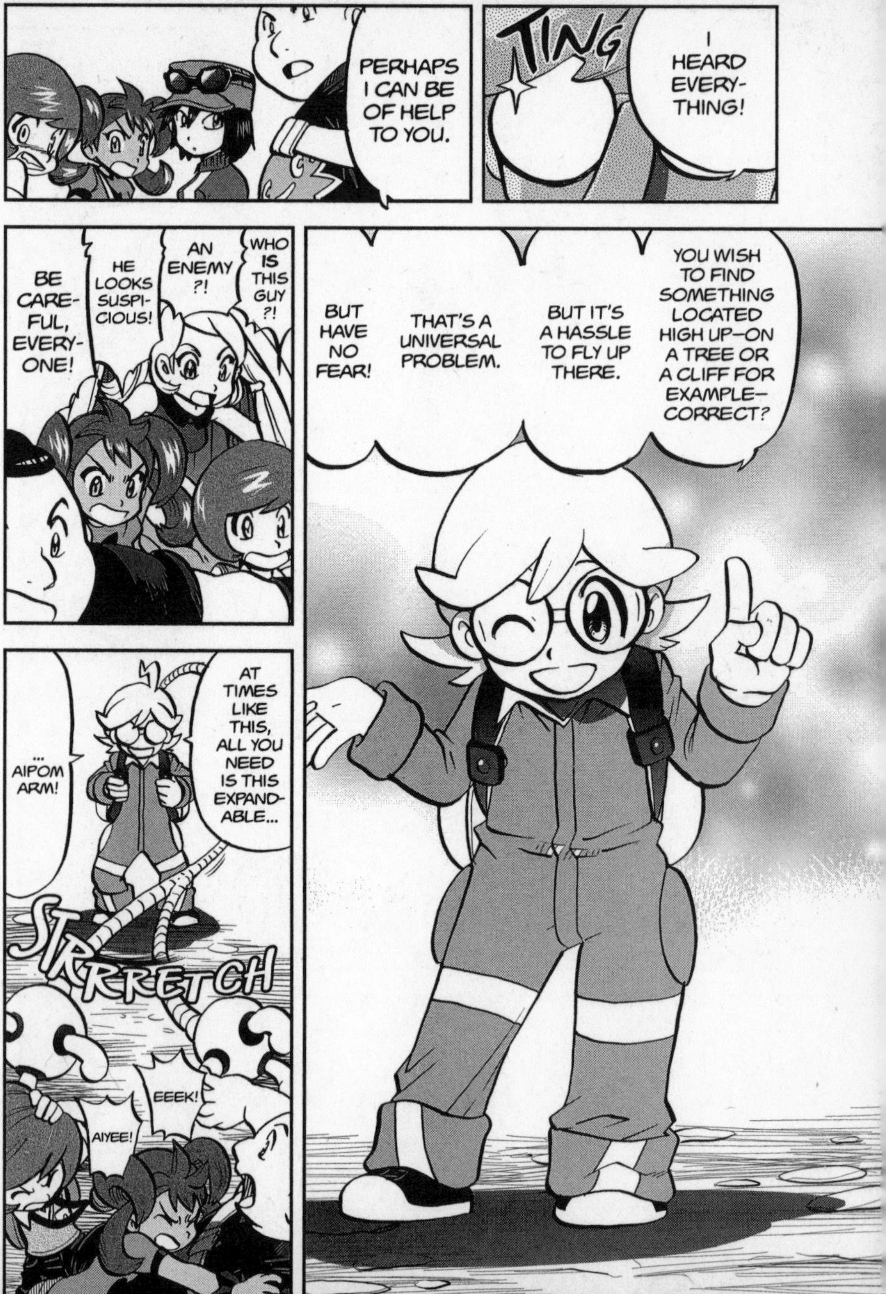
TING
I HEARD EVERYTHING!
PERHAPS I CAN BE OF HELP TO YOU.
YOU WISH TO FIND SOMETHING LOCATED HIGH UP—ON A TREE OR A CLIFF FOR EXAMPLE—CORRECT?
BUT IT'S A HASSLE TO FLY UP THERE.
THAT'S A UNIVERSAL PROBLEM.
BUT HAVE NO FEAR!
WHO IS THIS GUY?!
AN ENEMY?!
HE LOOKS SUSPICIOUS!
BE CAREFUL, EVERYONE!
AT TIMES LIKE THIS, ALL YOU NEED IS THIS EXPANDABLE...
...AIPOM ARM!
STRRRETCH
EEEK!
AIYEE!

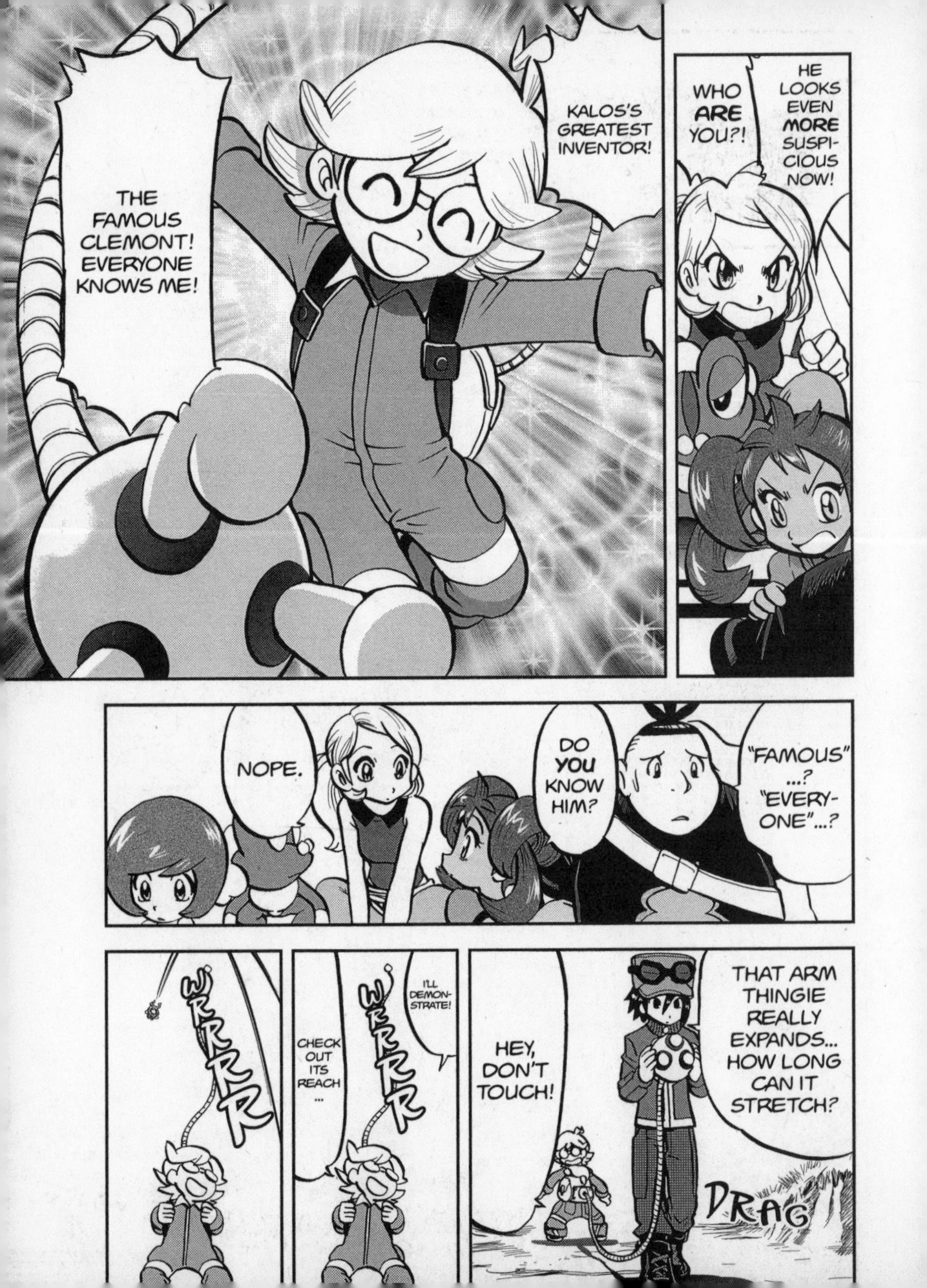
HE LOOKS EVEN MORE SUSPICIOUS NOW!
WHO ARE YOU?!
KALOS'S GREATEST INVENTOR!
THE FAMOUS CLEMONT! EVERYONE KNOWS ME!
"FAMOUS"...? "EVERYONE"...?
DO YOU KNOW HIM?
NOPE.
THAT ARM THINGIE REALLY EXPANDS... HOW LONG CAN IT STRETCH?
DRAG
HEY, DON'T TOUCH!
I'LL DEMONSTRATE!
CHECK OUT ITS REACH...
WRRRR
WRRRR

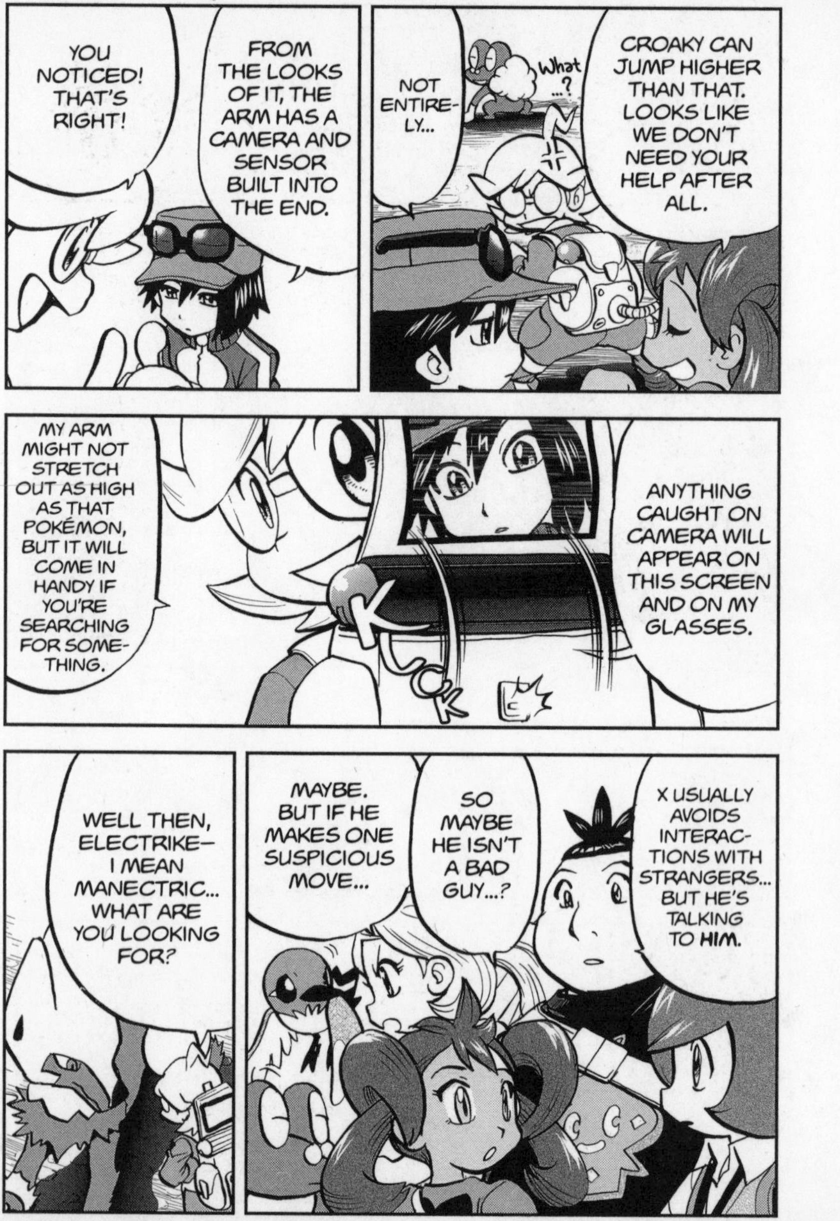
CROAKY CAN JUMP HIGHER THAN THAT. LOOKS LIKE WE DON'T NEED YOUR HELP AFTER ALL.
What ...?
NOT ENTIRE-LY...
FROM THE LOOKS OF IT, THE ARM HAS A CAMERA AND SENSOR BUILT INTO THE END.
YOU NOTICED! THAT'S RIGHT!
MY ARM MIGHT NOT STRETCH OUT AS HIGH AS THAT POKÉMON, BUT IT WILL COME IN HANDY IF YOU'RE SEARCHING FOR SOME-THING.
ANYTHING CAUGHT ON CAMERA WILL APPEAR ON THIS SCREEN AND ON MY GLASSES.
X USUALLY AVOIDS INTERAC-TIONS WITH STRANGERS... BUT HE'S TALKING TO **HIM**.
SO MAYBE HE ISN'T A BAD GUY...?
MAYBE. BUT IF HE MAKES ONE SUSPICIOUS MOVE...
WELL THEN, ELECTRIKE— I MEAN MANECTRIC... WHAT ARE YOU LOOKING FOR?

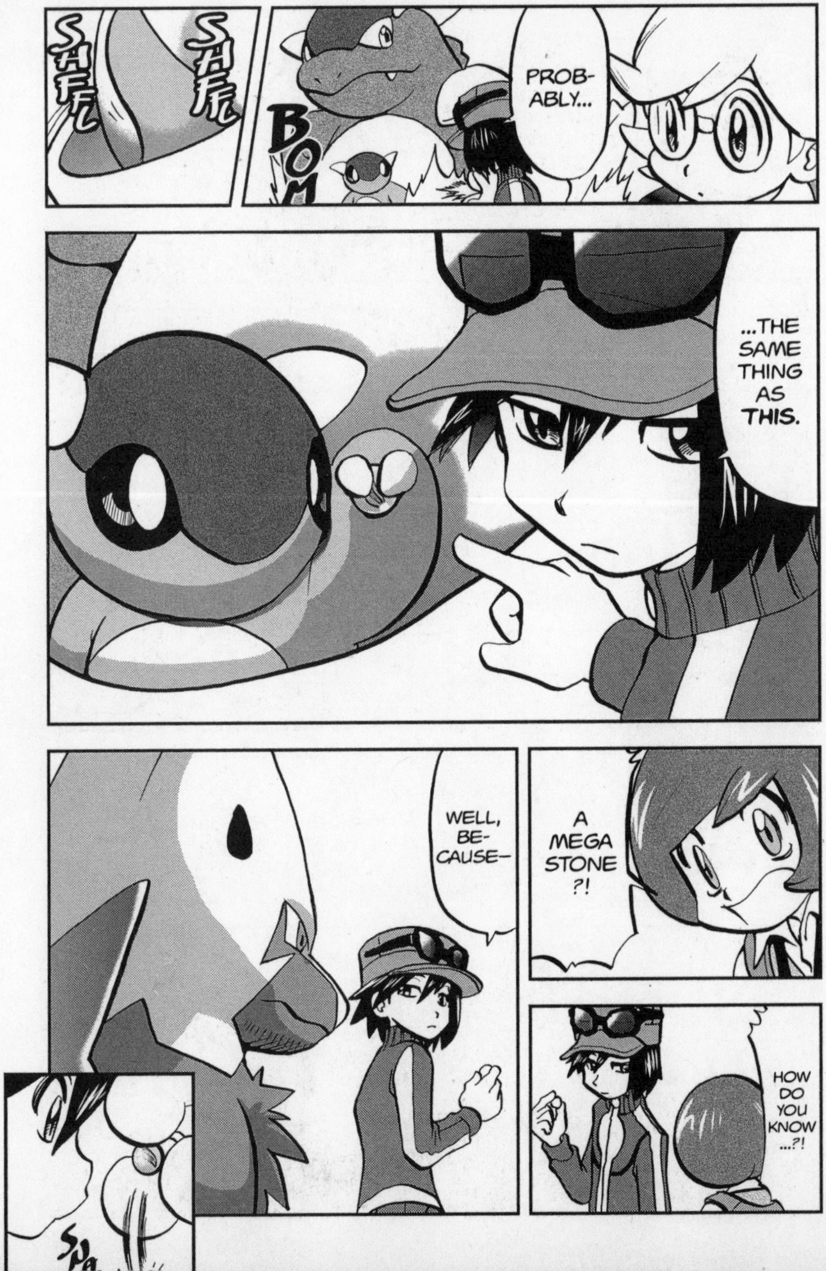
PROB-
ABLY...
BOM
SHFFL
SHFFL
...THE SAME THING AS THIS.
A MEGA STONE ?!
HOW DO YOU KNOW ...?!
WELL, BE-CAUSE—

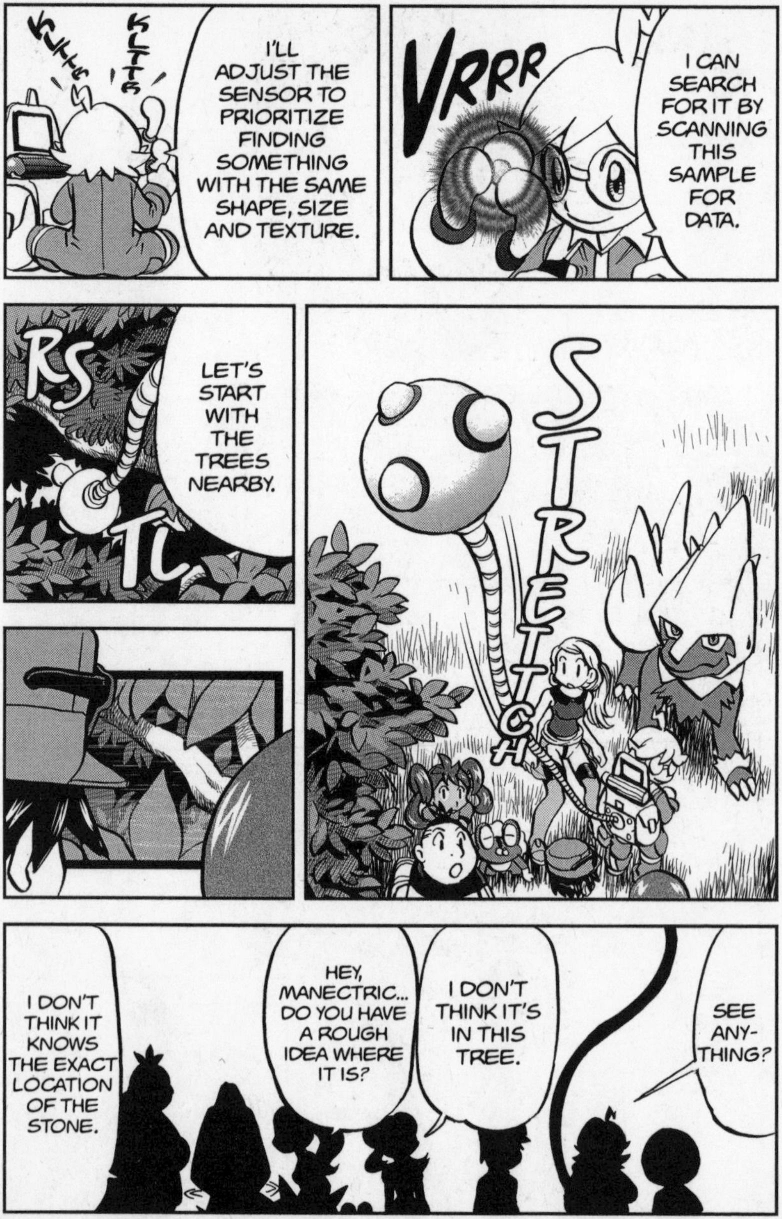
VRRR
I CAN SEARCH FOR IT BY SCANNING THIS SAMPLE FOR DATA.
I'LL ADJUST THE SENSOR TO PRIORITIZE FINDING SOMETHING WITH THE SAME SHAPE, SIZE AND TEXTURE.
STRETCH
RS
TL
LET'S START WITH THE TREES NEARBY.
SEE ANY-THING?
I DON'T THINK IT'S IN THIS TREE.
HEY, MANECTRIC... DO YOU HAVE A ROUGH IDEA WHERE IT IS?
I DON'T THINK IT KNOWS THE EXACT LOCATION OF THE STONE.

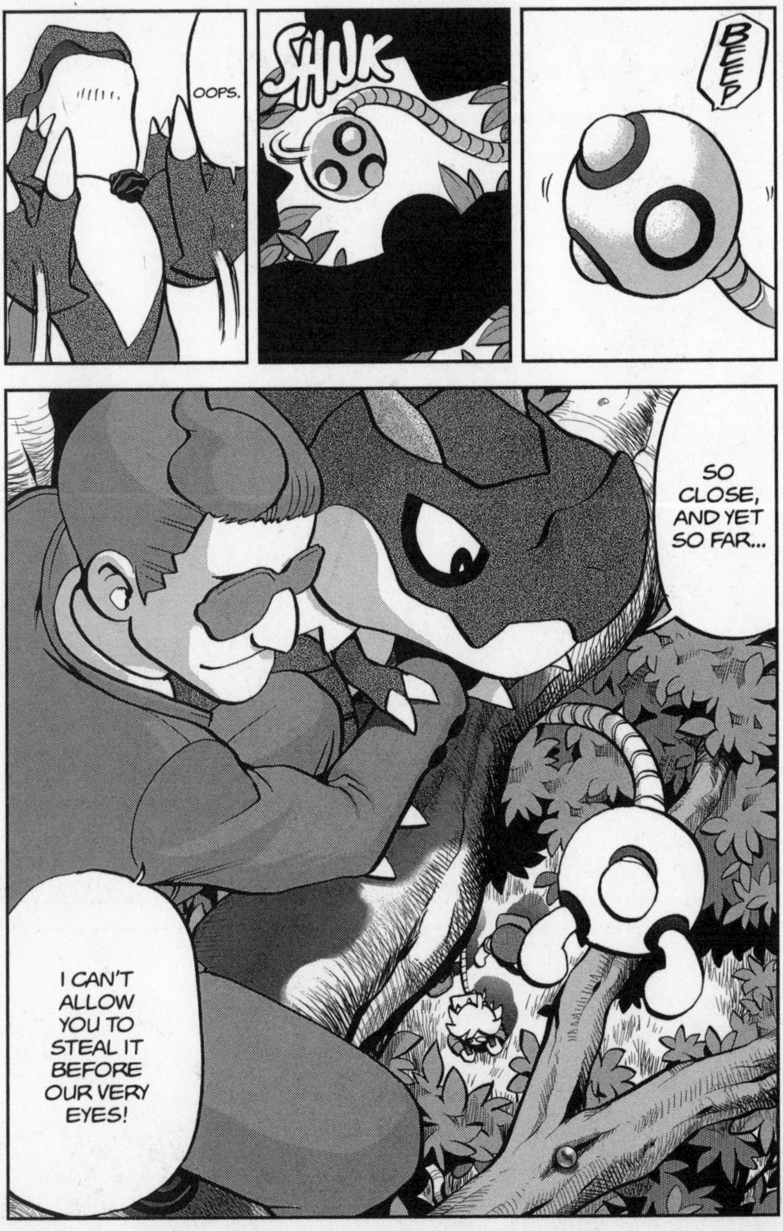
BEEP
SHNK
OOPS.
SO CLOSE, AND YET SO FAR...
I CAN'T ALLOW YOU TO STEAL IT BEFORE OUR VERY EYES!

Current Location

Route 5
Versant Road

Roller Skaters from across the Kalos region gather on this hilly path to demonstrate their best skills.

Adventure 13 Overthrowing a Tyrunt

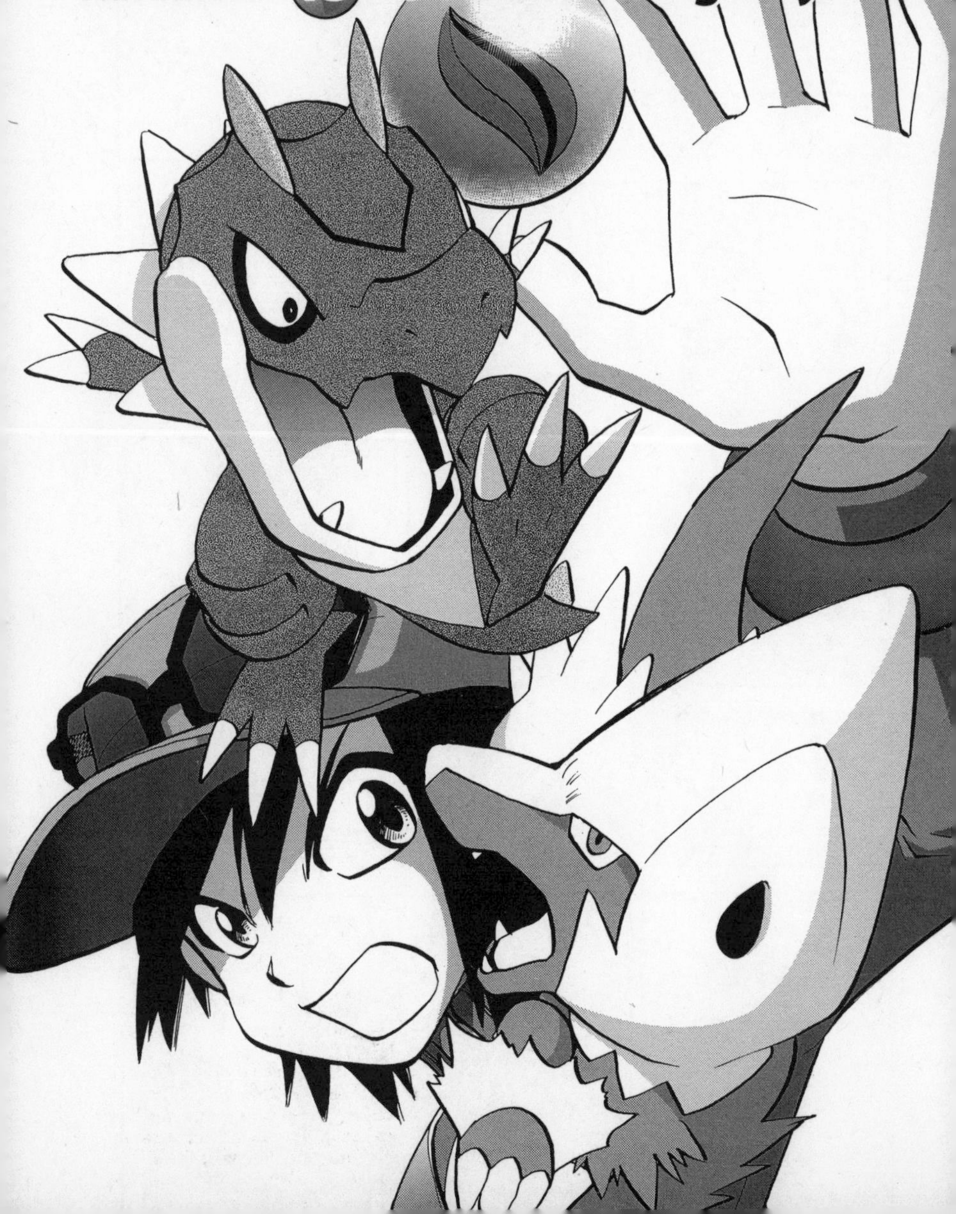

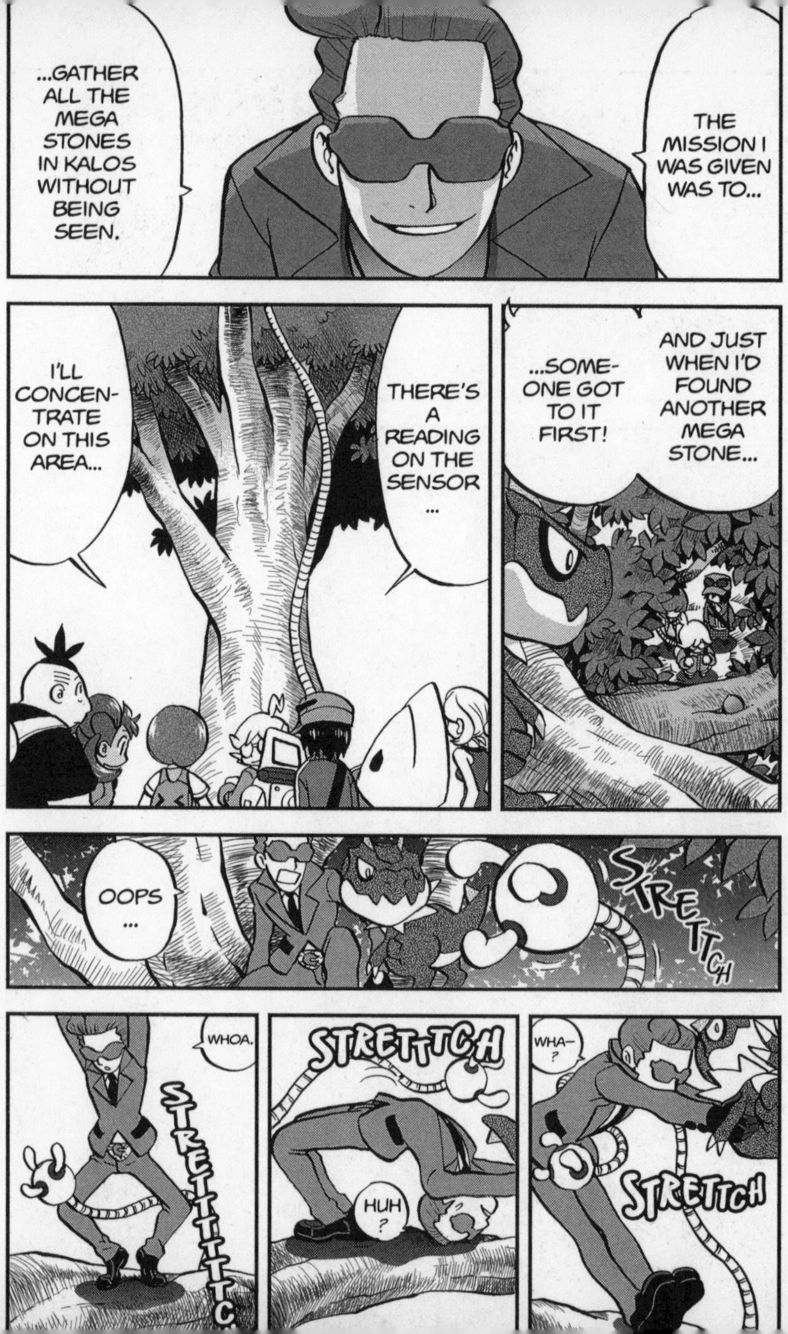
THE MISSION I WAS GIVEN WAS TO...
...GATHER ALL THE MEGA STONES IN KALOS WITHOUT BEING SEEN.
AND JUST WHEN I'D FOUND ANOTHER MEGA STONE...
...SOME-ONE GOT TO IT FIRST!
THERE'S A READING ON THE SENSOR ...
I'LL CONCEN-TRATE ON THIS AREA...
STRETTCH
OOPS ...
WHA- ?
STRETTCH
STRETTTCH
HUH ?
WHOA.
STRETTTTTTC

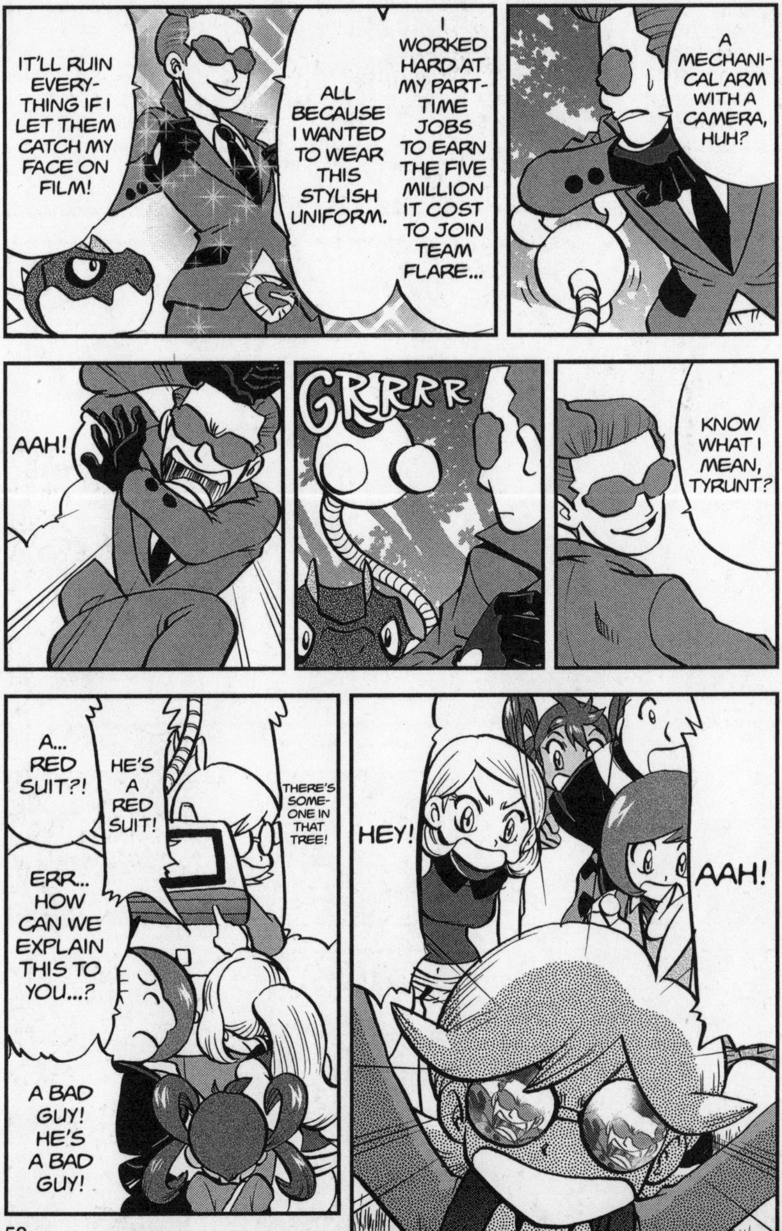
A MECHANICAL ARM WITH A CAMERA, HUH?
I WORKED HARD AT MY PART-TIME JOBS TO EARN THE FIVE MILLION IT COST TO JOIN TEAM FLARE...
ALL BECAUSE I WANTED TO WEAR THIS STYLISH UNIFORM.
IT'LL RUIN EVERYTHING IF I LET THEM CATCH MY FACE ON FILM!
KNOW WHAT I MEAN, TYRUNT?
GRRRR
AAH!
HEY!
AAH!
THERE'S SOMEONE IN THAT TREE!
HE'S A RED SUIT!
A... RED SUIT?!
ERR... HOW CAN WE EXPLAIN THIS TO YOU...?
A BAD GUY! HE'S A BAD GUY!

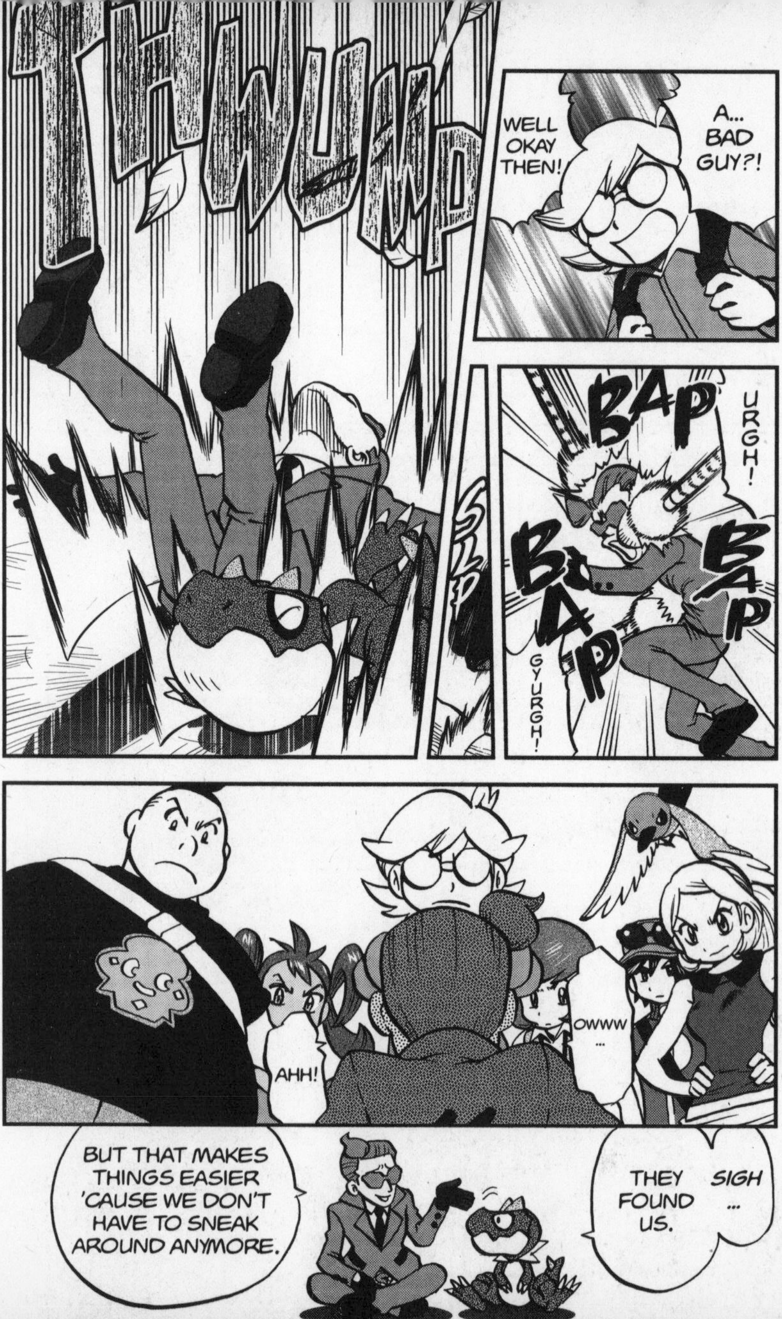
A... BAD GUY?!
WELL OKAY THEN!
BAP
URGH!
BAP
B... BAP
GYURGH!
THWUMP
SLIP
OWWW...
AHH!
SIGH...
THEY FOUND US.
BUT THAT MAKES THINGS EASIER 'CAUSE WE DON'T HAVE TO SNEAK AROUND ANYMORE.

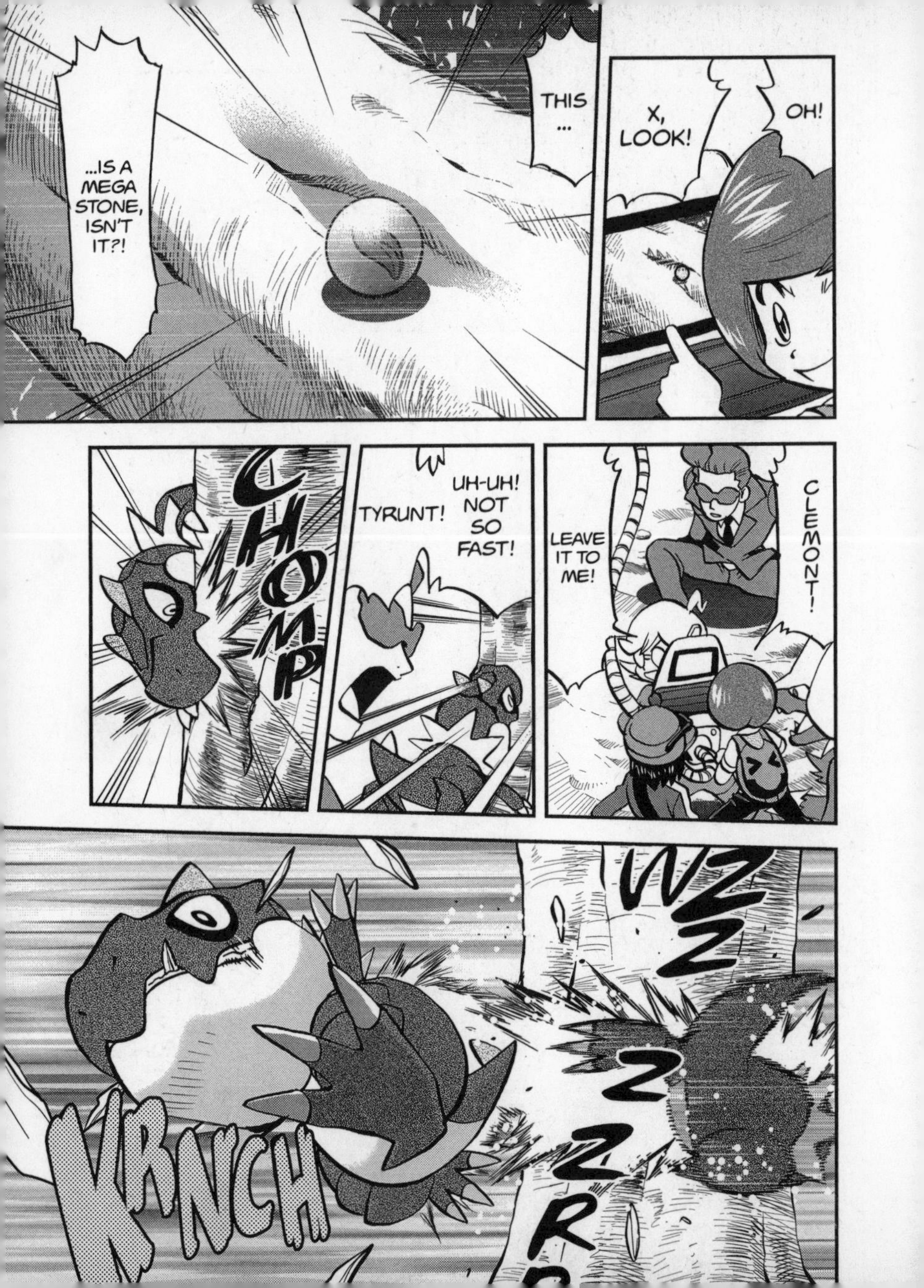
OH!
X, LOOK!
THIS ...
...IS A MEGA STONE, ISN'T IT?!
CLEMONT!
LEAVE IT TO ME!
UH-UH! NOT SO FAST!
TYRUNT!
CHOMP
WZZZZR
KRNCH

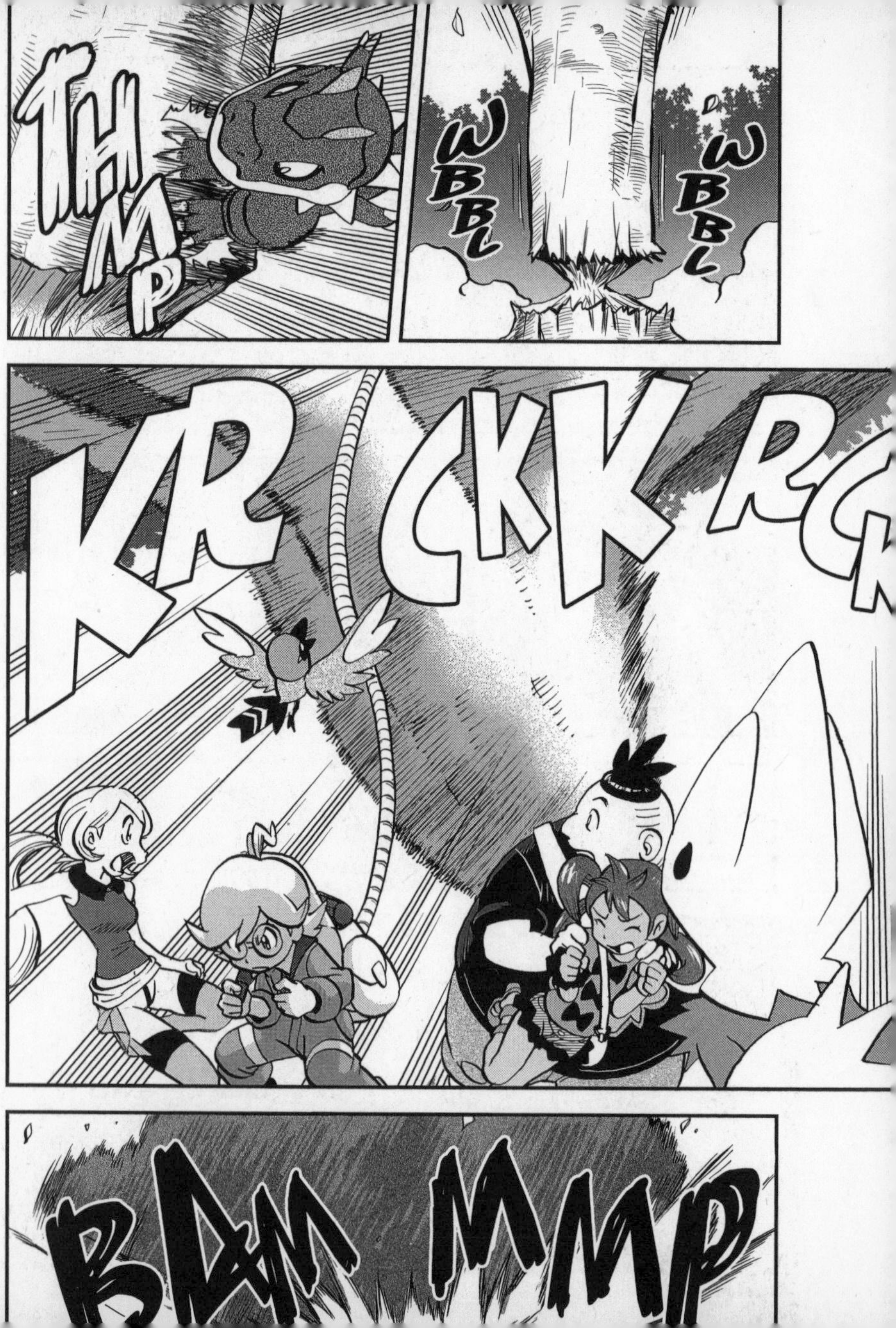
WBBL
WBBL
THMP
KRACKK
BAMMMP

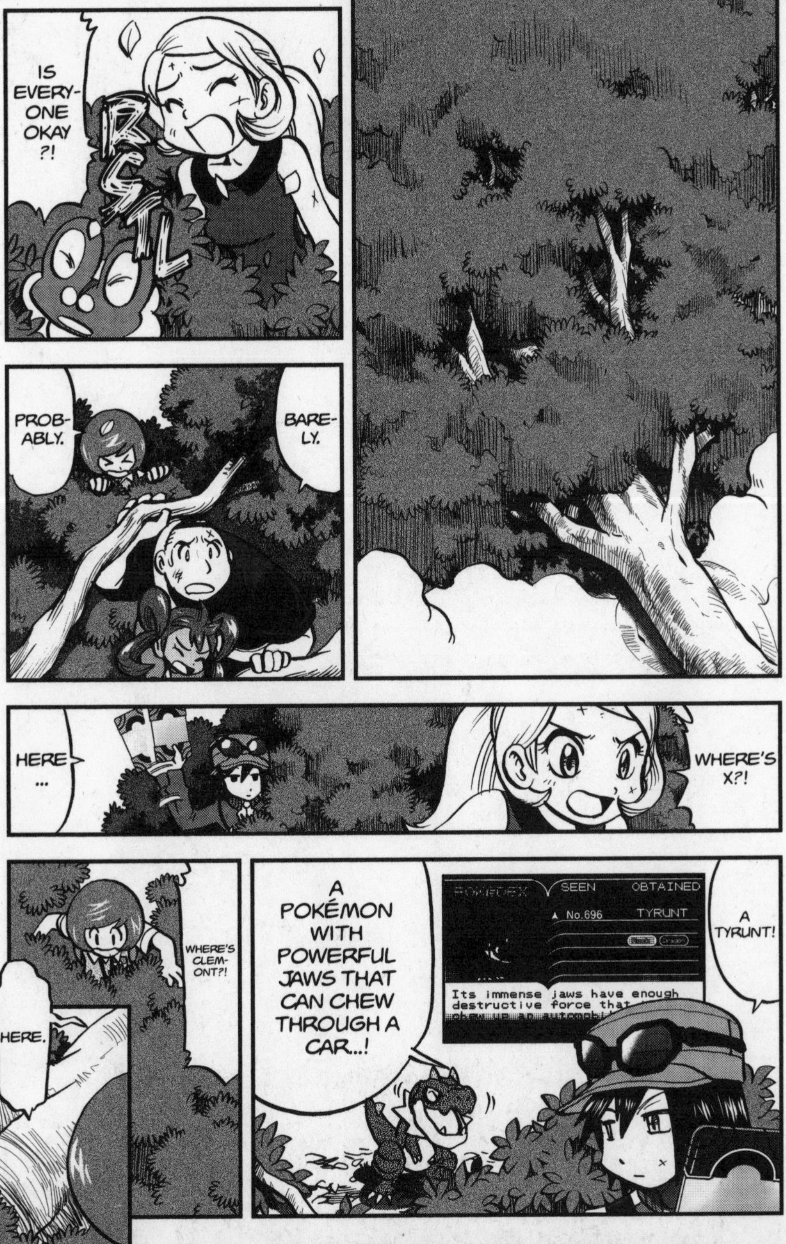
IS EVERY-ONE OKAY ?!
BARE-LY.
PROB-ABLY.
WHERE'S X?!
HERE ...
A TYRUNT!
SEEN OBTAINED
No.696 TYRUNT
Its immense jaws have enough destructive force that
A POKÉMON WITH POWERFUL JAWS THAT CAN CHEW THROUGH A CAR...!
WHERE'S CLEM-ONT?!
HERE.

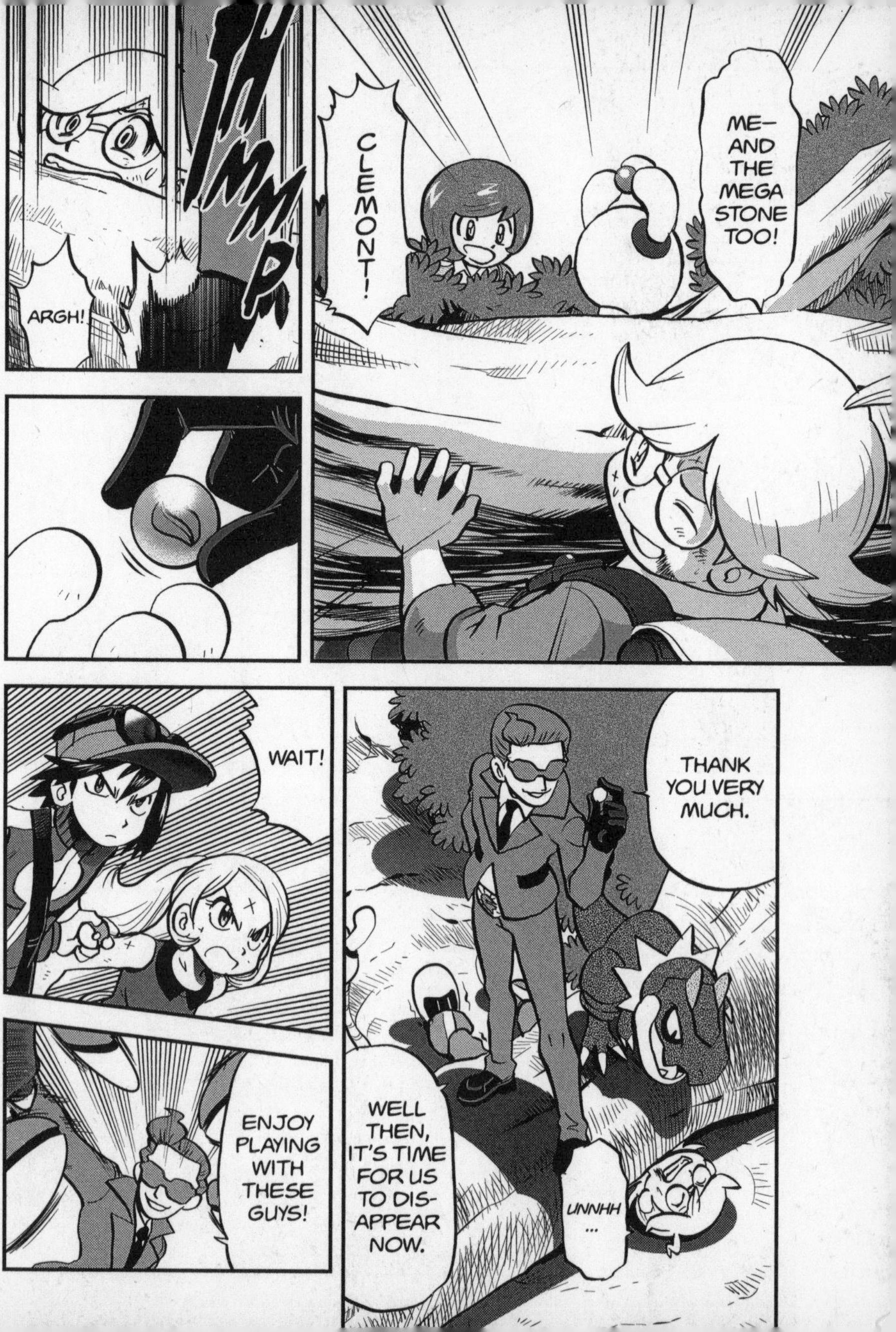

ME— AND THE MEGA STONE TOO!
CLEMONT!
THMMP
ARGH!
THANK YOU VERY MUCH.
WELL THEN, IT'S TIME FOR US TO DIS-APPEAR NOW.
UNNHH ...
WAIT!
ENJOY PLAYING WITH THESE GUYS!

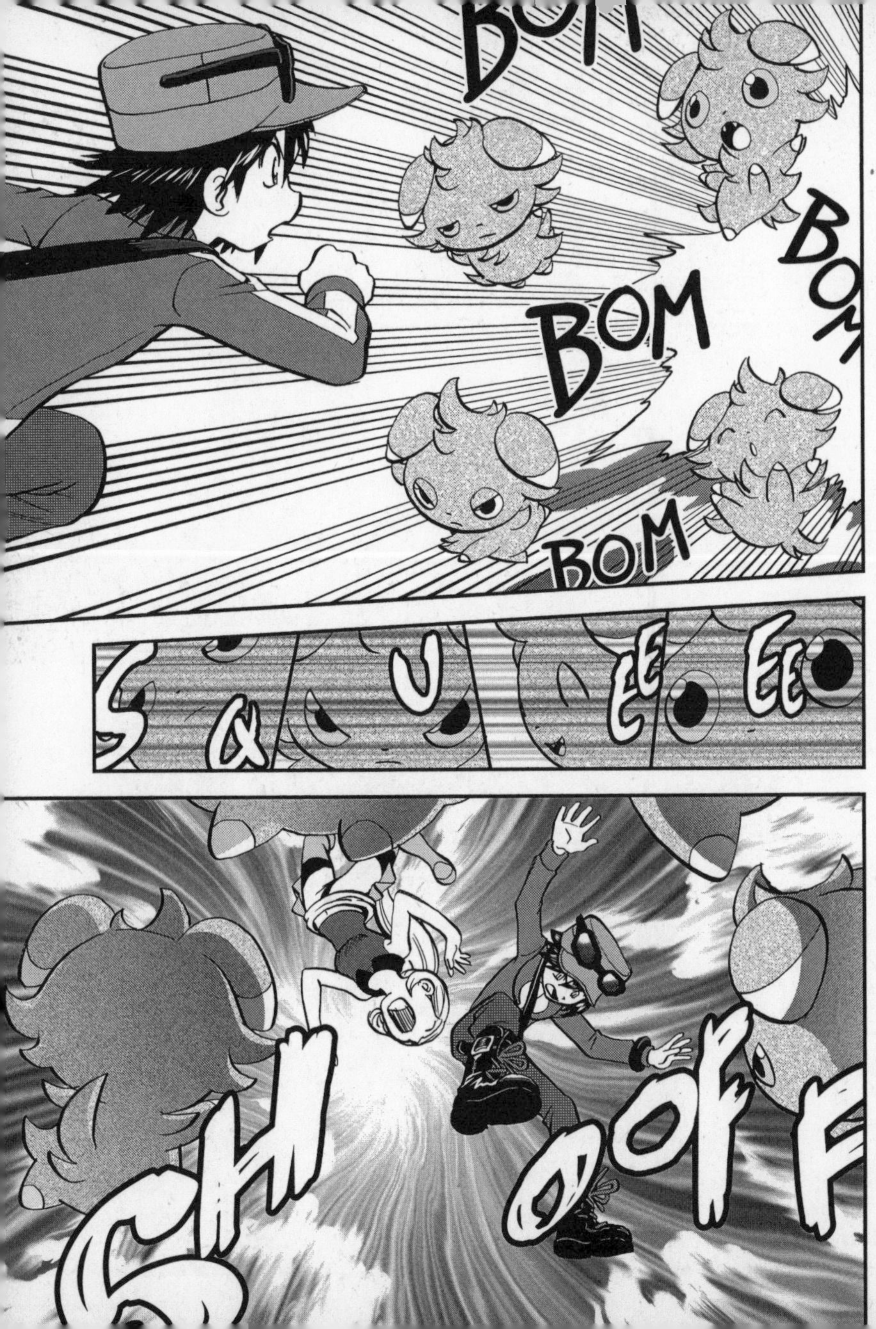
BOM
BOM
BOM
BOM
SQUEEEE
SHOOFF

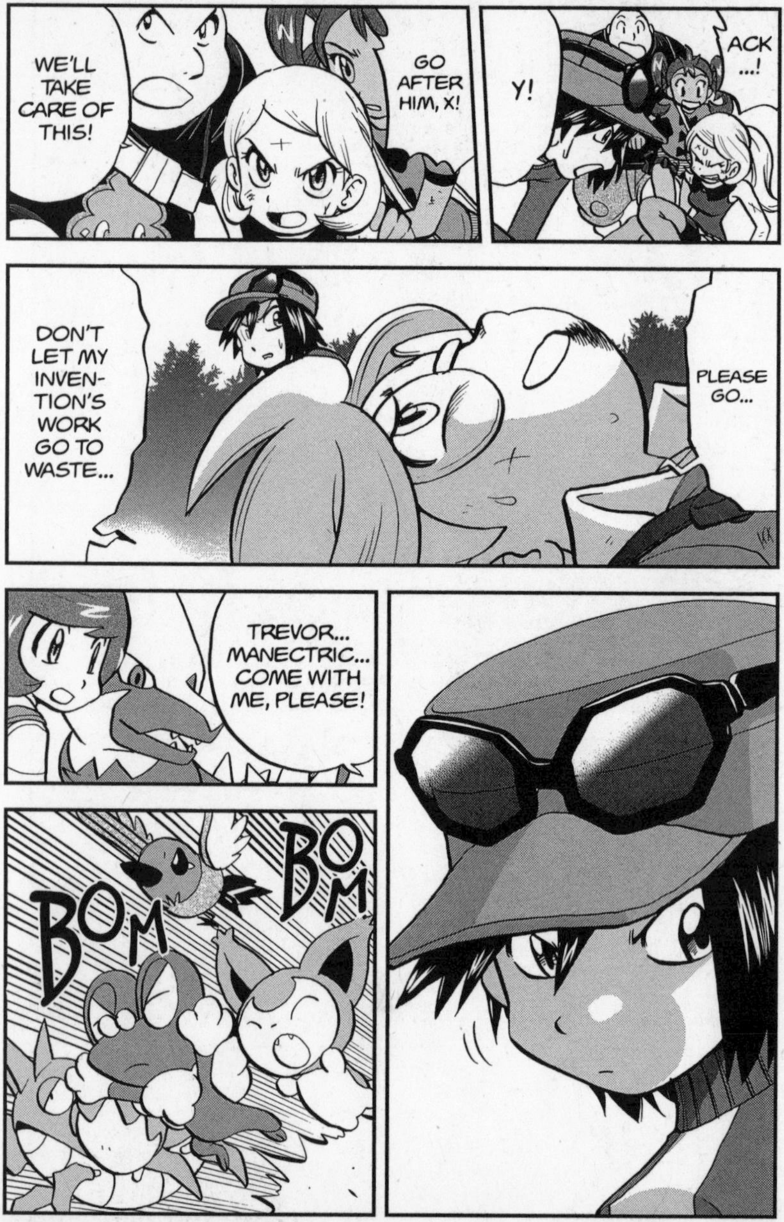
ACK ...!
Y!
GO AFTER HIM, X!
WE'LL TAKE CARE OF THIS!
PLEASE GO...
DON'T LET MY INVEN-TION'S WORK GO TO WASTE...
TREVOR... MANECTRIC... COME WITH ME, PLEASE!
BOM
BOM

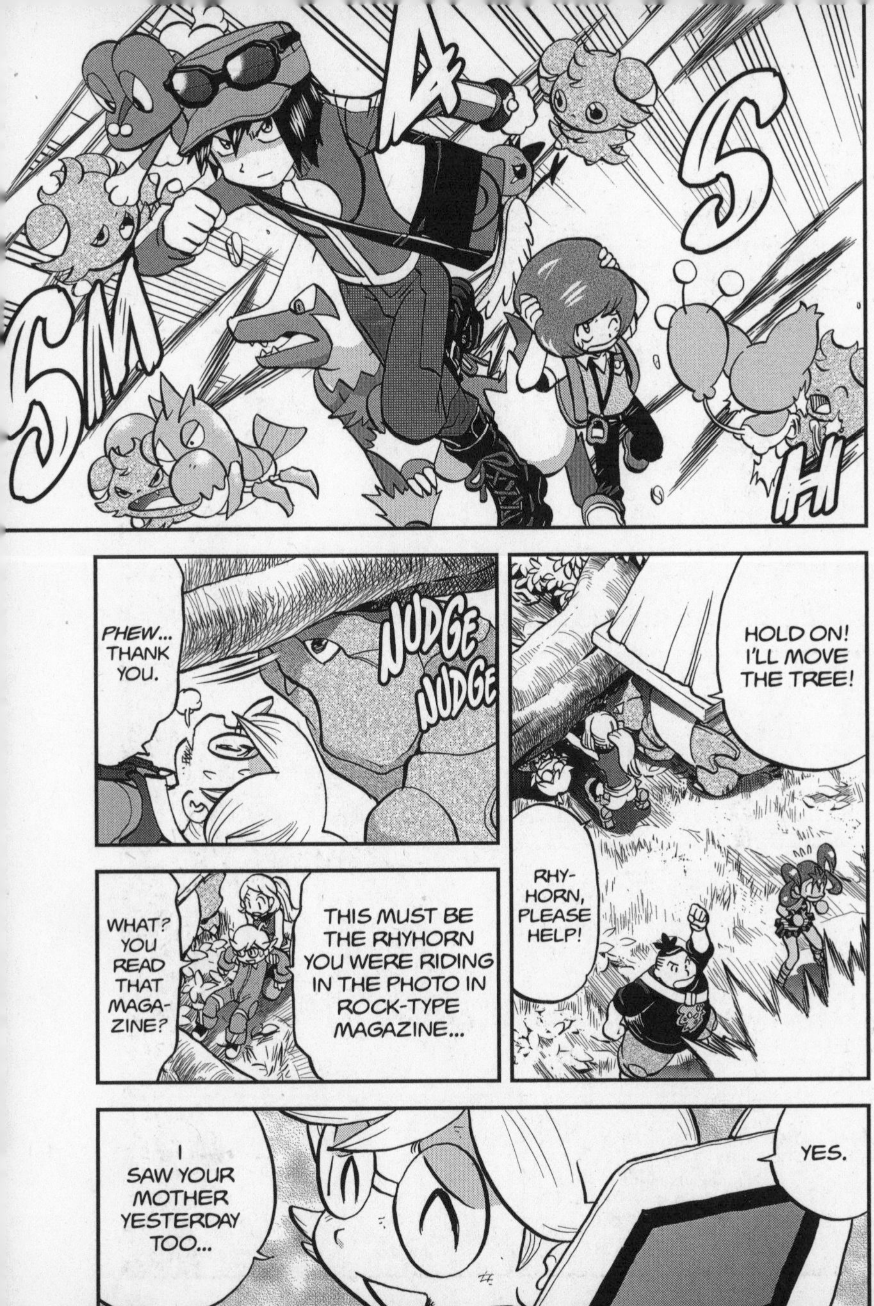
SMASH
HOLD ON! I'LL MOVE THE TREE!
RHY-HORN, PLEASE HELP!
NUDGE NUDGE
PHEW... THANK YOU.
THIS MUST BE THE RHYHORN YOU WERE RIDING IN THE PHOTO IN ROCK-TYPE MAGAZINE...
WHAT? YOU READ THAT MAGAZINE?
YES.
I SAW YOUR MOTHER YESTERDAY TOO...

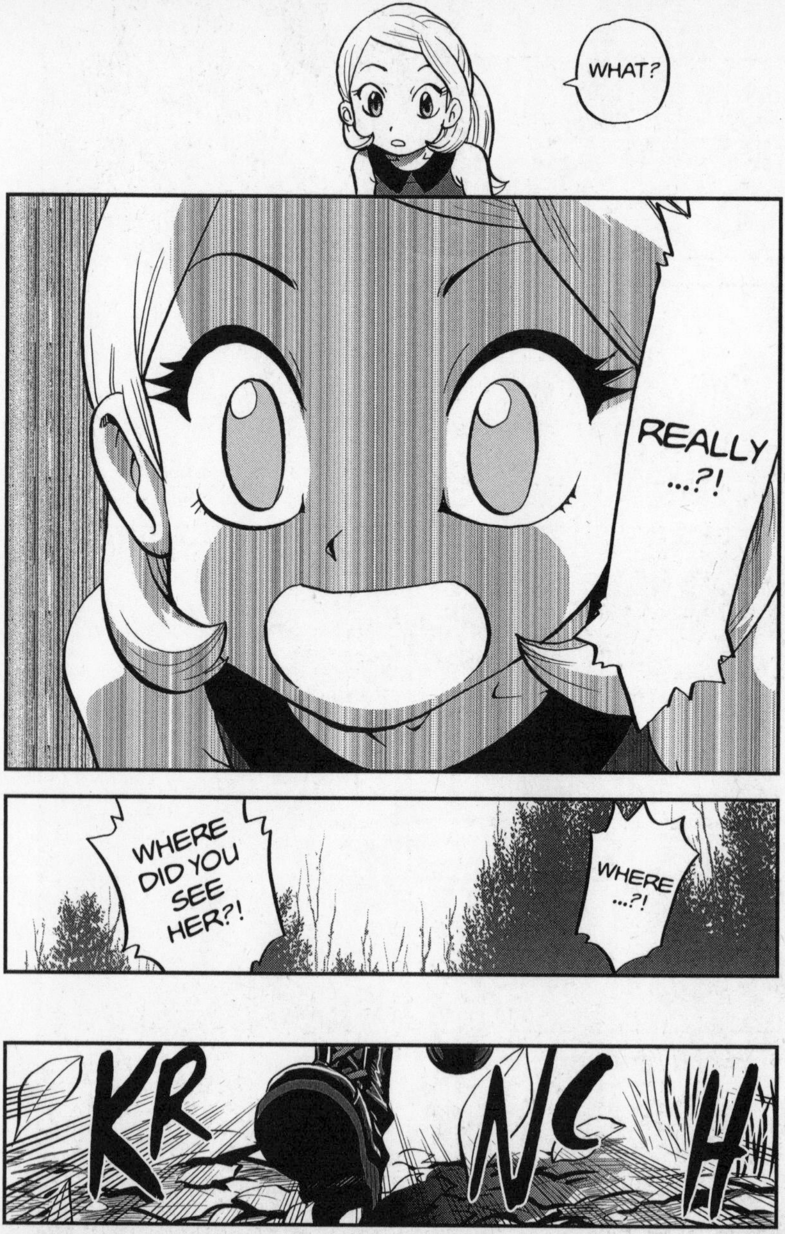
WHAT?
REALLY ...?!
WHERE ...?!
WHERE DID YOU SEE HER?!
KRNCH

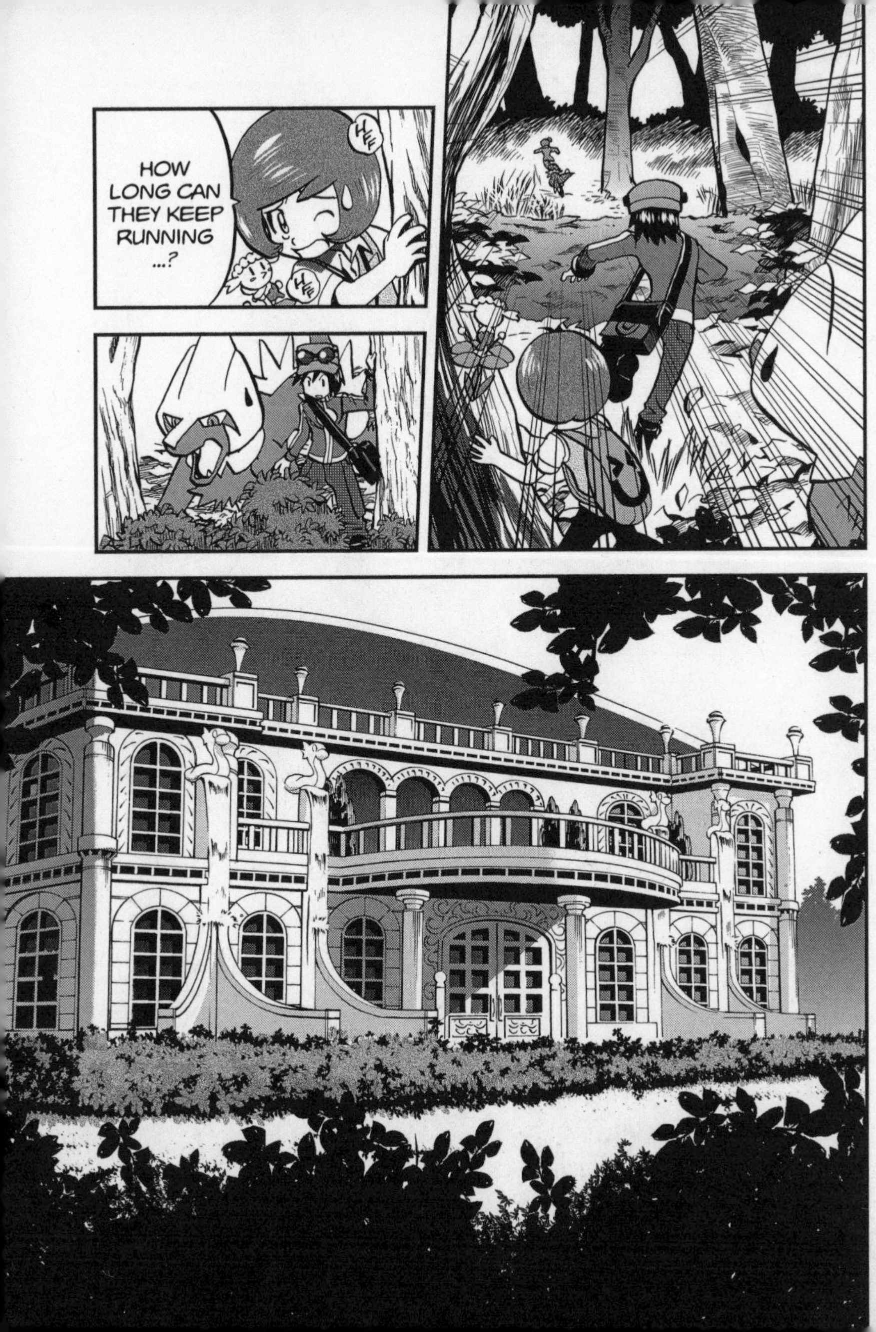
HFF
HOW LONG CAN THEY KEEP RUNNING ...?
!
HFF

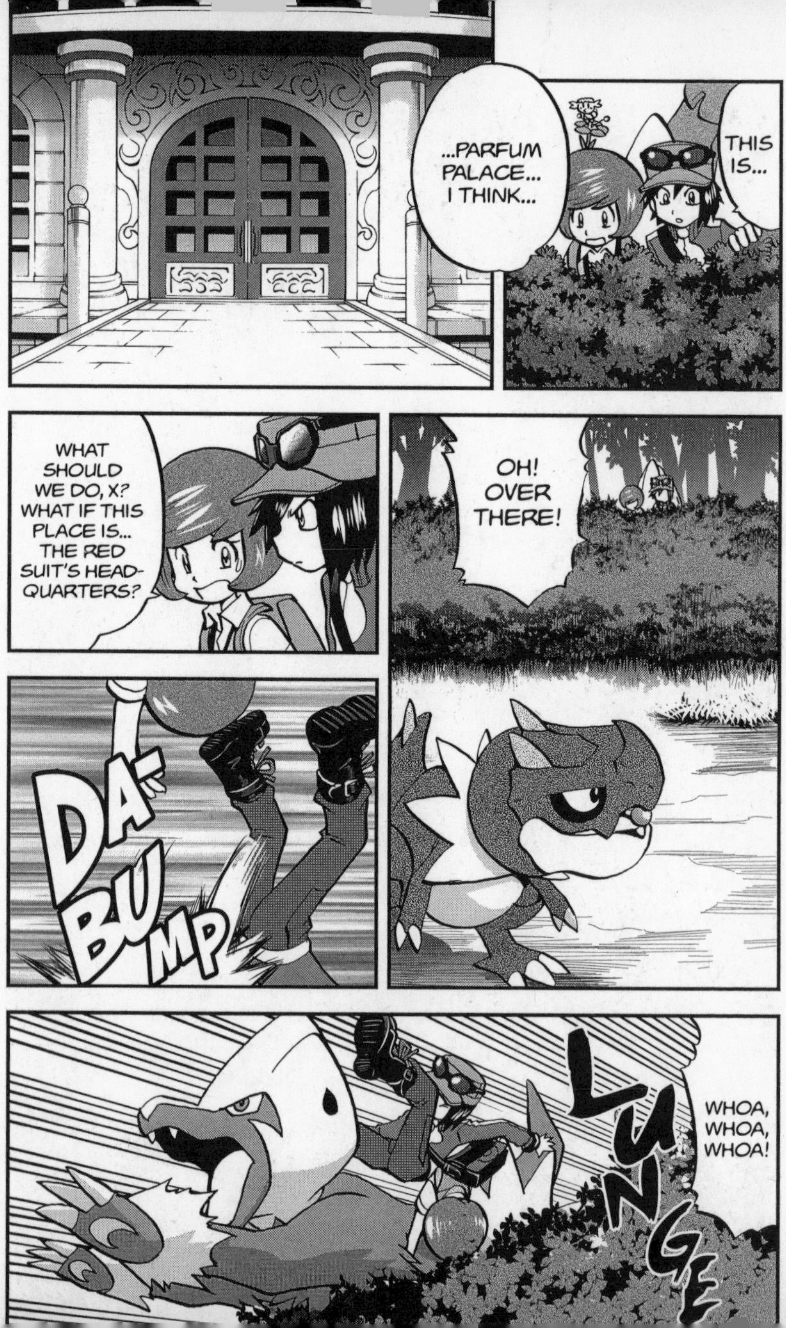
THIS IS...
...PARFUM PALACE... I THINK...
WHAT SHOULD WE DO, X? WHAT IF THIS PLACE IS... THE RED SUIT'S HEAD-QUARTERS?
OH! OVER THERE!
DA-BUMP
LUNGE
WHOA, WHOA, WHOA!

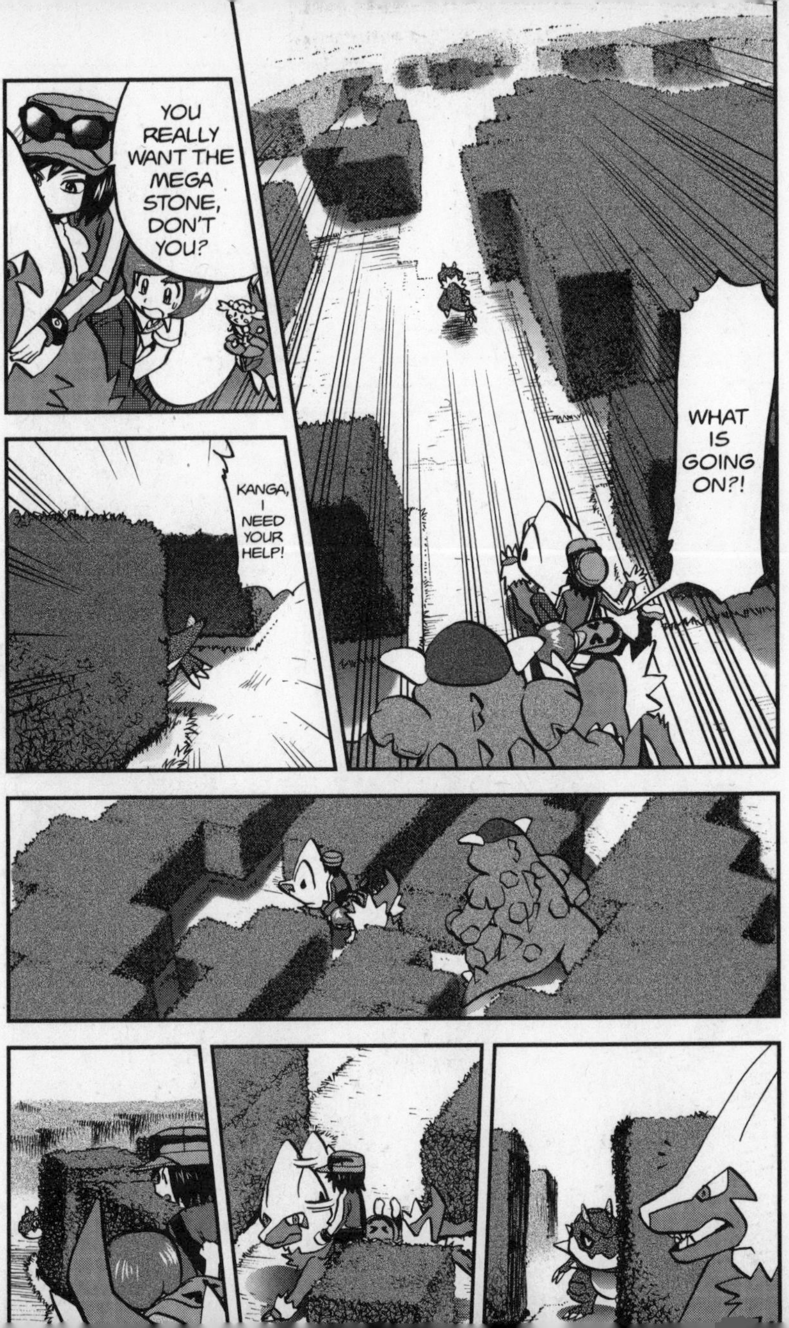
WHAT IS GOING ON?!
YOU REALLY WANT THE MEGA STONE, DON'T YOU?
KANGA, I NEED YOUR HELP!

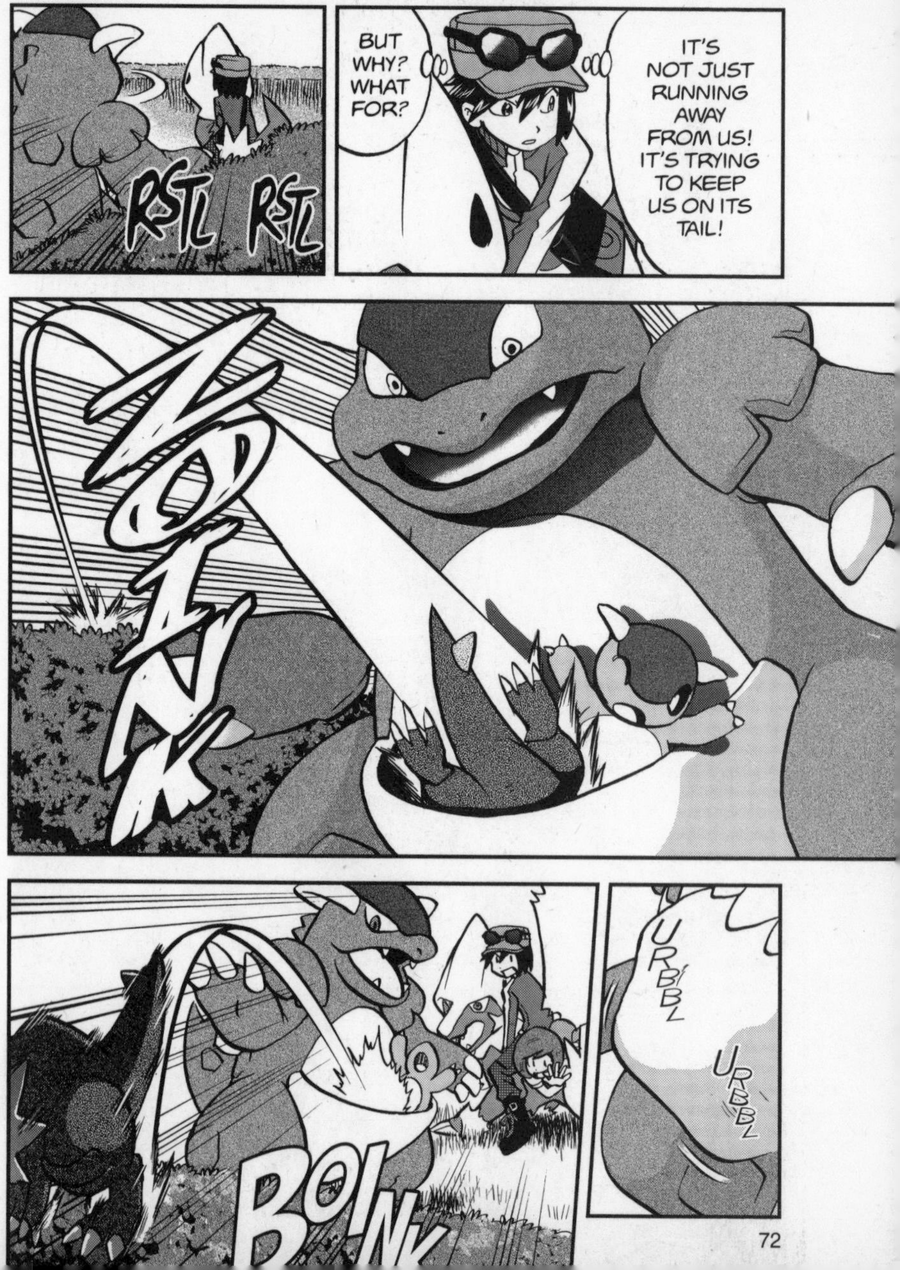
BUT WHY? WHAT FOR?
IT'S NOT JUST RUNNING AWAY FROM US! IT'S TRYING TO KEEP US ON ITS TAIL!
RSTL RSTL
ZOINK
URBBL
URBBL
BOINK

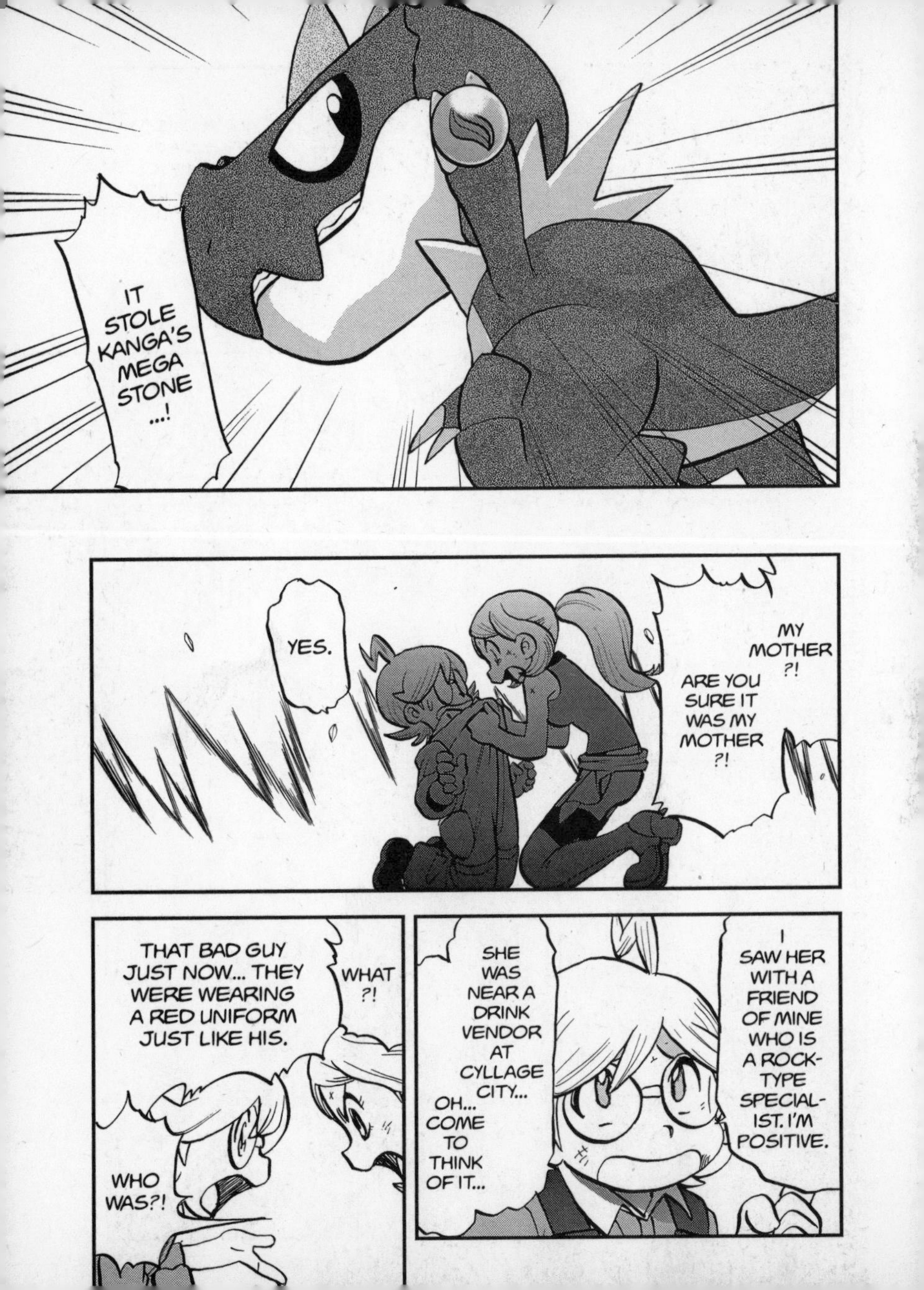
IT STOLE KANGA'S MEGA STONE ...!
MY MOTHER ?!
ARE YOU SURE IT WAS MY MOTHER ?!
YES.
I SAW HER WITH A FRIEND OF MINE WHO IS A ROCK-TYPE SPECIALIST. I'M POSITIVE.
SHE WAS NEAR A DRINK VENDOR AT CYLLAGE CITY...
OH... COME TO THINK OF IT...
THAT BAD GUY JUST NOW... THEY WERE WEARING A RED UNIFORM JUST LIKE HIS.
WHAT ?!
WHO WAS?!

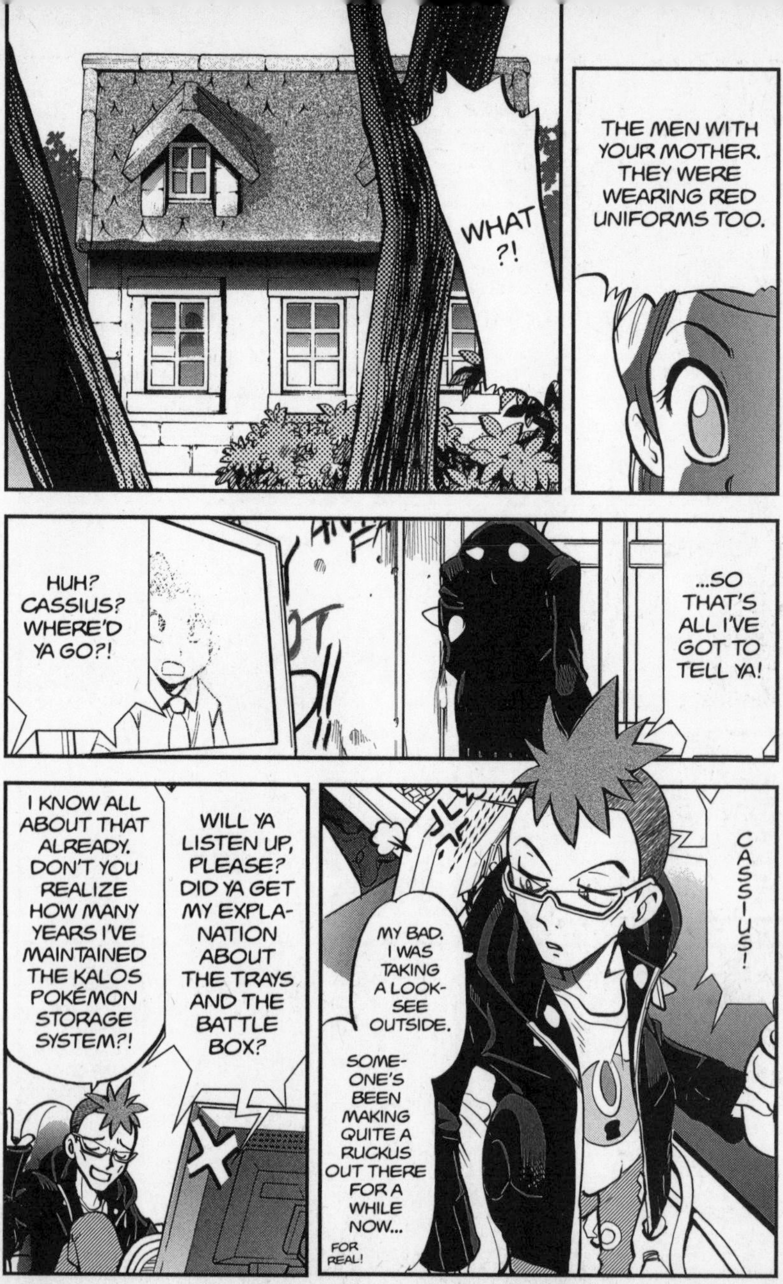
THE MEN WITH YOUR MOTHER. THEY WERE WEARING RED UNIFORMS TOO.
WHAT ?!
...SO THAT'S ALL I'VE GOT TO TELL YA!
HUH? CASSIUS? WHERE'D YA GO?!
CASSIUS!
MY BAD. I WAS TAKING A LOOK-SEE OUTSIDE.
SOME-ONE'S BEEN MAKING QUITE A RUCKUS OUT THERE FOR A WHILE NOW...
FOR REAL!
WILL YA LISTEN UP, PLEASE? DID YA GET MY EXPLA-NATION ABOUT THE TRAYS AND THE BATTLE BOX?
I KNOW ALL ABOUT THAT ALREADY. DON'T YOU REALIZE HOW MANY YEARS I'VE MAINTAINED THE KALOS POKÉMON STORAGE SYSTEM?!

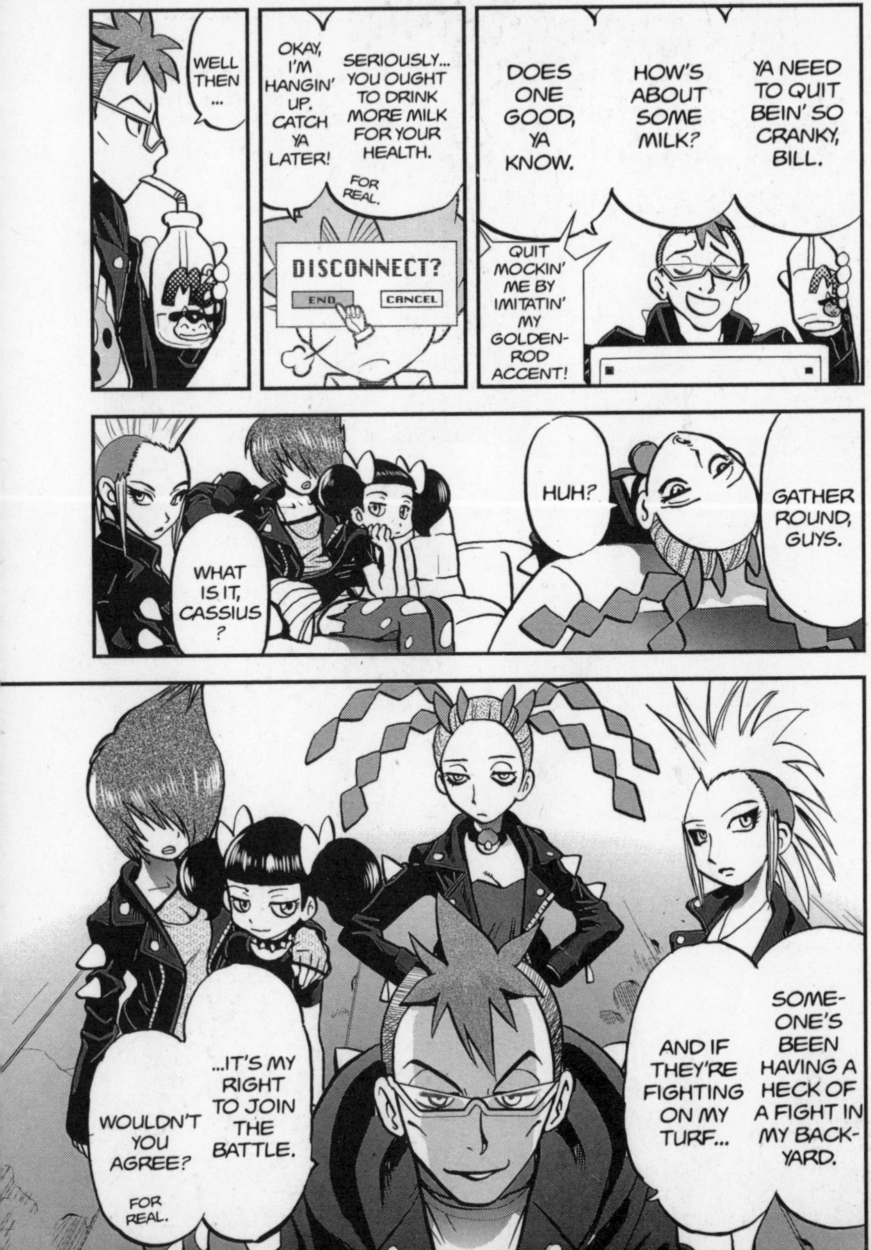
YA NEED TO QUIT BEIN' SO CRANKY, BILL.
HOW'S ABOUT SOME MILK?
DOES ONE GOOD, YA KNOW.
QUIT MOCKIN' ME BY IMITATIN' MY GOLDENROD ACCENT!
SERIOUSLY... YOU OUGHT TO DRINK MORE MILK FOR YOUR HEALTH.
OKAY, I'M HANGIN' UP. CATCH YA LATER!
FOR REAL.
DISCONNECT?
END
CANCEL
WELL THEN...
GATHER ROUND, GUYS.
HUH?
WHAT IS IT, CASSIUS?
SOMEONE'S BEEN HAVING A HECK OF A FIGHT IN MY BACKYARD.
AND IF THEY'RE FIGHTING ON MY TURF...
...IT'S MY RIGHT TO JOIN THE BATTLE.
WOULDN'T YOU AGREE?
FOR REAL.

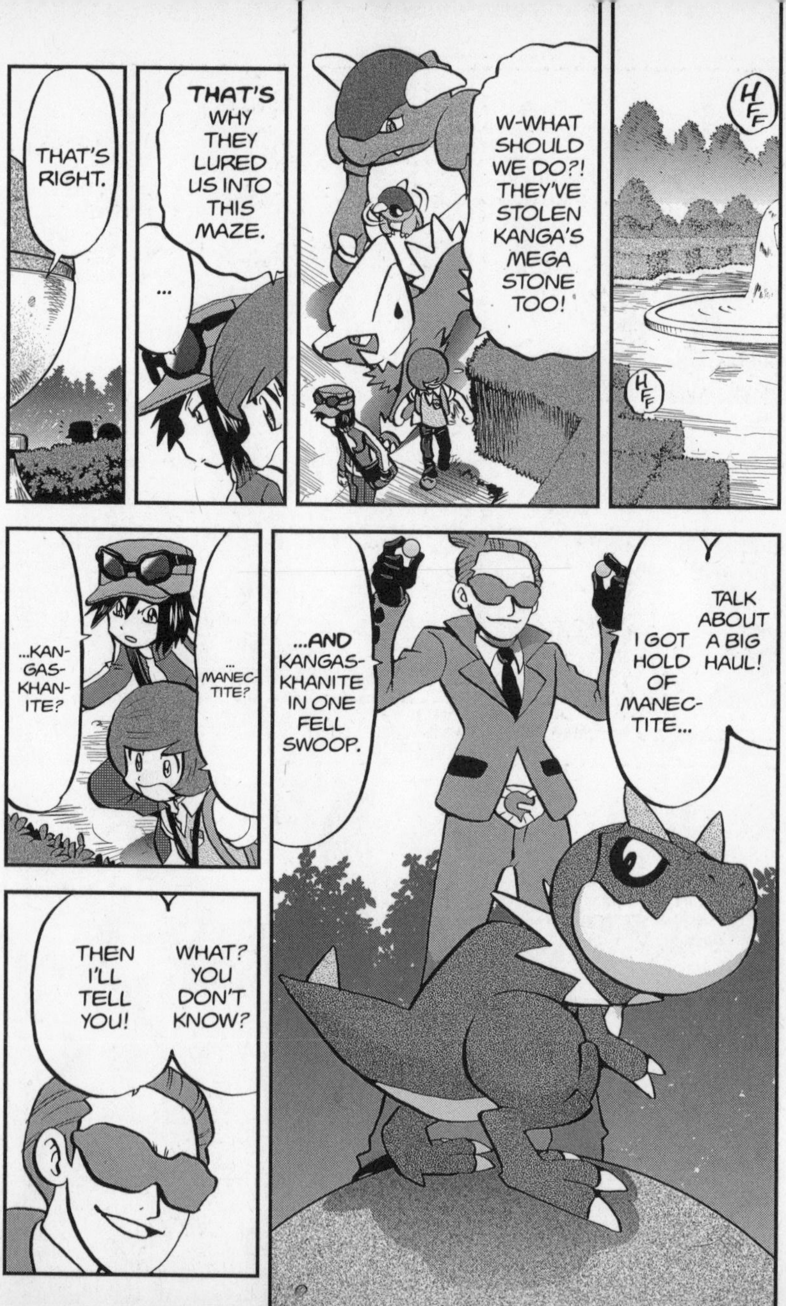
HFF
HFF
W-WHAT SHOULD WE DO?! THEY'VE STOLEN KANGA'S MEGA STONE TOO!
THAT'S WHY THEY LURED US INTO THIS MAZE.
...
THAT'S RIGHT.
TALK ABOUT A BIG HAUL!
I GOT HOLD OF MANEC-TITE...
...AND KANGAS-KHANITE IN ONE FELL SWOOP.
...MANEC-TITE?
...KAN-GAS-KHAN-ITE?
WHAT? YOU DON'T KNOW?
THEN I'LL TELL YOU!

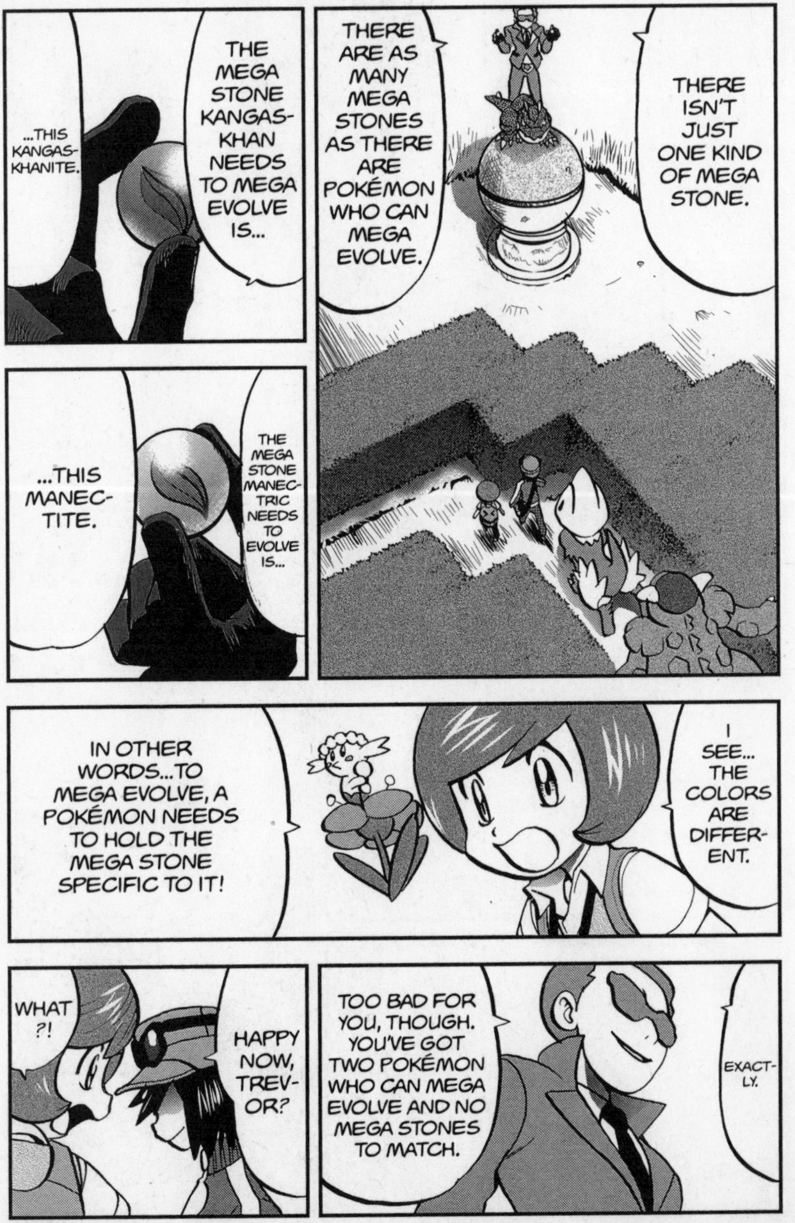
THERE ISN'T JUST ONE KIND OF MEGA STONE.
THERE ARE AS MANY MEGA STONES AS THERE ARE POKÉMON WHO CAN MEGA EVOLVE.
THE MEGA STONE KANGASKHAN NEEDS TO MEGA EVOLVE IS...
...THIS KANGASKHANITE.
THE MEGA STONE MANECTRIC NEEDS TO EVOLVE IS...
...THIS MANECTITE.
I SEE... THE COLORS ARE DIFFERENT.
IN OTHER WORDS...TO MEGA EVOLVE, A POKÉMON NEEDS TO HOLD THE MEGA STONE SPECIFIC TO IT!
EXACTLY.
TOO BAD FOR YOU, THOUGH. YOU'VE GOT TWO POKÉMON WHO CAN MEGA EVOLVE AND NO MEGA STONES TO MATCH.
HAPPY NOW, TREVOR?
WHAT?!

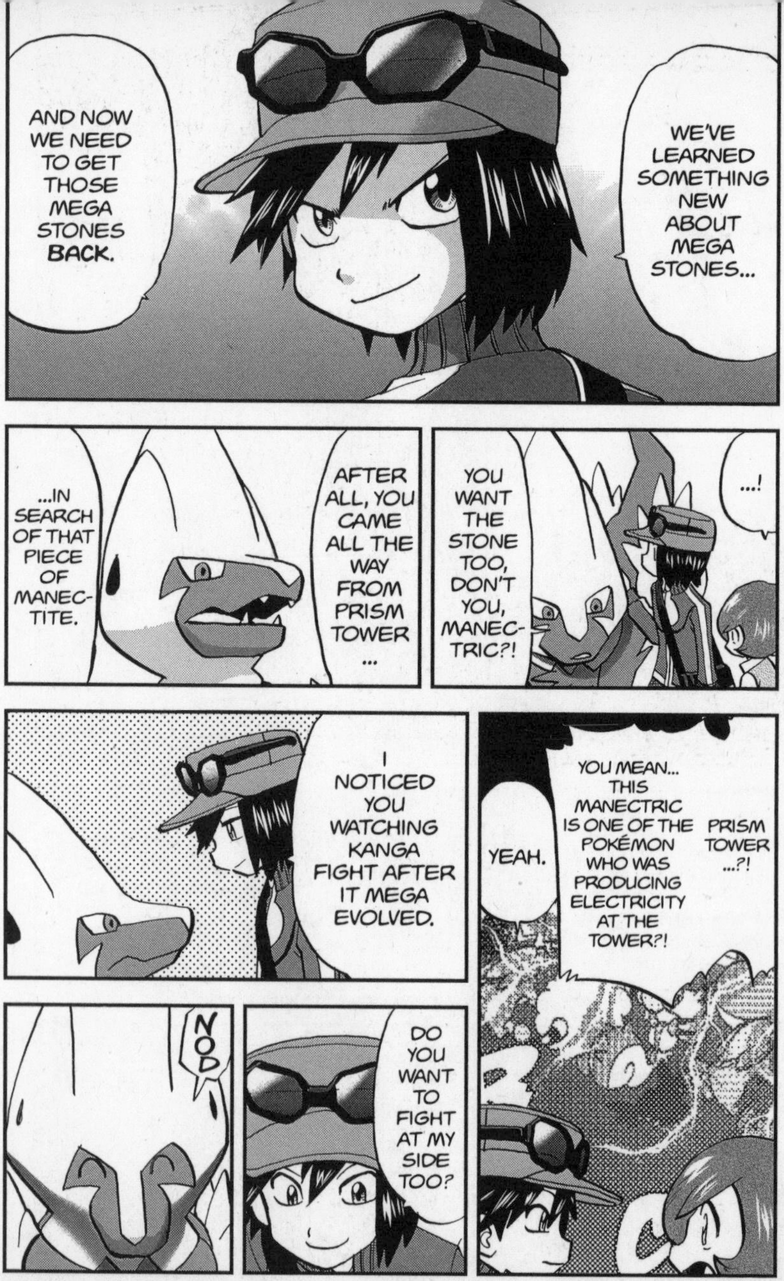
WE'VE LEARNED SOMETHING NEW ABOUT MEGA STONES...
AND NOW WE NEED TO GET THOSE MEGA STONES BACK.
...!
YOU WANT THE STONE TOO, DON'T YOU, MANECTRIC?!
AFTER ALL, YOU CAME ALL THE WAY FROM PRISM TOWER...
...IN SEARCH OF THAT PIECE OF MANECTITE.
PRISM TOWER...?!
YOU MEAN... THIS MANECTRIC IS ONE OF THE POKÉMON WHO WAS PRODUCING ELECTRICITY AT THE TOWER?!
YEAH.
I NOTICED YOU WATCHING KANGA FIGHT AFTER IT MEGA EVOLVED.
DO YOU WANT TO FIGHT AT MY SIDE TOO?
NOD

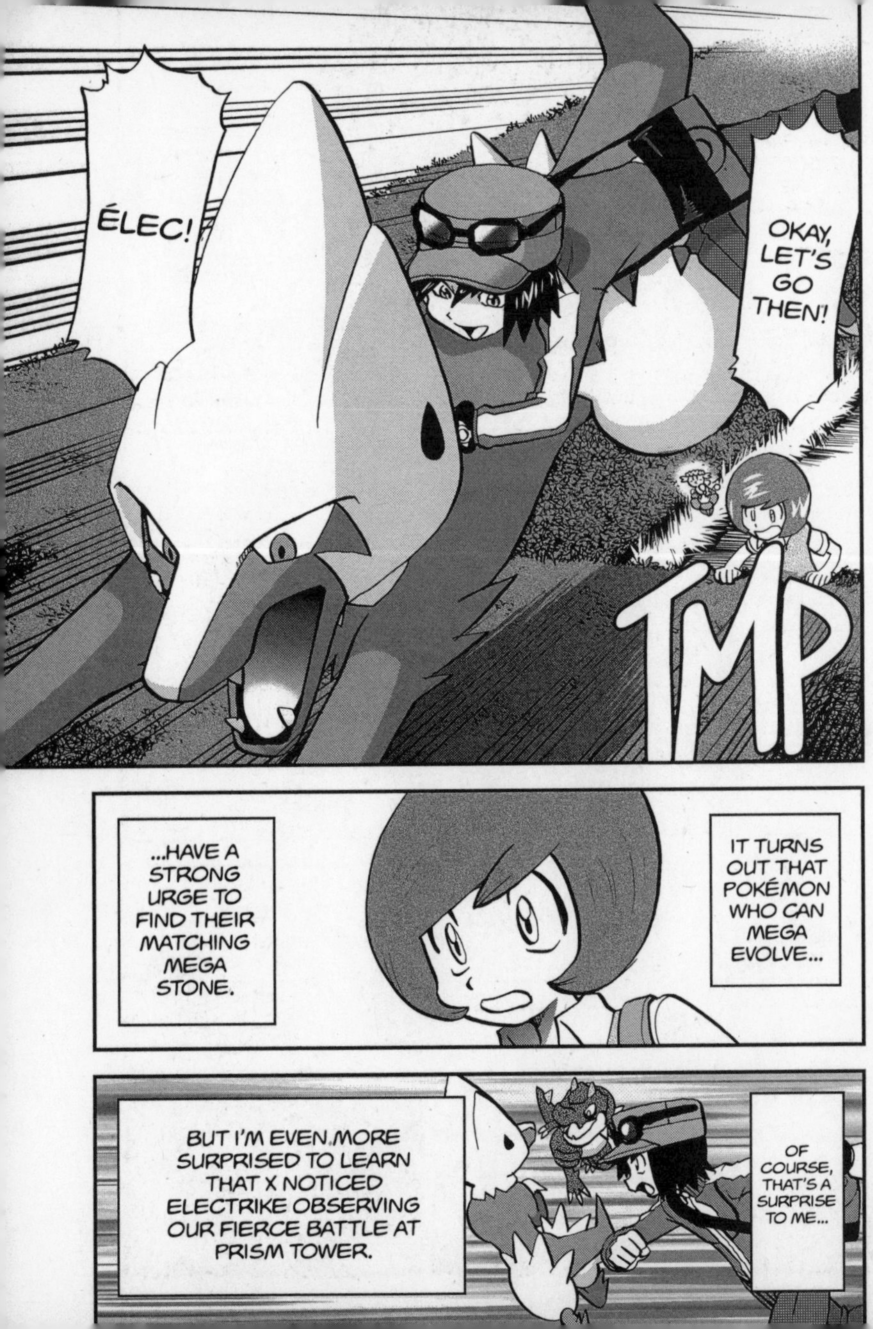
OKAY, LET'S GO THEN!
ÉLEC!
TMP
IT TURNS OUT THAT POKÉMON WHO CAN MEGA EVOLVE...
...HAVE A STRONG URGE TO FIND THEIR MATCHING MEGA STONE.
OF COURSE, THAT'S A SURPRISE TO ME...
BUT I'M EVEN MORE SURPRISED TO LEARN THAT X NOTICED ELECTRIKE OBSERVING OUR FIERCE BATTLE AT PRISM TOWER.

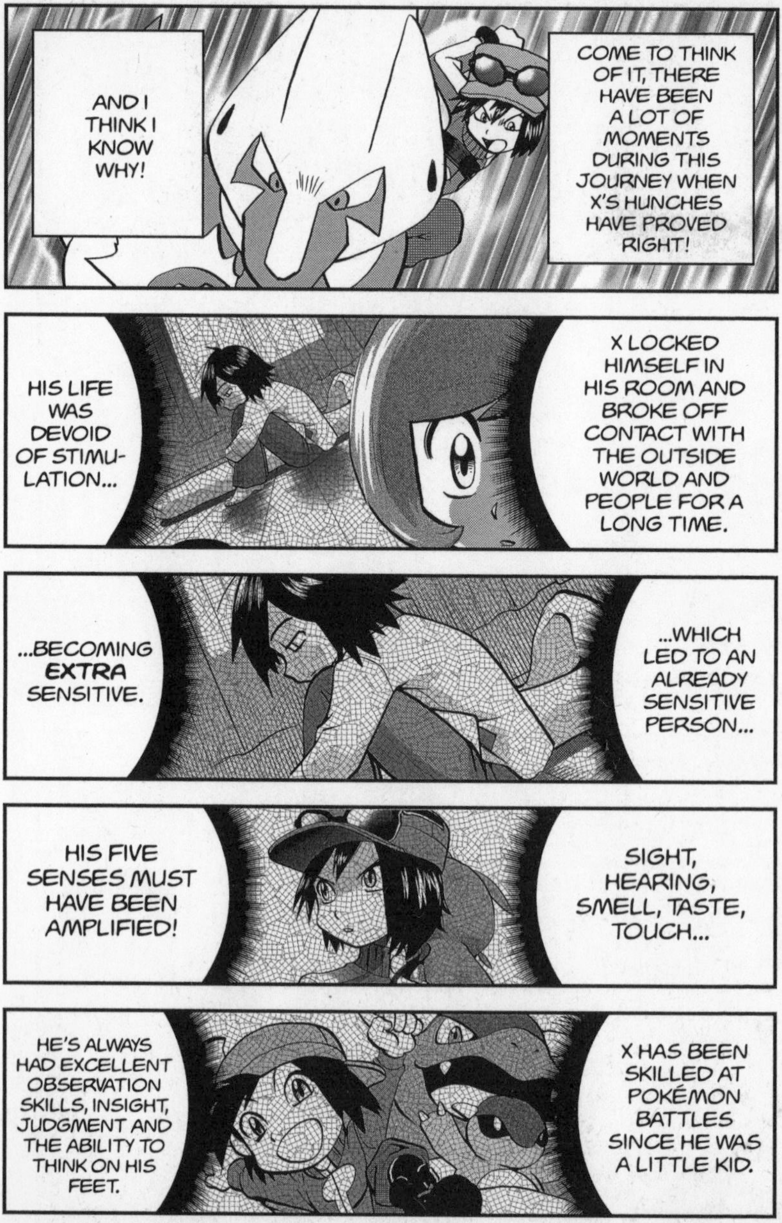
COME TO THINK OF IT, THERE HAVE BEEN A LOT OF MOMENTS DURING THIS JOURNEY WHEN X'S HUNCHES HAVE PROVED RIGHT!
AND I THINK I KNOW WHY!
X LOCKED HIMSELF IN HIS ROOM AND BROKE OFF CONTACT WITH THE OUTSIDE WORLD AND PEOPLE FOR A LONG TIME.
HIS LIFE WAS DEVOID OF STIMU-LATION...
...WHICH LED TO AN ALREADY SENSITIVE PERSON...
...BECOMING EXTRA SENSITIVE.
SIGHT, HEARING, SMELL, TASTE, TOUCH...
HIS FIVE SENSES MUST HAVE BEEN AMPLIFIED!
X HAS BEEN SKILLED AT POKÉMON BATTLES SINCE HE WAS A LITTLE KID.
HE'S ALWAYS HAD EXCELLENT OBSERVATION SKILLS, INSIGHT, JUDGMENT AND THE ABILITY TO THINK ON HIS FEET.

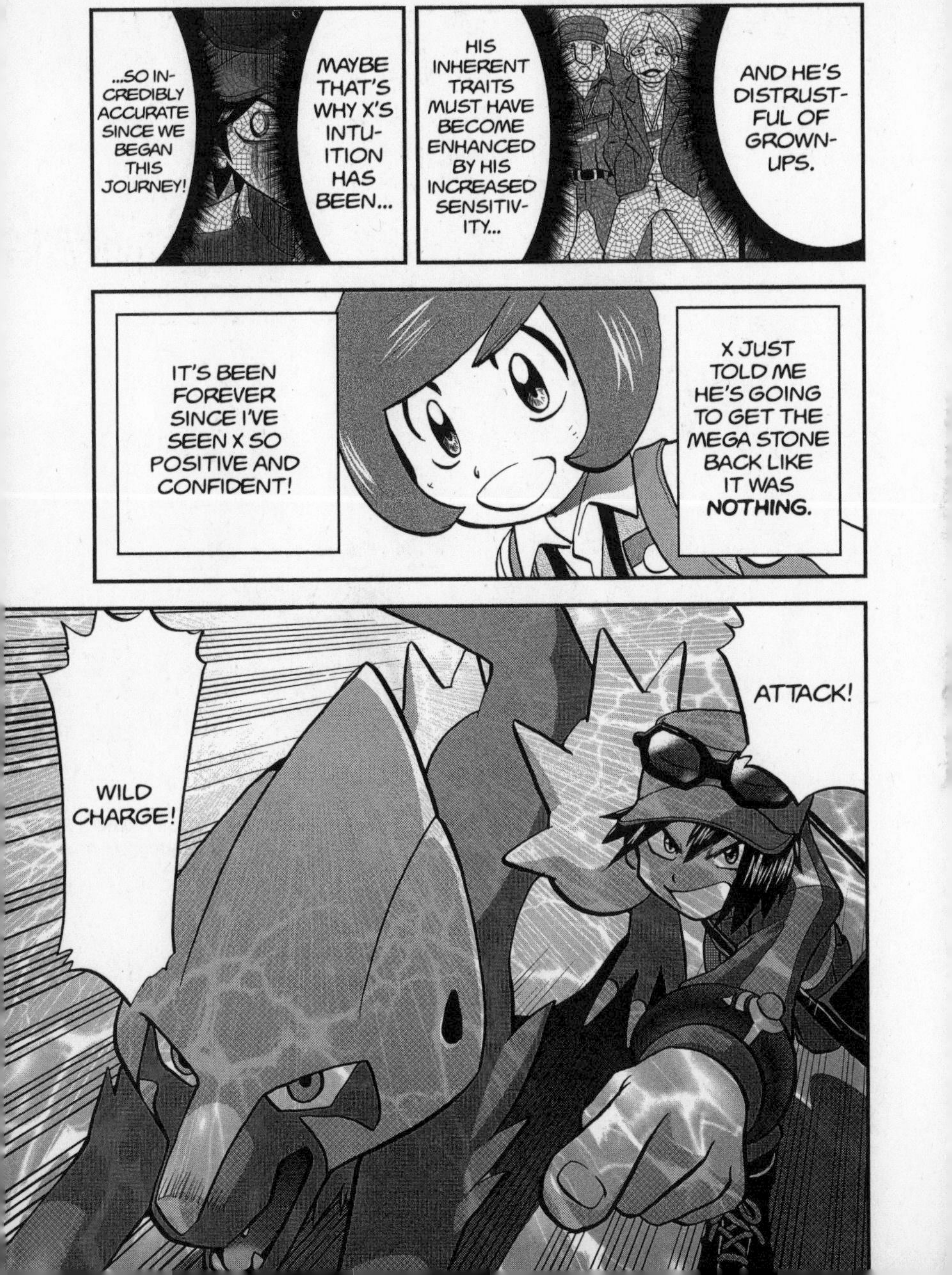
AND HE'S DISTRUST-FUL OF GROWN-UPS.
HIS INHERENT TRAITS MUST HAVE BECOME ENHANCED BY HIS INCREASED SENSITIV-ITY...
MAYBE THAT'S WHY X'S INTU-ITION HAS BEEN...
...SO IN-CREDIBLY ACCURATE SINCE WE BEGAN THIS JOURNEY!
X JUST TOLD ME HE'S GOING TO GET THE MEGA STONE BACK LIKE IT WAS **NOTHING.**
IT'S BEEN FOREVER SINCE I'VE SEEN X SO POSITIVE AND CONFIDENT!
ATTACK!
WILD CHARGE!

Current Location

Route 5
Versant Road

Roller Skaters from across the Kalos region gather on this hilly path to demonstrate their best skills.

▼

Camphrier Town

This ancient town was once famous for the long-neglected manor home of a noble family.

▼

Route 6
Palais Lane

This tree-lined path was once covered with grass as tall as a man, but it was cleared by the palace.

▼

Parfum Palace

A luxurious palace constructed 300 years ago by a king who wished to display his power to all.

Adventure 14 Morphing Manectric

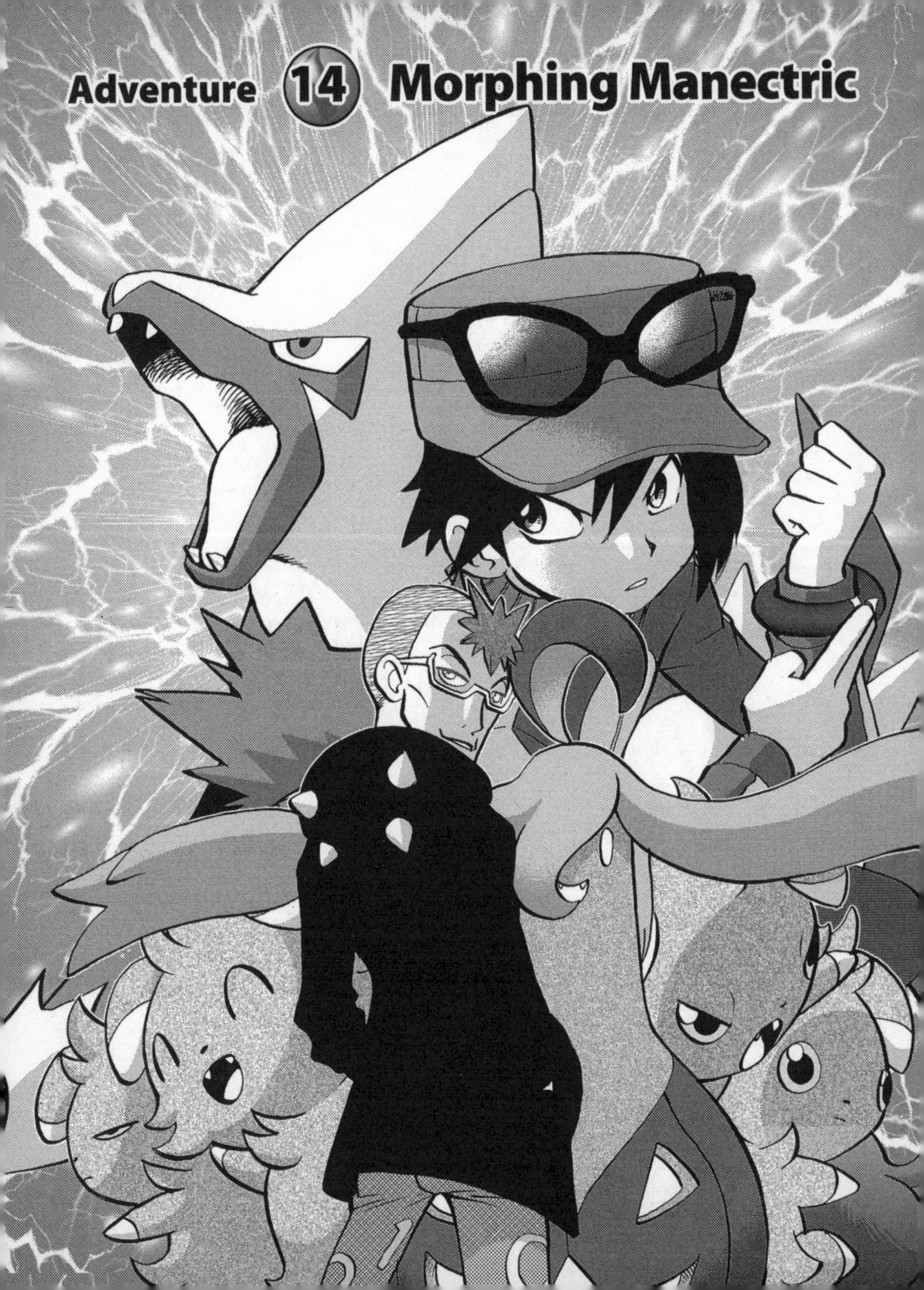

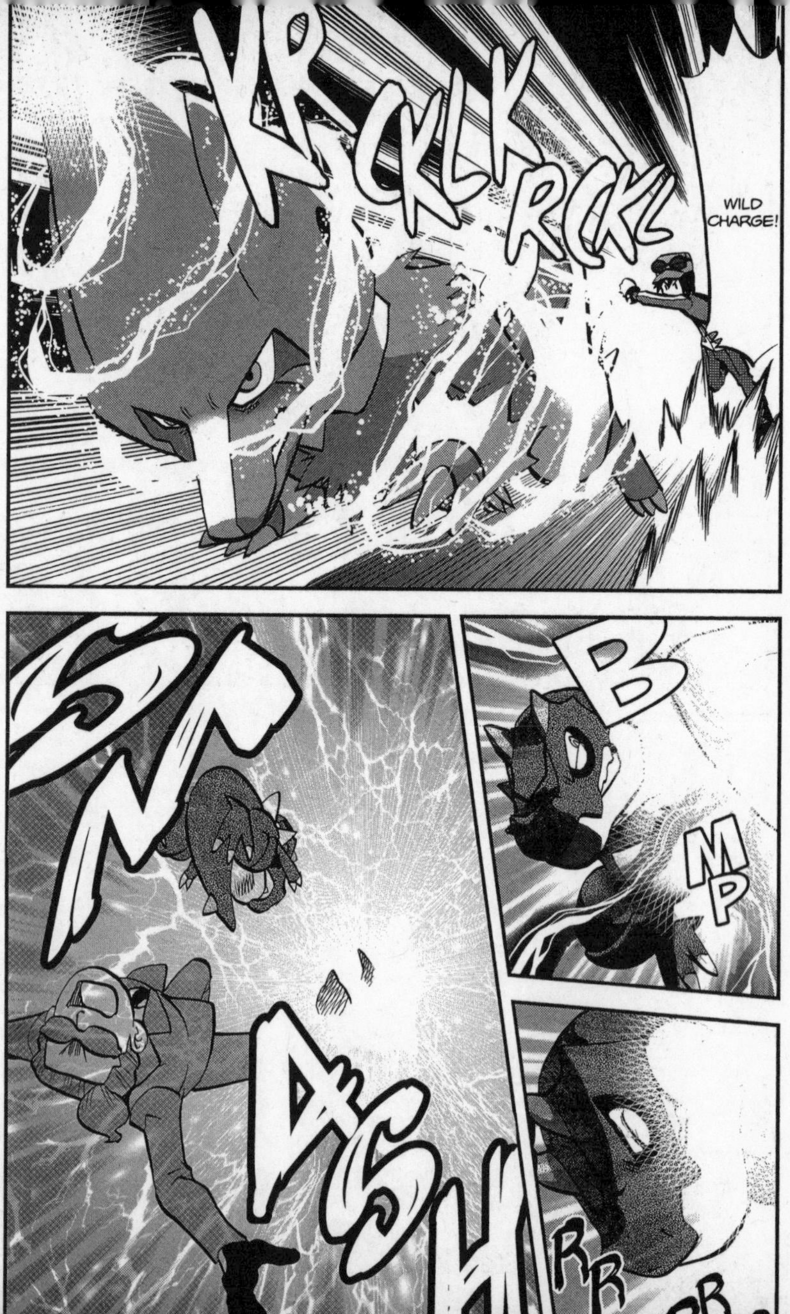
WILD CHARGE!

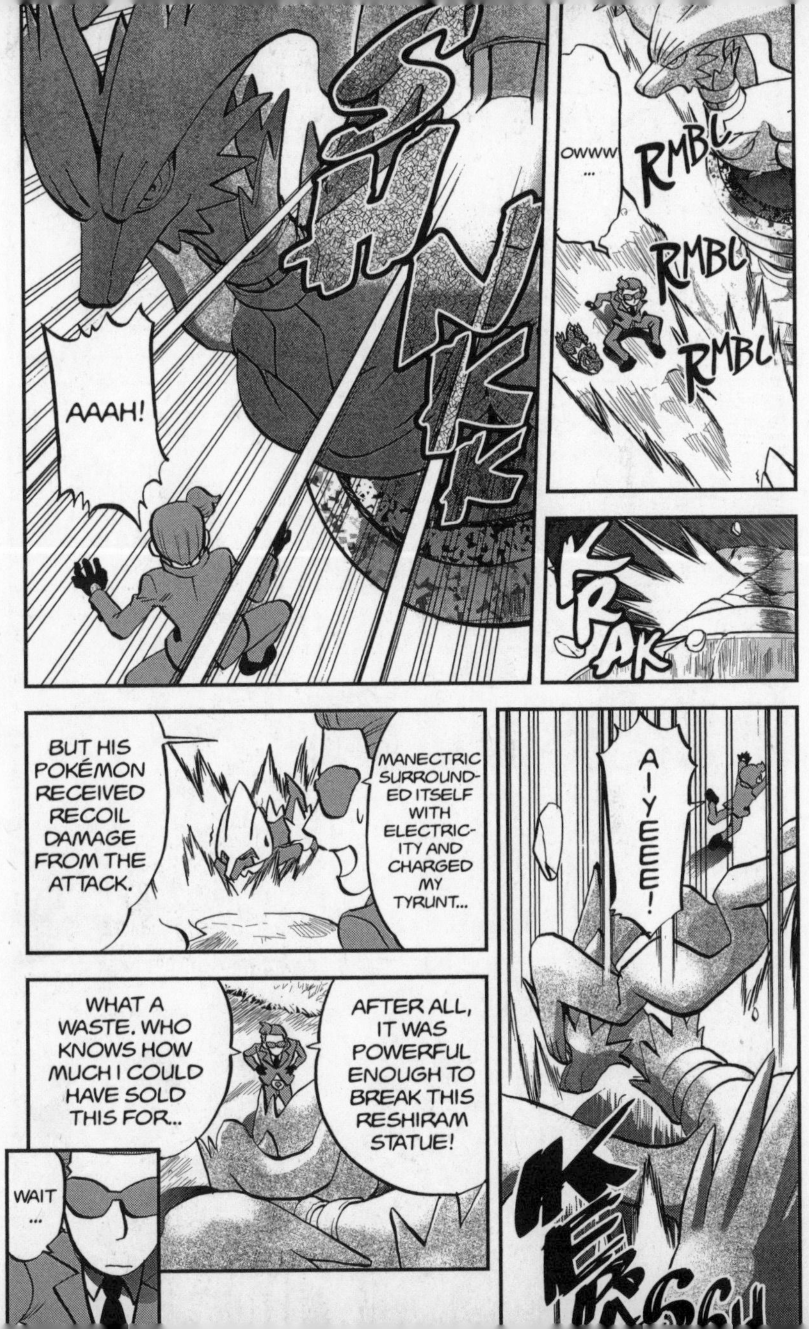
OWWW...
RMBL
RMBL
RMBL
KRAK
SHNKK
AAAH!
AIYEEE!
MANECTRIC SURROUNDED ITSELF WITH ELECTRICITY AND CHARGED MY TYRUNT...
BUT HIS POKÉMON RECEIVED RECOIL DAMAGE FROM THE ATTACK.
AFTER ALL, IT WAS POWERFUL ENOUGH TO BREAK THIS RESHIRAM STATUE!
WHAT A WASTE. WHO KNOWS HOW MUCH I COULD HAVE SOLD THIS FOR...
WAIT...

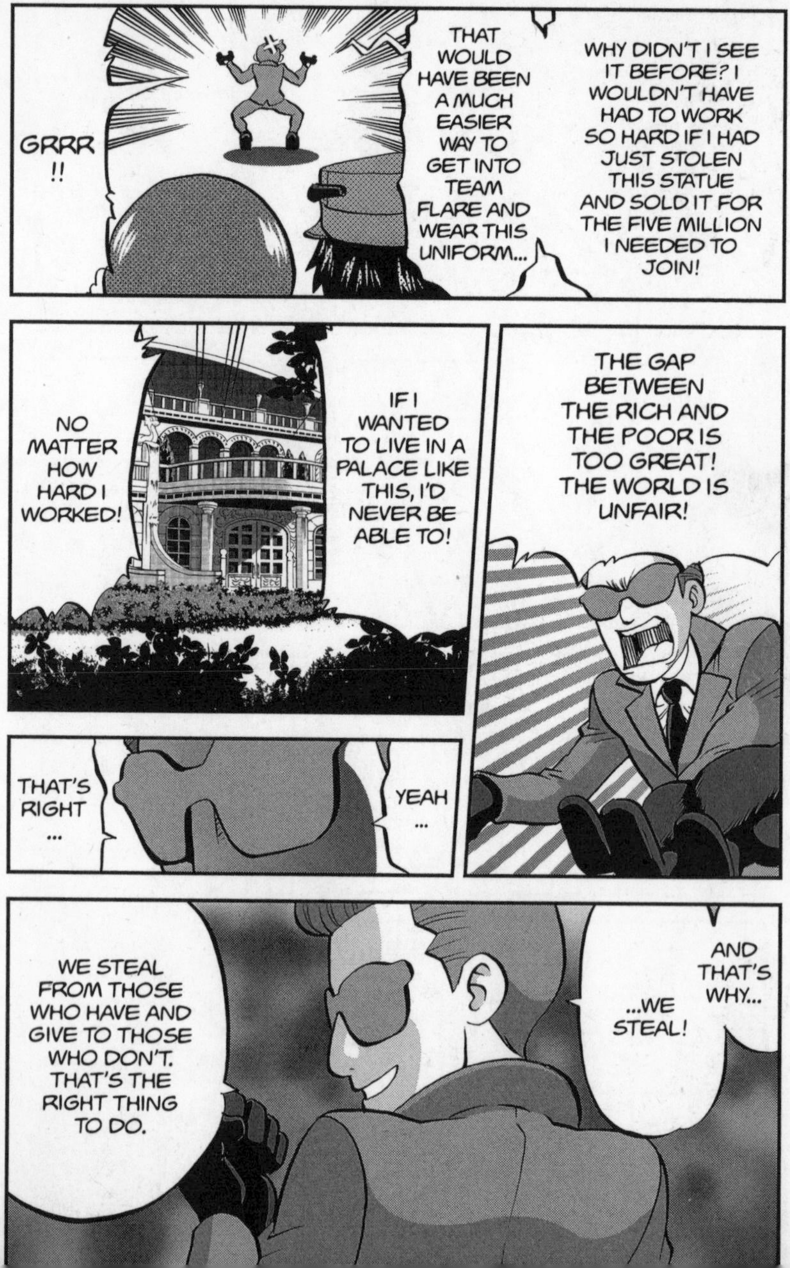
WHY DIDN'T I SEE IT BEFORE? I WOULDN'T HAVE HAD TO WORK SO HARD IF I HAD JUST STOLEN THIS STATUE AND SOLD IT FOR THE FIVE MILLION I NEEDED TO JOIN!
THAT WOULD HAVE BEEN A MUCH EASIER WAY TO GET INTO TEAM FLARE AND WEAR THIS UNIFORM...
GRRR!!
THE GAP BETWEEN THE RICH AND THE POOR IS TOO GREAT! THE WORLD IS UNFAIR!
IF I WANTED TO LIVE IN A PALACE LIKE THIS, I'D NEVER BE ABLE TO!
NO MATTER HOW HARD I WORKED!
YEAH...
THAT'S RIGHT...
AND THAT'S WHY...
...WE STEAL!
WE STEAL FROM THOSE WHO HAVE AND GIVE TO THOSE WHO DON'T. THAT'S THE RIGHT THING TO DO.

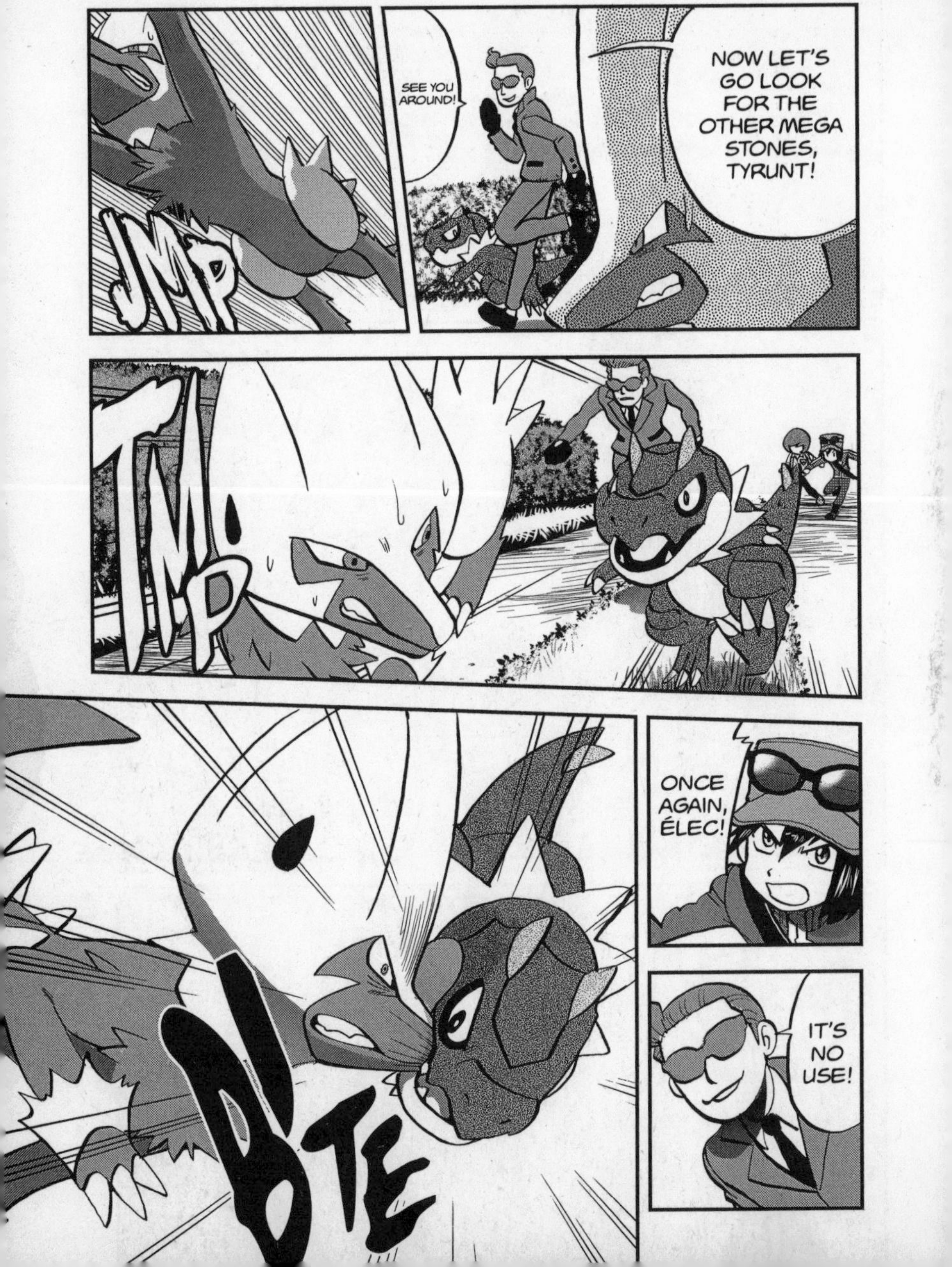
JMP
SEE YOU AROUND!
NOW LET'S GO LOOK FOR THE OTHER MEGA STONES, TYRUNT!
TMP
BITE
ONCE AGAIN, ÉLEC!
IT'S NO USE!

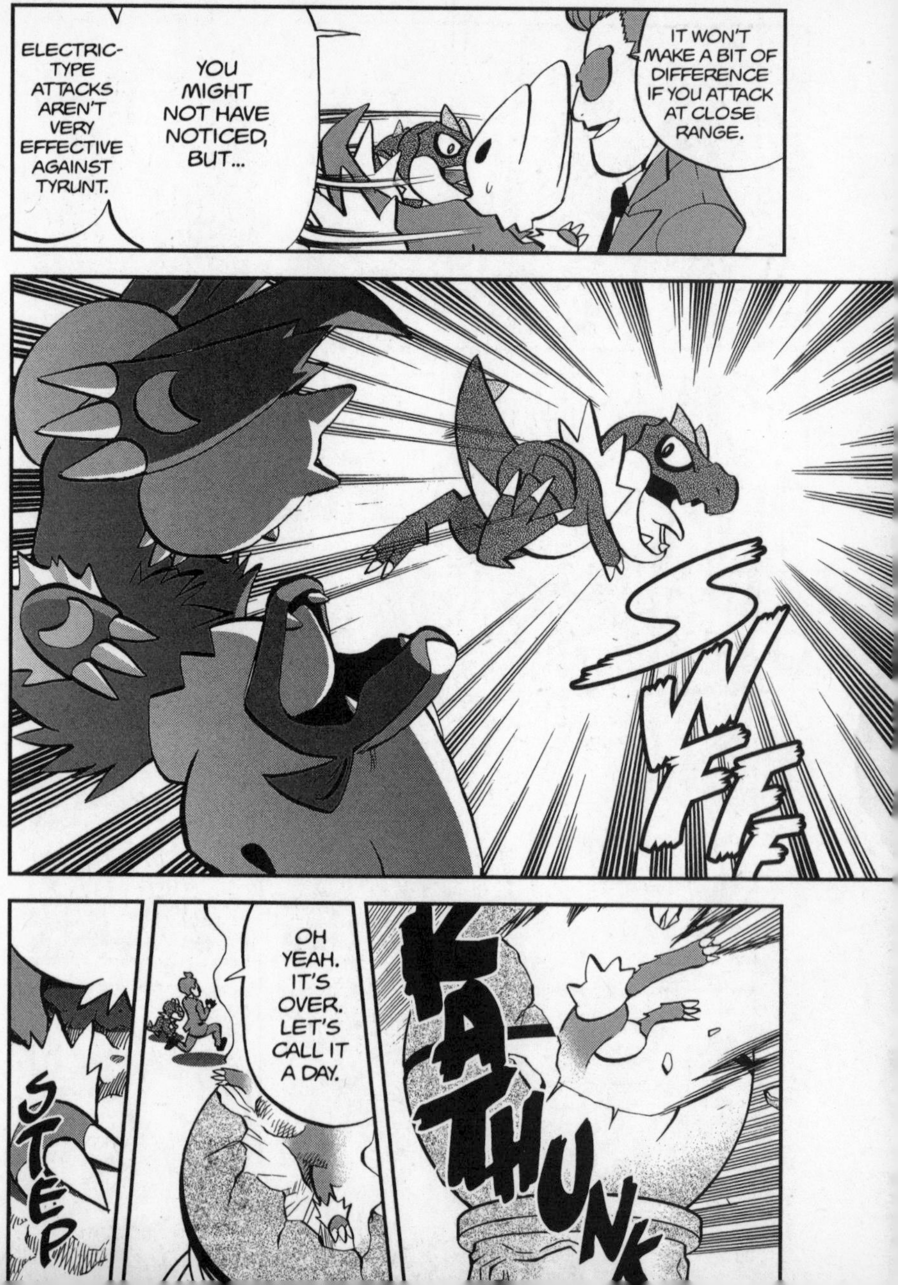
ELECTRIC-TYPE ATTACKS AREN'T VERY EFFECTIVE AGAINST TYRUNT.
YOU MIGHT NOT HAVE NOTICED, BUT...
IT WON'T MAKE A BIT OF DIFFERENCE IF YOU ATTACK AT CLOSE RANGE.
SWFF
STEP
OH YEAH. IT'S OVER. LET'S CALL IT A DAY.
KATHUNK

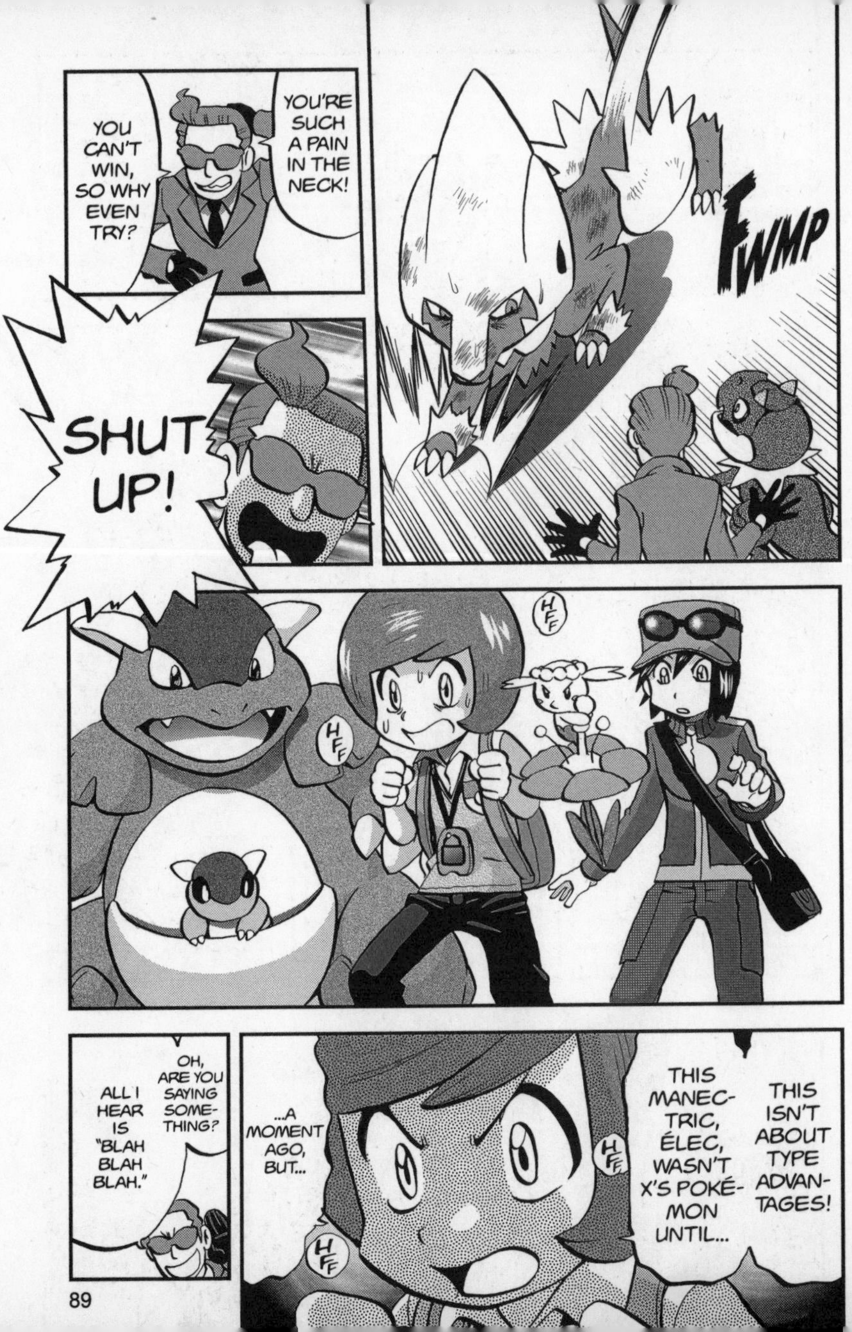
FWMP
YOU'RE SUCH A PAIN IN THE NECK!
YOU CAN'T WIN, SO WHY EVEN TRY?
SHUT UP!
HFF
HFF
THIS ISN'T ABOUT TYPE ADVANTAGES!
THIS MANECTRIC, ÉLEC, WASN'T X'S POKÉMON UNTIL...
...A MOMENT AGO, BUT...
HFF
HFF
OH, ARE YOU SAYING SOMETHING?
ALL I HEAR IS "BLAH BLAH BLAH."

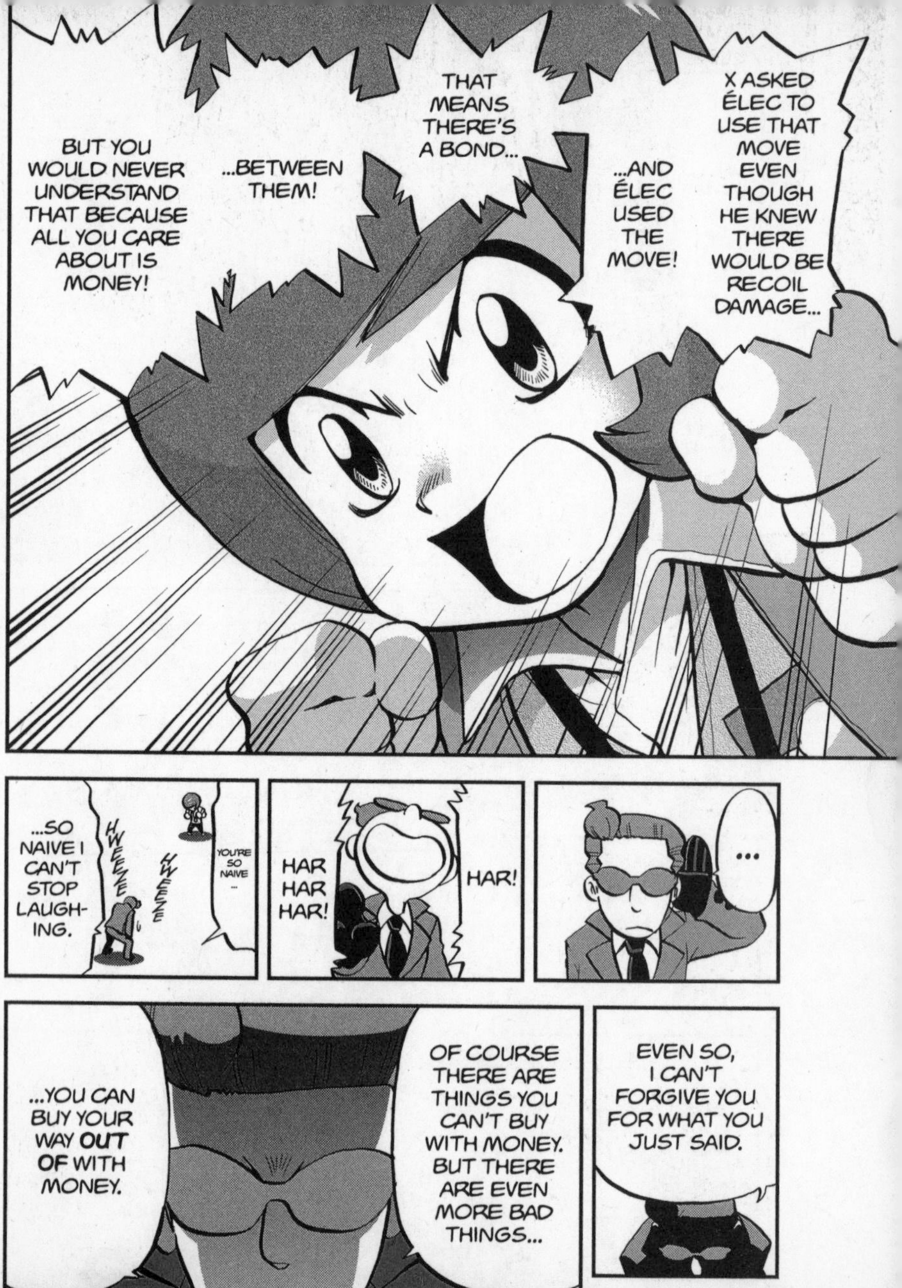
X ASKED ÉLEC TO USE THAT MOVE EVEN THOUGH HE KNEW THERE WOULD BE RECOIL DAMAGE...
...AND ÉLEC USED THE MOVE!
THAT MEANS THERE'S A BOND...
...BETWEEN THEM!
BUT YOU WOULD NEVER UNDERSTAND THAT BECAUSE ALL YOU CARE ABOUT IS MONEY!
...
HAR!
HAR HAR HAR!
YOU'RE SO NAIVE...
HWEEZE
HWEEZE
...SO NAIVE I CAN'T STOP LAUGH-ING.
EVEN SO, I CAN'T FORGIVE YOU FOR WHAT YOU JUST SAID.
OF COURSE THERE ARE THINGS YOU CAN'T BUY WITH MONEY. BUT THERE ARE EVEN MORE BAD THINGS...
...YOU CAN BUY YOUR WAY **OUT OF** WITH MONEY.

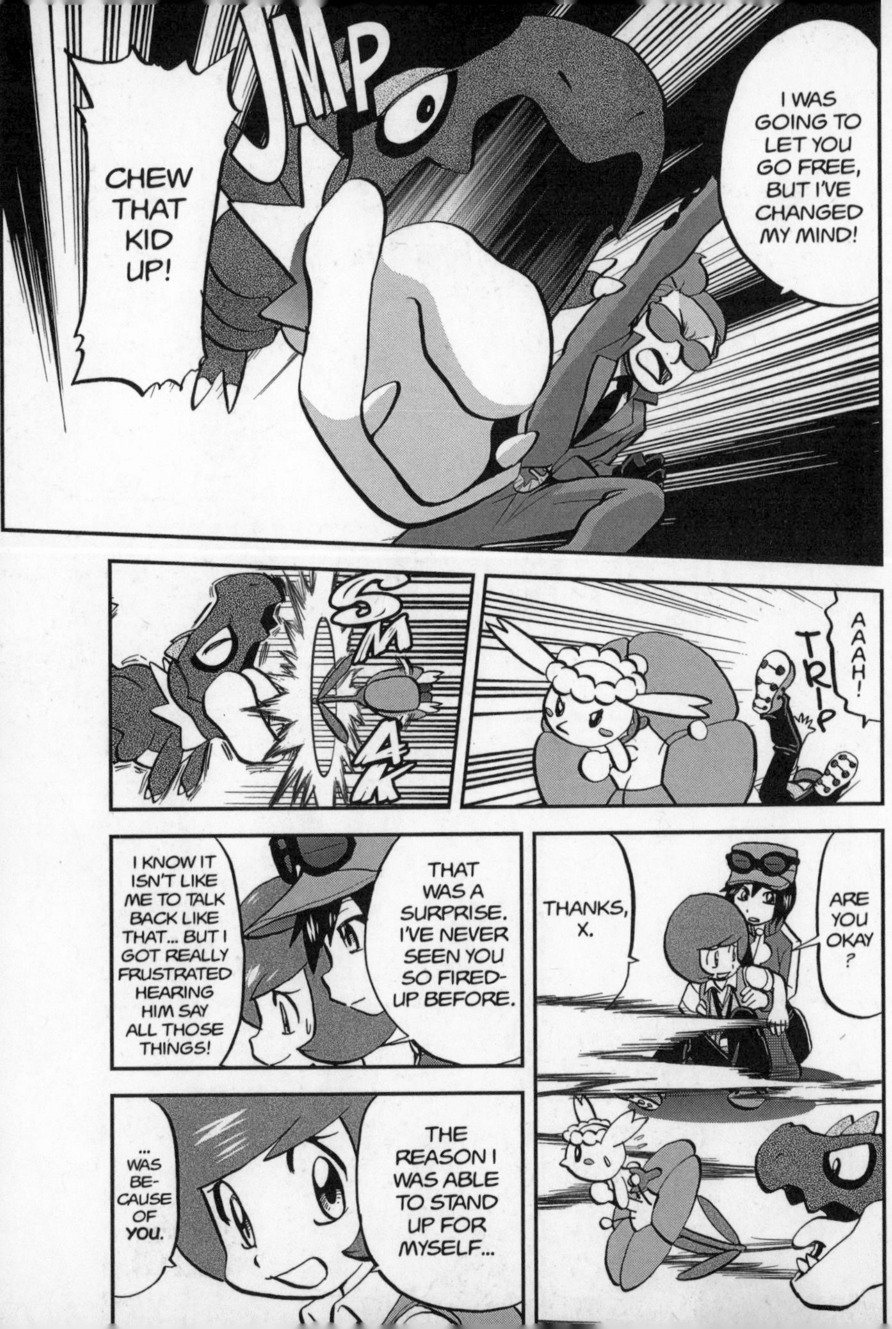
I WAS GOING TO LET YOU GO FREE, BUT I'VE CHANGED MY MIND!
JMP
CHEW THAT KID UP!
AAAAH!
TRIP
SMAK
ARE YOU OKAY?
THANKS, X.
THAT WAS A SURPRISE. I'VE NEVER SEEN YOU SO FIRED-UP BEFORE.
I KNOW IT ISN'T LIKE ME TO TALK BACK LIKE THAT... BUT I GOT REALLY FRUSTRATED HEARING HIM SAY ALL THOSE THINGS!
THE REASON I WAS ABLE TO STAND UP FOR MYSELF...
...WAS BE-CAUSE OF YOU.

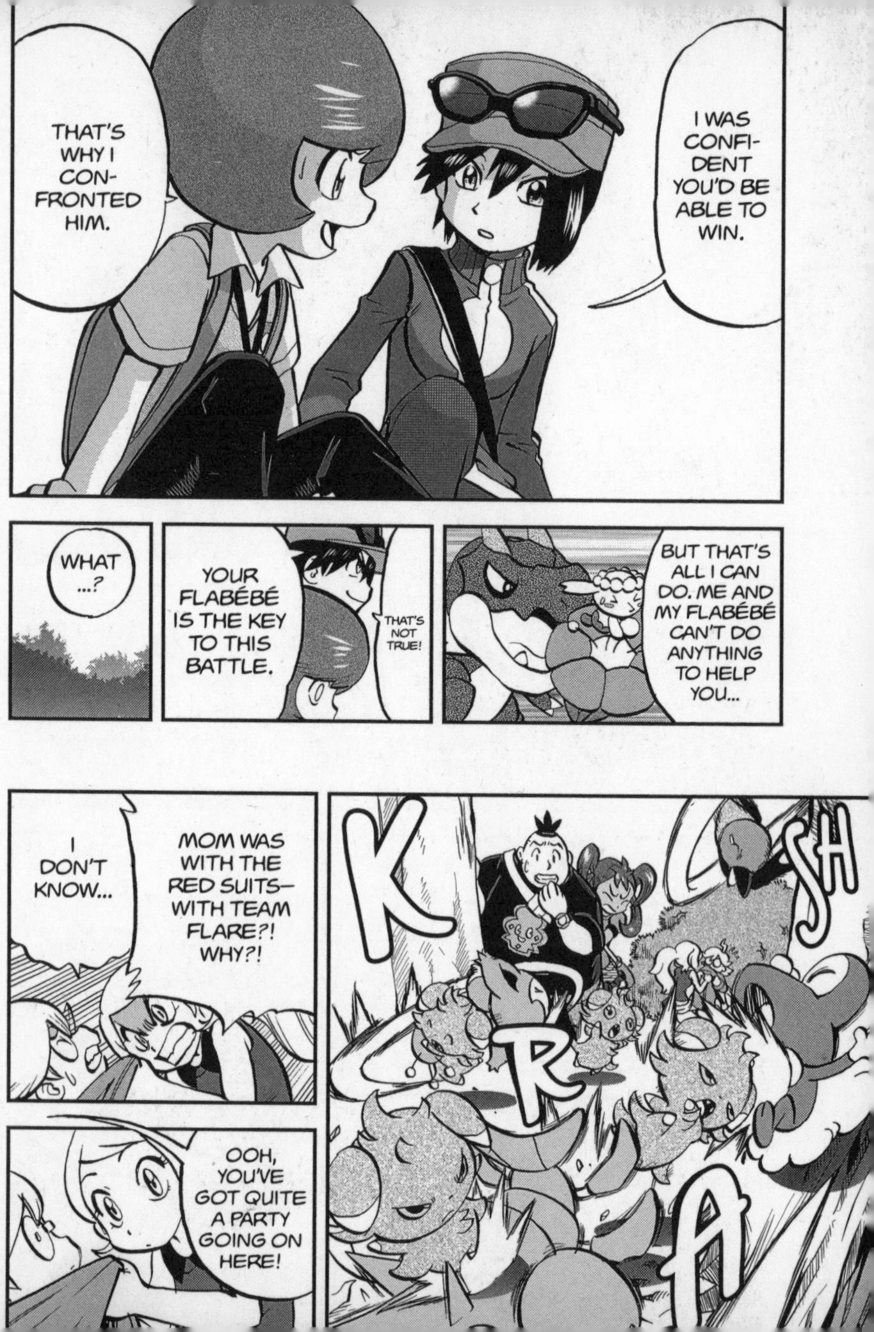
I WAS CONFIDENT YOU'D BE ABLE TO WIN.
THAT'S WHY I CONFRONTED HIM.
BUT THAT'S ALL I CAN DO. ME AND MY FLABÉBÉ CAN'T DO ANYTHING TO HELP YOU...
THAT'S NOT TRUE!
YOUR FLABÉBÉ IS THE KEY TO THIS BATTLE.
WHAT ...?
KRASH
MOM WAS WITH THE RED SUITS—WITH TEAM FLARE?! WHY?!
I DON'T KNOW...
OOH, YOU'VE GOT QUITE A PARTY GOING ON HERE!

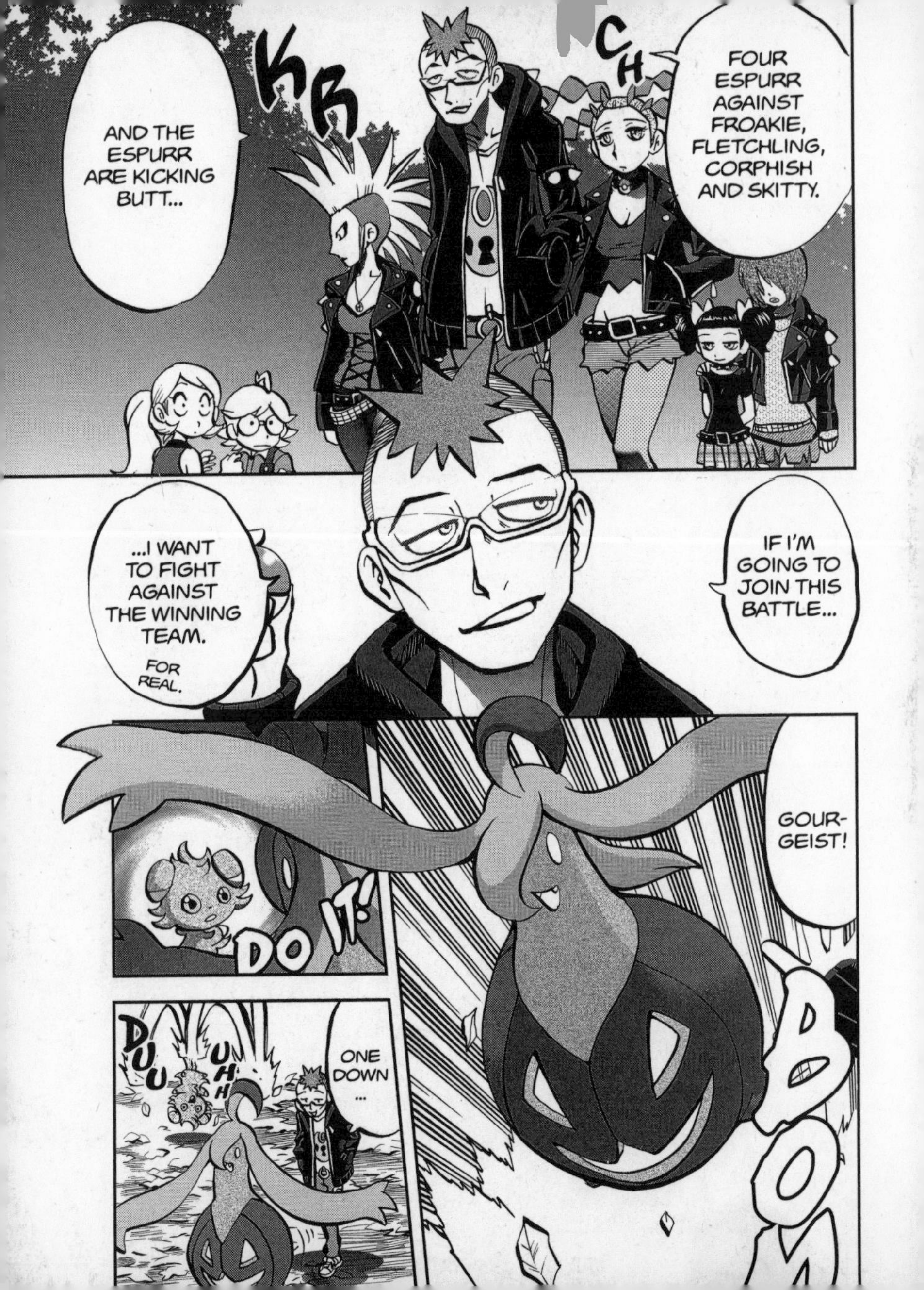
FOUR ESPURR AGAINST FROAKIE, FLETCHLING, CORPHISH AND SKITTY.
CH
KR
AND THE ESPURR ARE KICKING BUTT...
IF I'M GOING TO JOIN THIS BATTLE...
...I WANT TO FIGHT AGAINST THE WINNING TEAM.
FOR REAL.
GOUR-GEIST!
DO IT!
BOOM
ONE DOWN ...
UHH
DUU

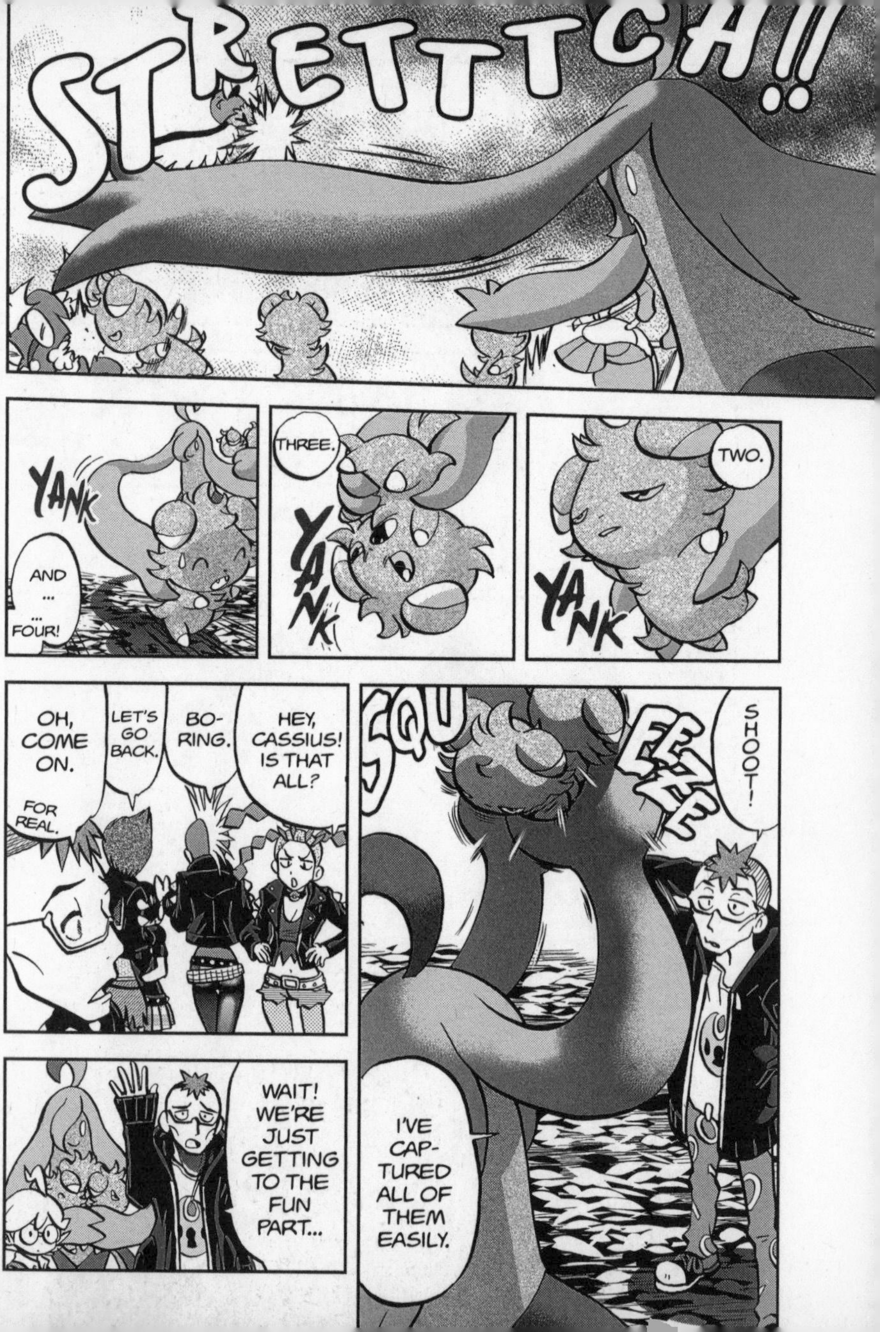
STRETTTCH!!
TWO.
YANK
THREE.
YANK
YANK
AND ... ... FOUR!
SQUEEZE
SHOOT!
I'VE CAPTURED ALL OF THEM EASILY.
HEY, CASSIUS! IS THAT ALL?
BO-RING.
LET'S GO BACK.
OH, COME ON.
FOR REAL.
WAIT! WE'RE JUST GETTING TO THE FUN PART...

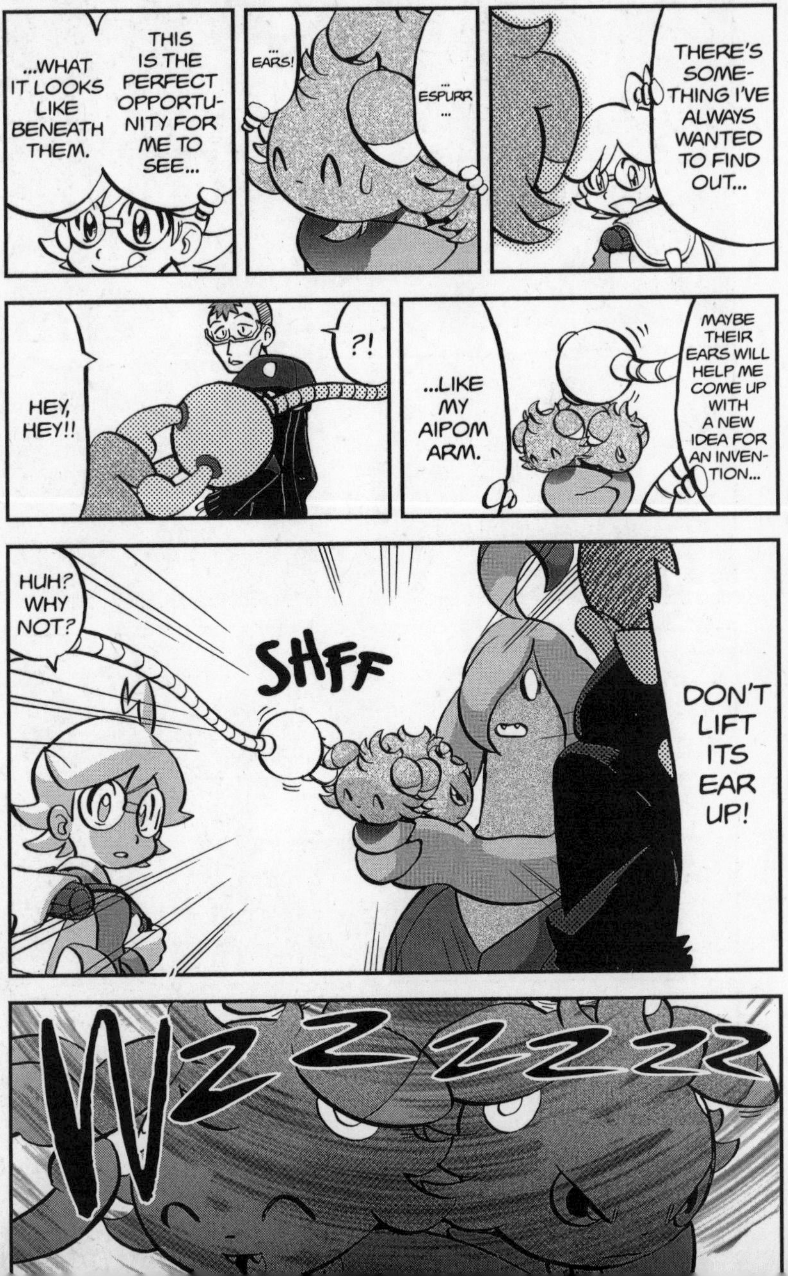
THERE'S SOME-THING I'VE ALWAYS WANTED TO FIND OUT...
... ESPURR ...
... EARS!
THIS IS THE PERFECT OPPORTU-NITY FOR ME TO SEE...
...WHAT IT LOOKS LIKE BENEATH THEM.
MAYBE THEIR EARS WILL HELP ME COME UP WITH A NEW IDEA FOR AN INVEN-TION...
...LIKE MY AIPOM ARM.
?!
HEY, HEY!!
DON'T LIFT ITS EAR UP!
SHFF
HUH? WHY NOT?
WZZZZZZ

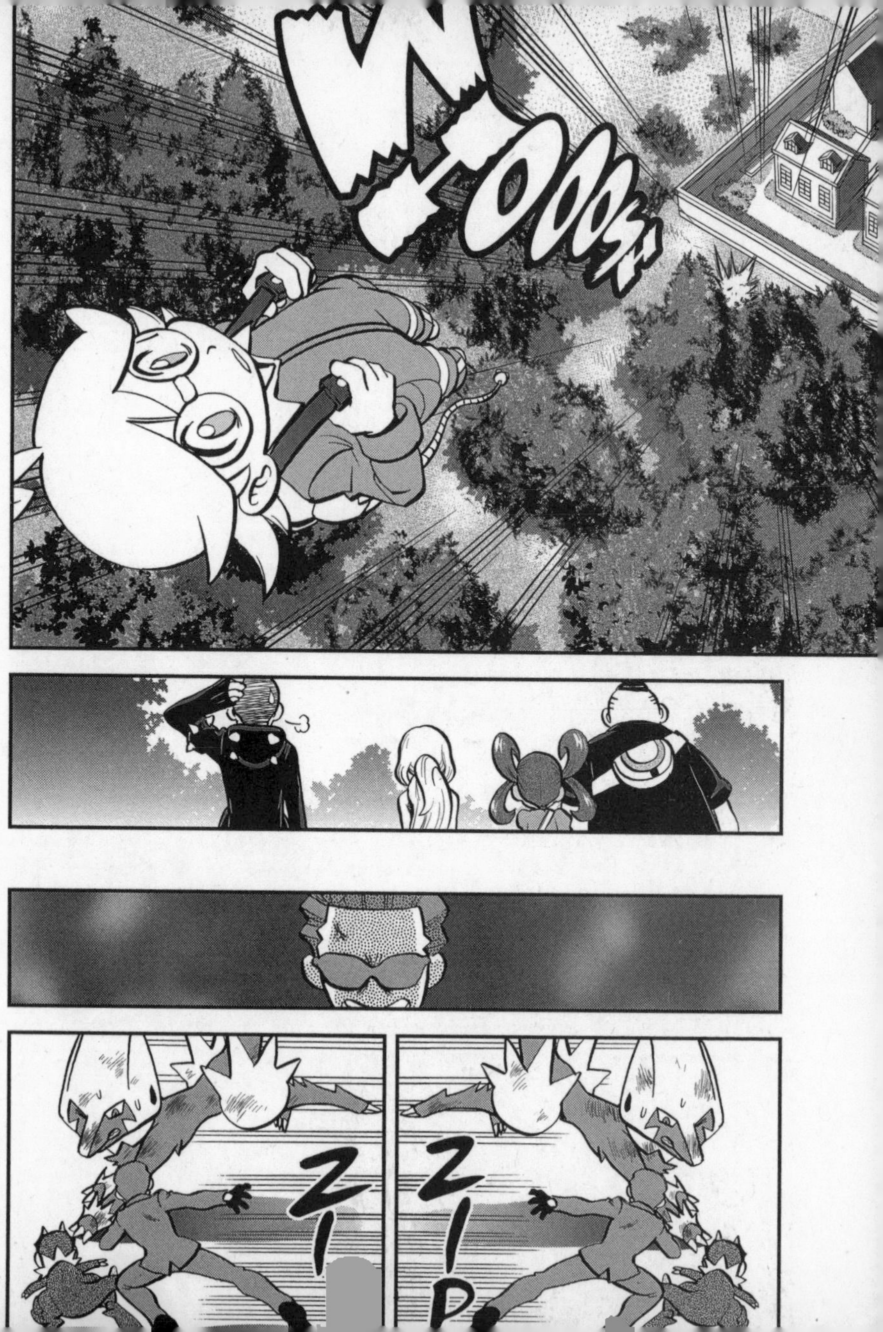
WHOOOSH
ZIP
ZI

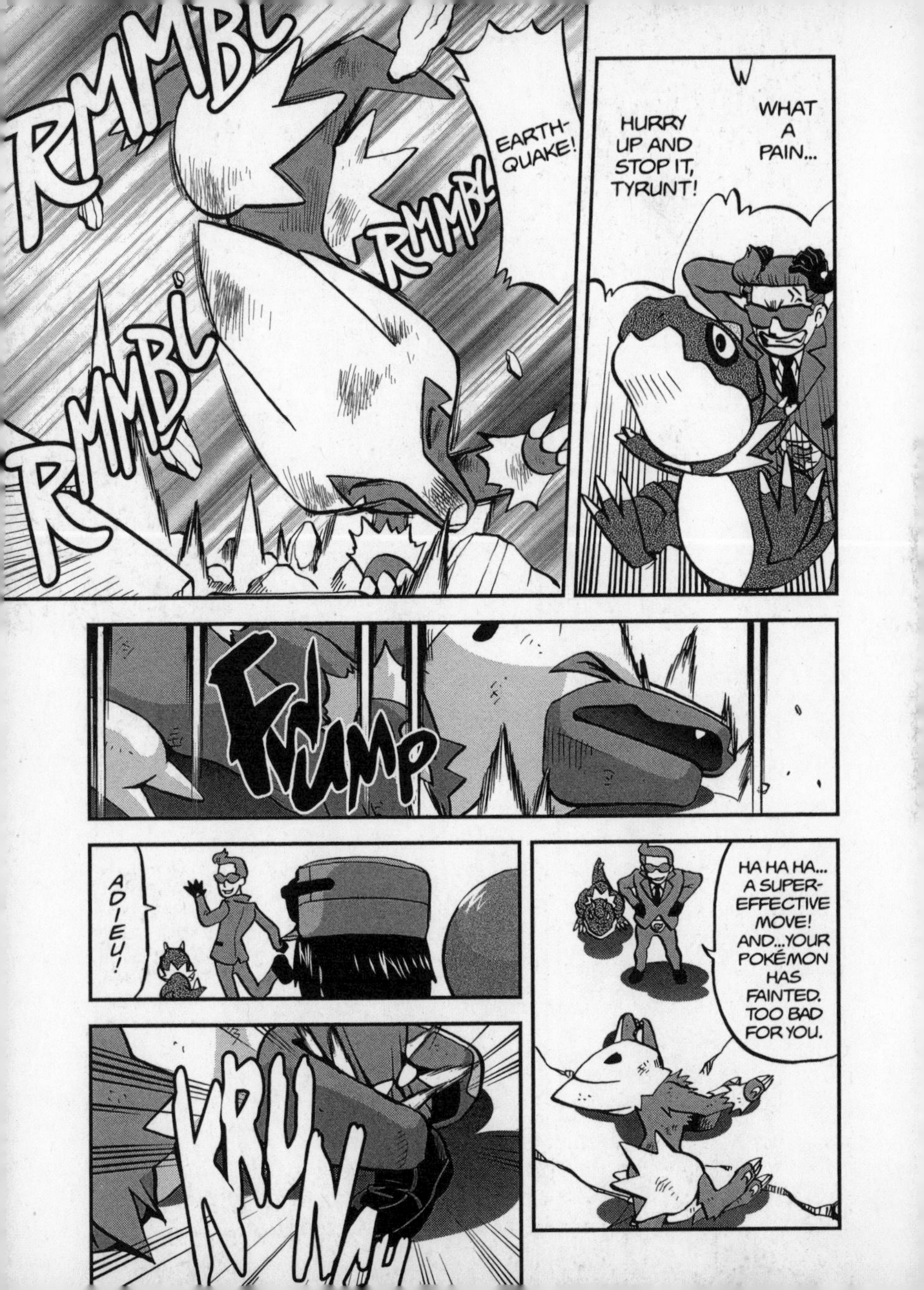
WHAT A PAIN...
HURRY UP AND STOP IT, TYRUNT!
EARTHQUAKE!
RMMBL
RMMBL
RMMBL
RMMBL
FVUMP
HA HA HA... A SUPER-EFFECTIVE MOVE! AND...YOUR POKÉMON HAS FAINTED. TOO BAD FOR YOU.
ADIEU!
KRUN

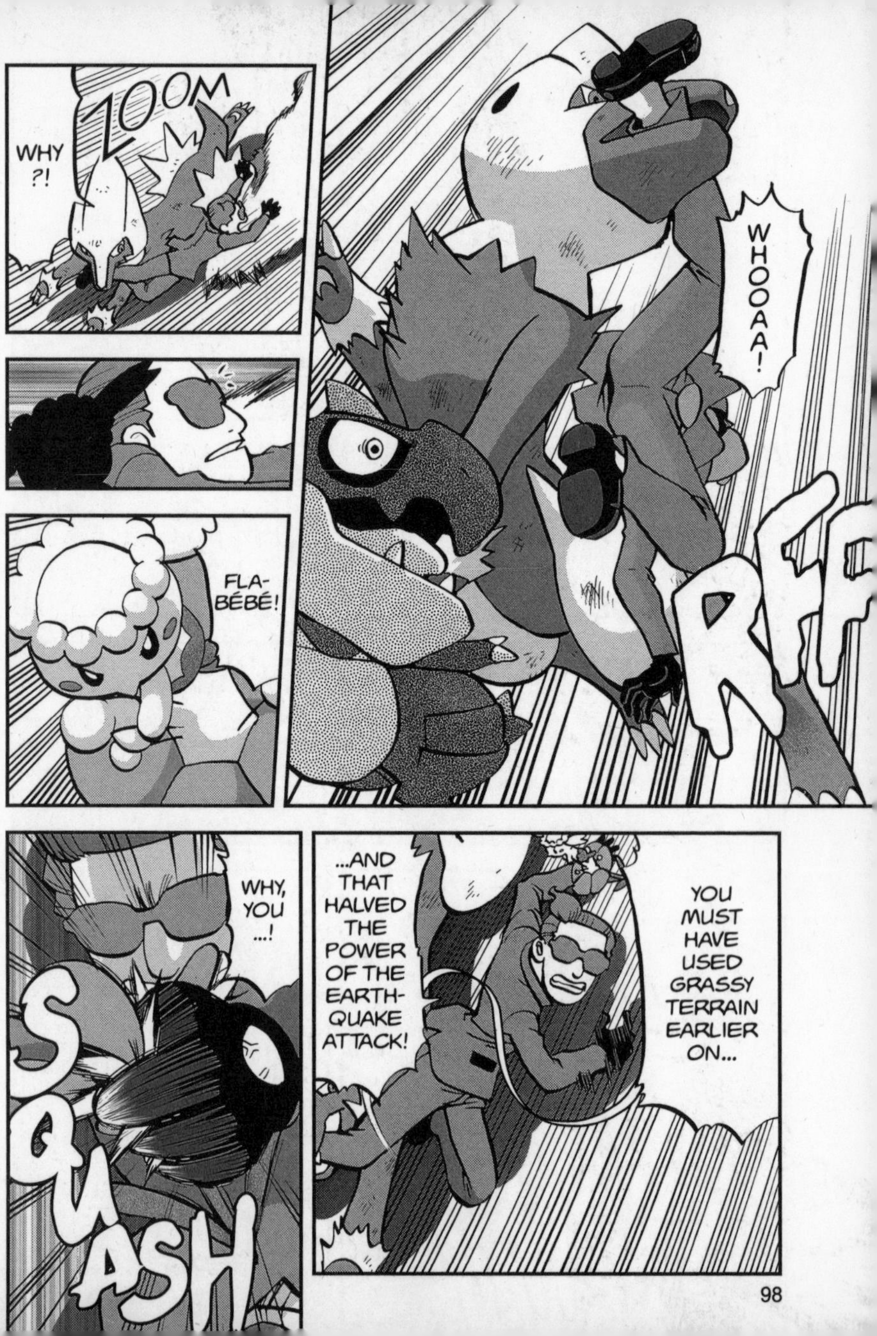
WHOOAA!
RFF
ZOOM
WHY?!
FLA-BÉBÉ!
YOU MUST HAVE USED GRASSY TERRAIN EARLIER ON...
...AND THAT HALVED THE POWER OF THE EARTH-QUAKE ATTACK!
WHY, YOU ...!
SQUASH

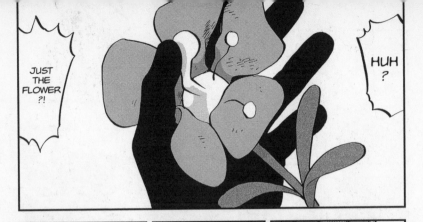

JUST THE FLOWER ?!

HUH ?

BOIN!

RSTL

RSTL

WHERE IS IT?!

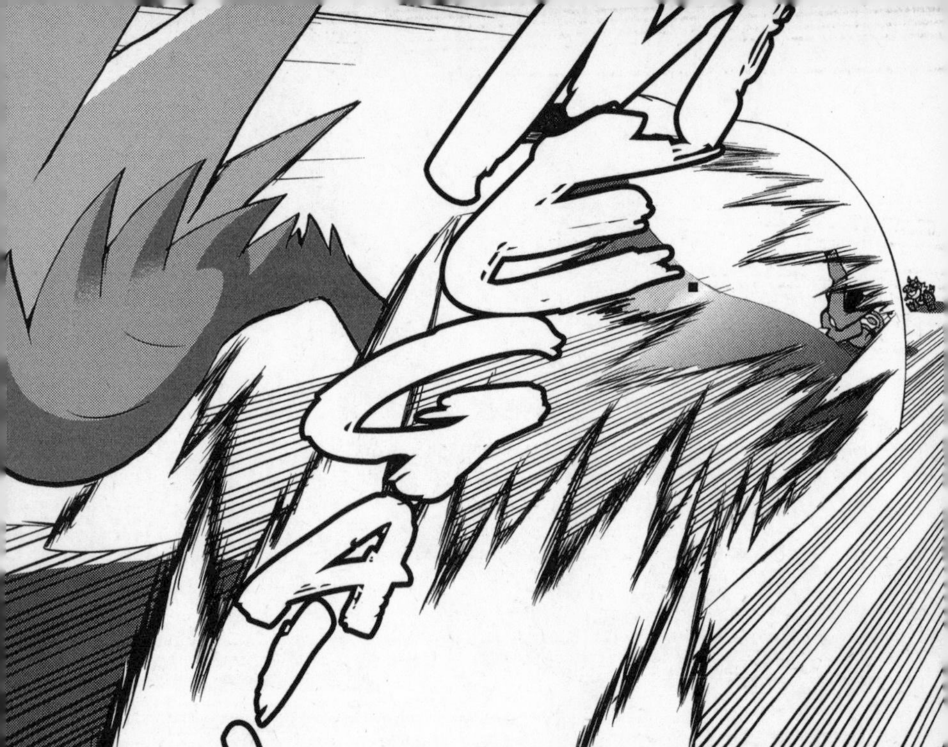

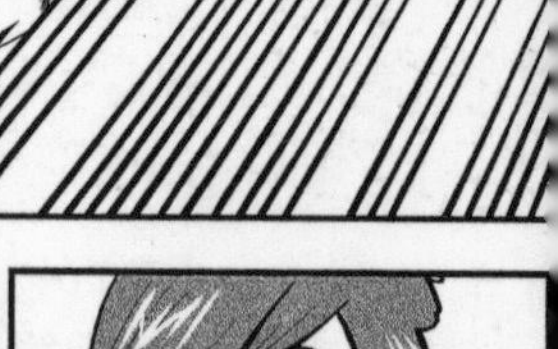
HE DID IT!

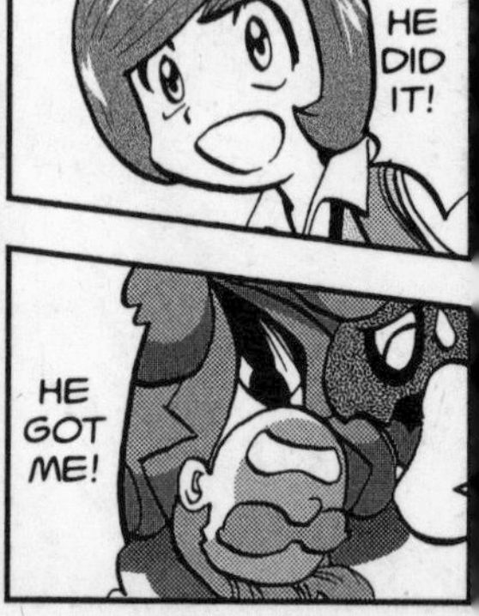
HE GOT ME!

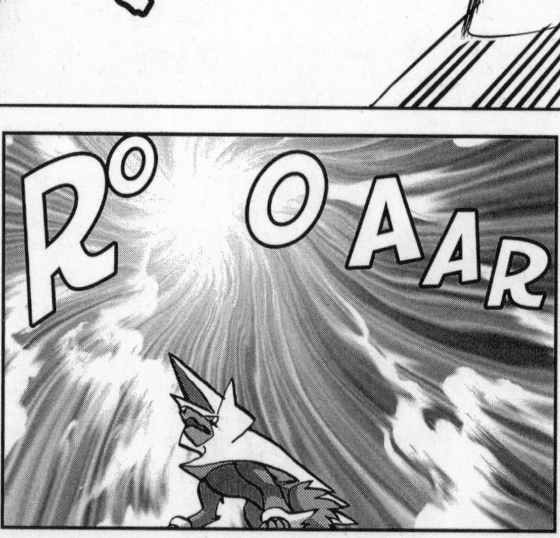
ROOAAR

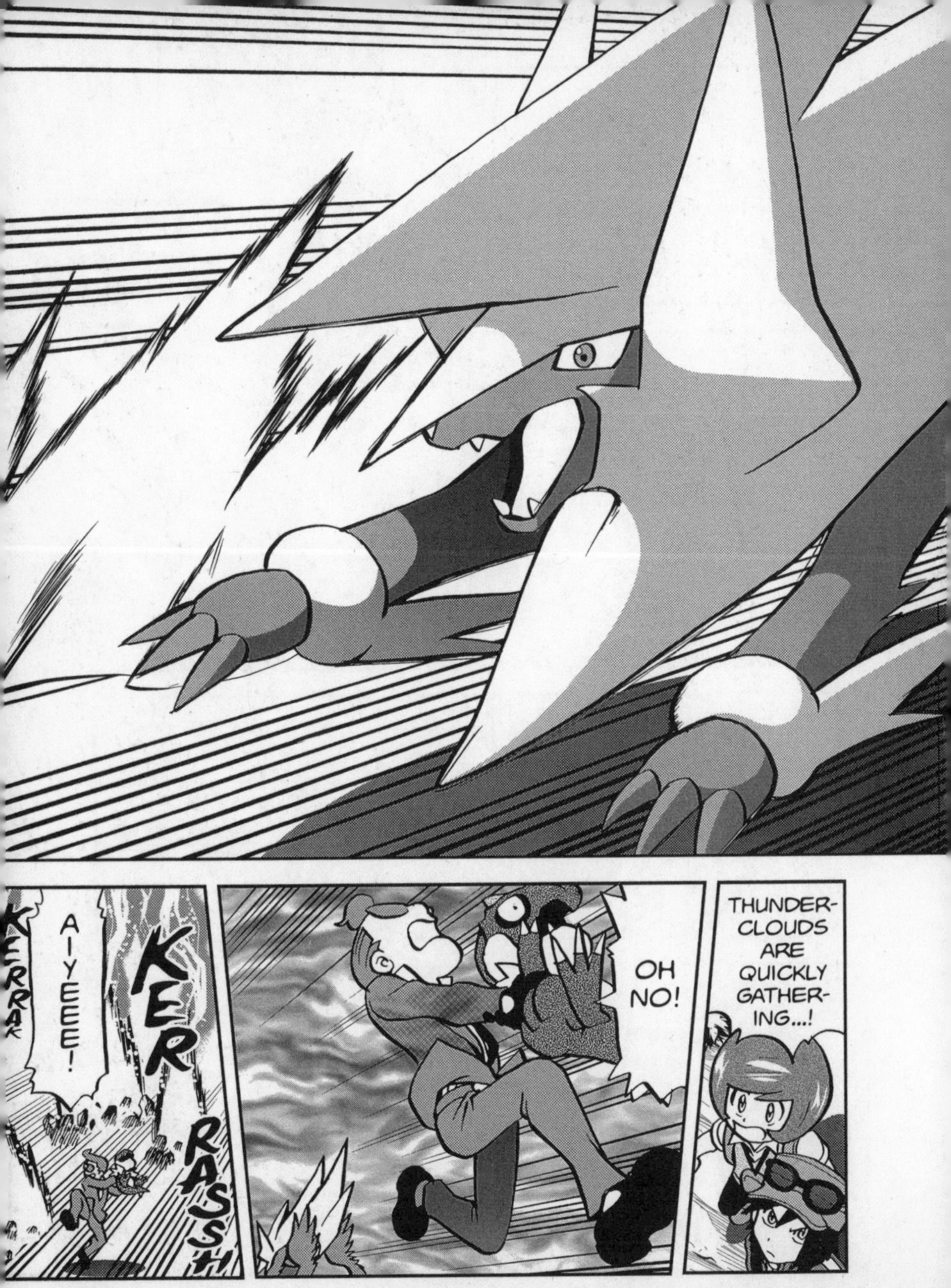
THUNDER-CLOUDS ARE QUICKLY GATHER-ING...!
OH NO!
KERRASSH!
AIYEEE!
KERRAK

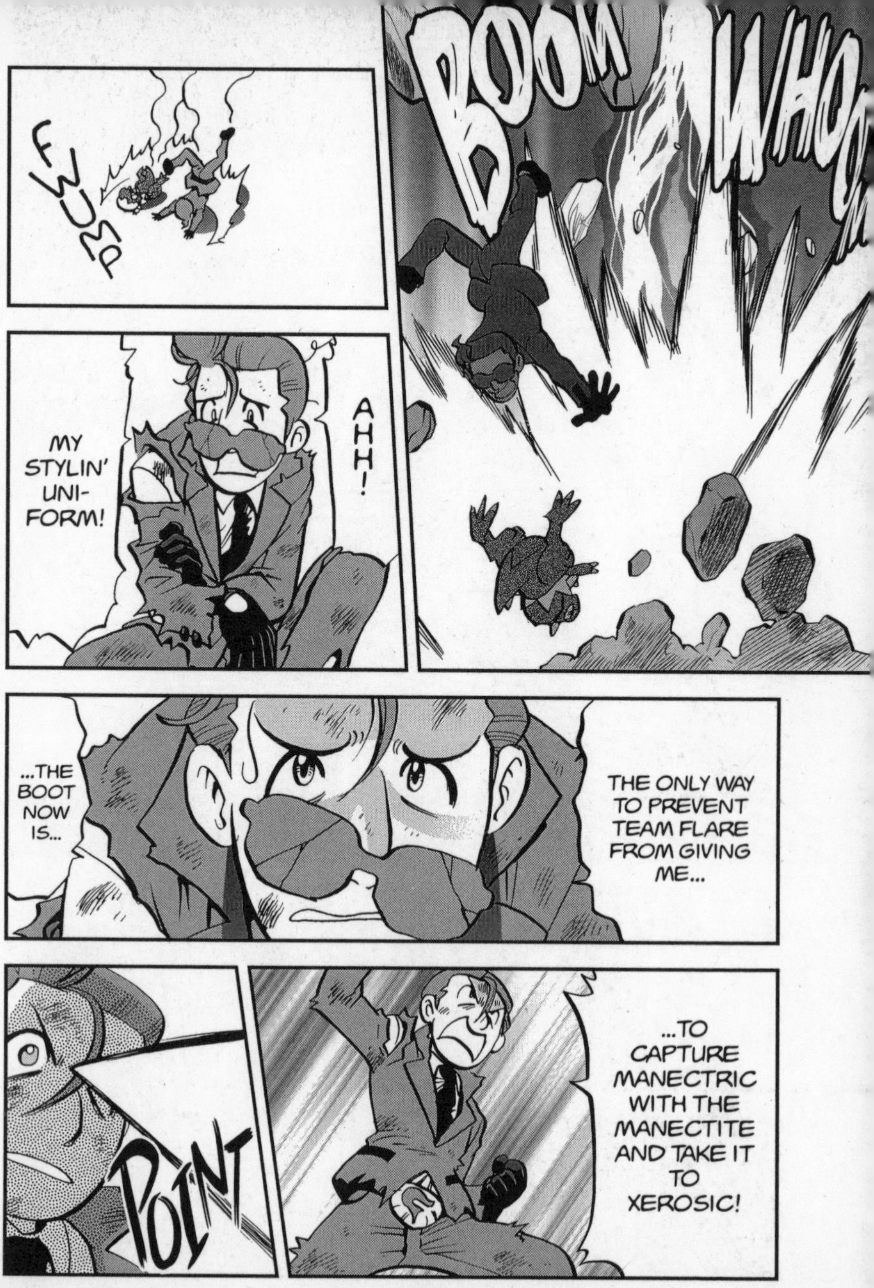
BOOM
WHOO
FWUMP
AHH!
MY STYLIN' UNI-FORM!
THE ONLY WAY TO PREVENT TEAM FLARE FROM GIVING ME...
...THE BOOT NOW IS...
...TO CAPTURE MANECTRIC WITH THE MANECTITE AND TAKE IT TO XEROSIC!
POINT

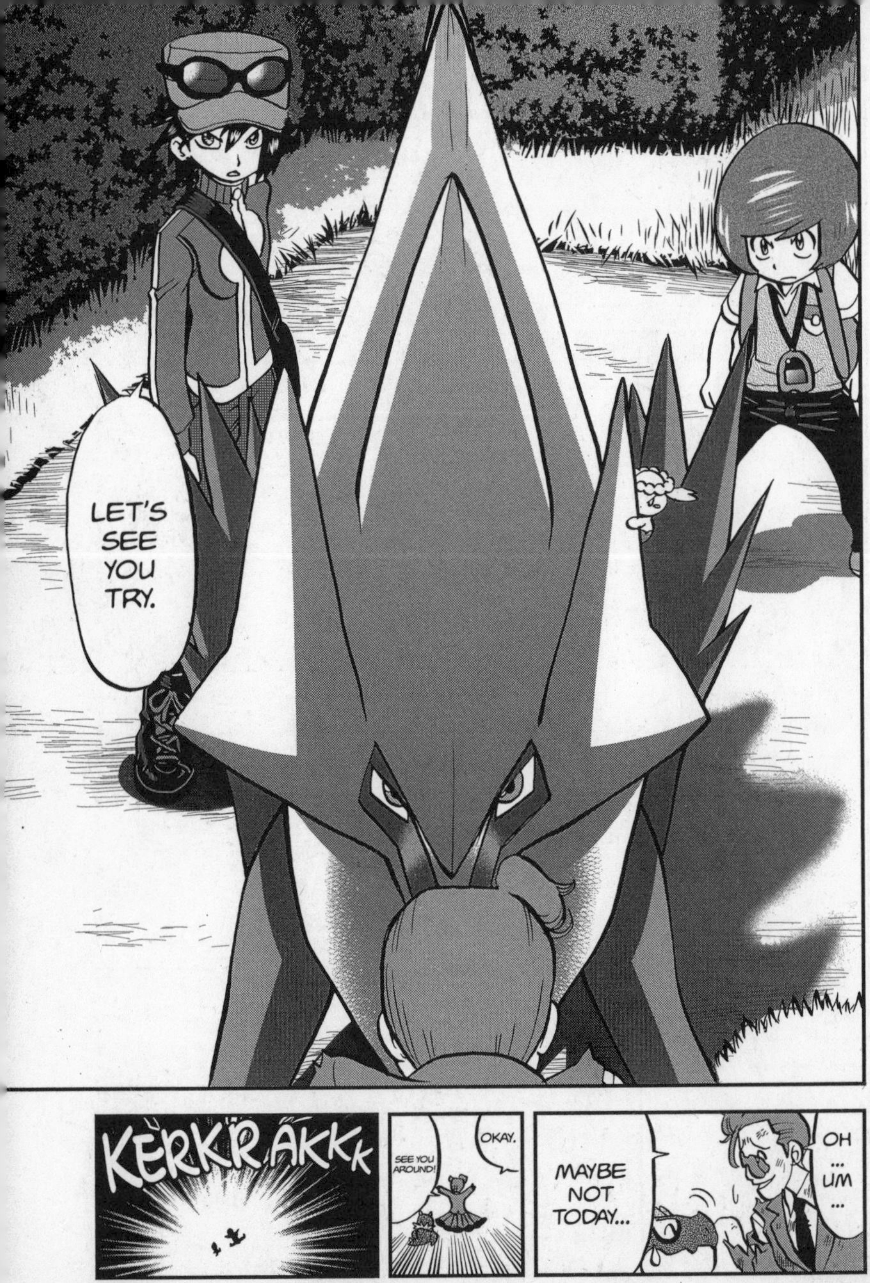
LET'S SEE YOU TRY.
OH ... UM ...
MAYBE NOT TODAY...
OKAY.
SEE YOU AROUND!
KERKRAKKK

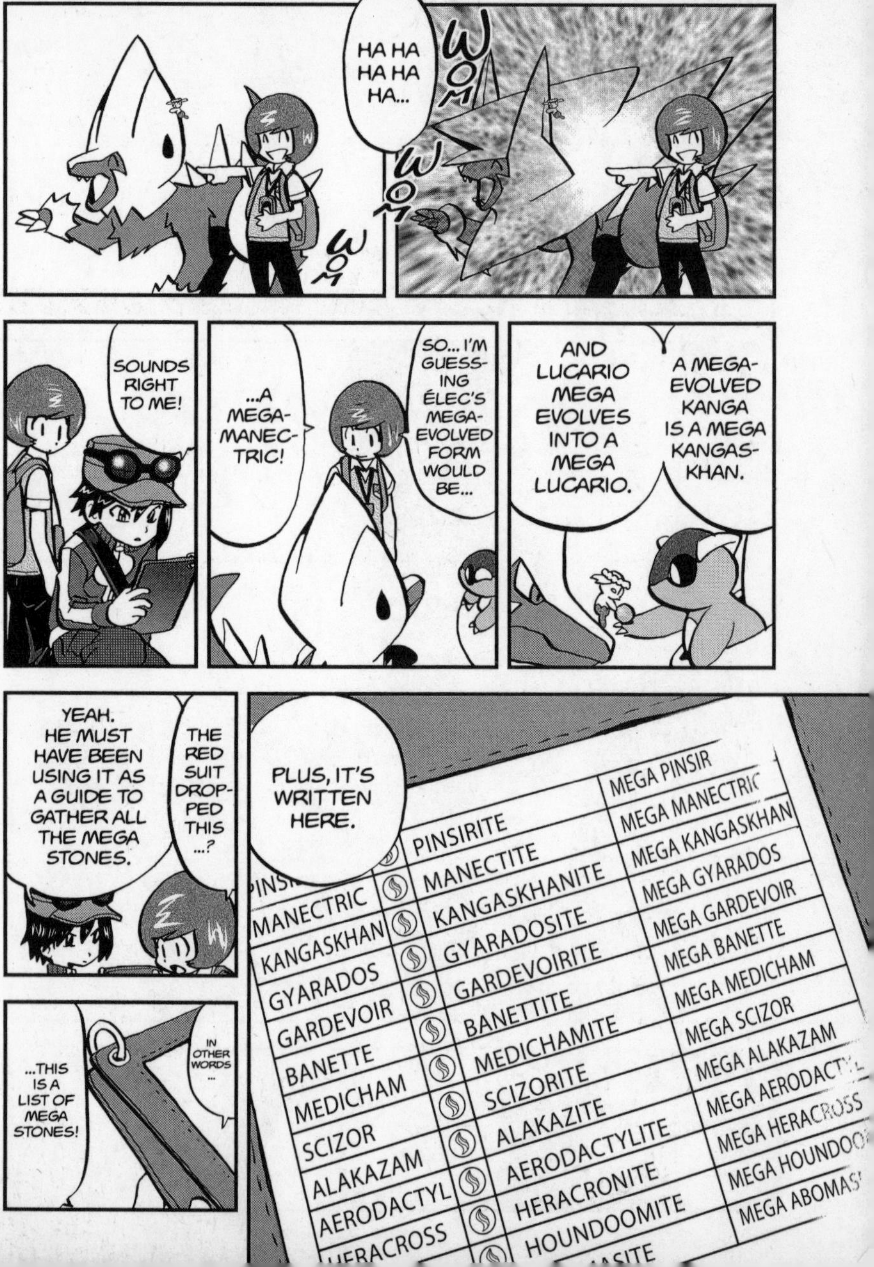
WOM
WOM
WOM
HA HA HA HA HA...
A MEGA-EVOLVED KANGA IS A MEGA KANGASKHAN.
AND LUCARIO MEGA EVOLVES INTO A MEGA LUCARIO.
SO... I'M GUESSING ÉLEC'S MEGA-EVOLVED FORM WOULD BE...
...A MEGA-MANECTRIC!
SOUNDS RIGHT TO ME!
PLUS, IT'S WRITTEN HERE.
MEGA PINSIR
PINSIRITE
MANECTRIC MANECTITE MEGA MANECTRIC
KANGASKHAN KANGASKHANITE MEGA KANGASKHAN
GYARADOS GYARADOSITE MEGA GYARADOS
GARDEVOIR GARDEVOIRITE MEGA GARDEVOIR
BANETTE BANETTITE MEGA BANETTE
MEDICHAM MEDICHAMITE MEGA MEDICHAM
SCIZOR SCIZORITE MEGA SCIZOR
ALAKAZAM ALAKAZITE MEGA ALAKAZAM
AERODACTYL AERODACTYLITE
HERACROSS HERACRONITE MEGA HERACROSS
HOUNDOOMITE
THE RED SUIT DROPPED THIS...?
YEAH. HE MUST HAVE BEEN USING IT AS A GUIDE TO GATHER ALL THE MEGA STONES.
IN OTHER WORDS...
...THIS IS A LIST OF MEGA STONES!

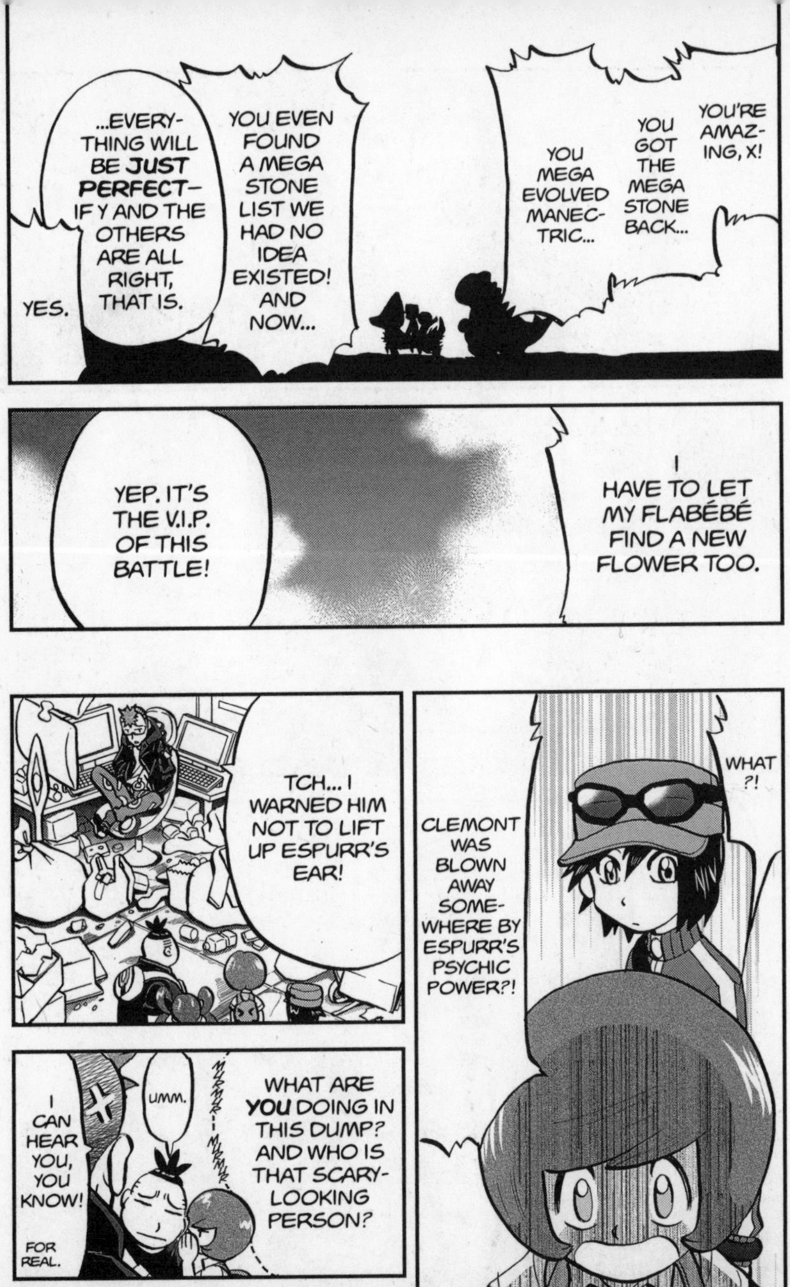
YOU'RE AMAZ-ING, X!
YOU GOT THE MEGA STONE BACK...
YOU MEGA EVOLVED MANEC-TRIC...
YOU EVEN FOUND A MEGA STONE LIST WE HAD NO IDEA EXISTED! AND NOW...
...EVERY-THING WILL BE **JUST PERFECT**—IF Y AND THE OTHERS ARE ALL RIGHT, THAT IS.
YES.
I HAVE TO LET MY FLABÉBÉ FIND A NEW FLOWER TOO.
YEP. IT'S THE V.I.P. OF THIS BATTLE!
WHAT?!
CLEMONT WAS BLOWN AWAY SOME-WHERE BY ESPURR'S PSYCHIC POWER?!
TCH... I WARNED HIM NOT TO LIFT UP ESPURR'S EAR!
WHAT ARE **YOU** DOING IN THIS DUMP? AND WHO IS THAT SCARY-LOOKING PERSON?
MURMUR MURMUR
UMM.
I CAN HEAR YOU, YOU KNOW!
FOR REAL.

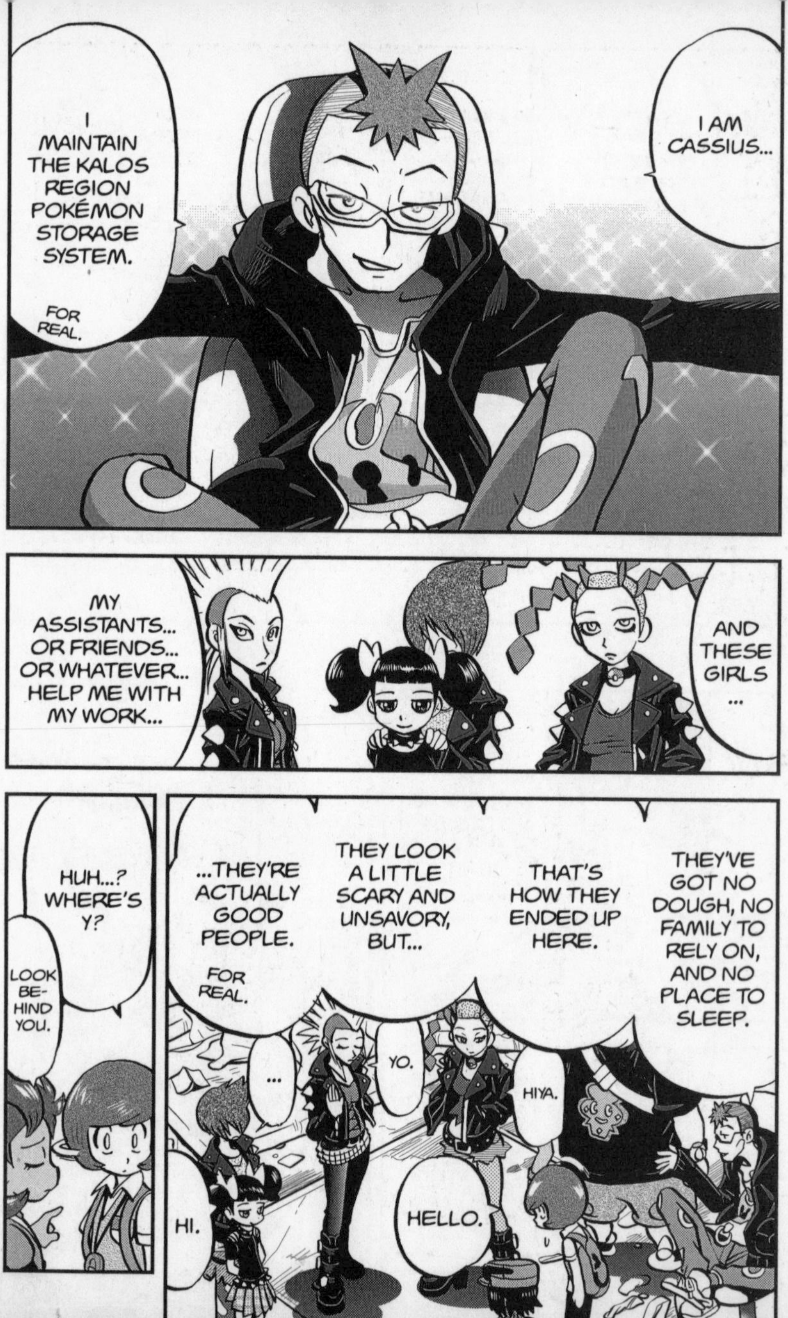
I AM CASSIUS...
I MAINTAIN THE KALOS REGION POKÉMON STORAGE SYSTEM.
FOR REAL.
AND THESE GIRLS ...
MY ASSISTANTS... OR FRIENDS... OR WHATEVER... HELP ME WITH MY WORK...
THEY'VE GOT NO DOUGH, NO FAMILY TO RELY ON, AND NO PLACE TO SLEEP.
THAT'S HOW THEY ENDED UP HERE.
THEY LOOK A LITTLE SCARY AND UNSAVORY, BUT...
...THEY'RE ACTUALLY GOOD PEOPLE.
FOR REAL.
HIYA.
YO.
...
HELLO.
HI.
HUH...? WHERE'S Y?
LOOK BE-HIND YOU.

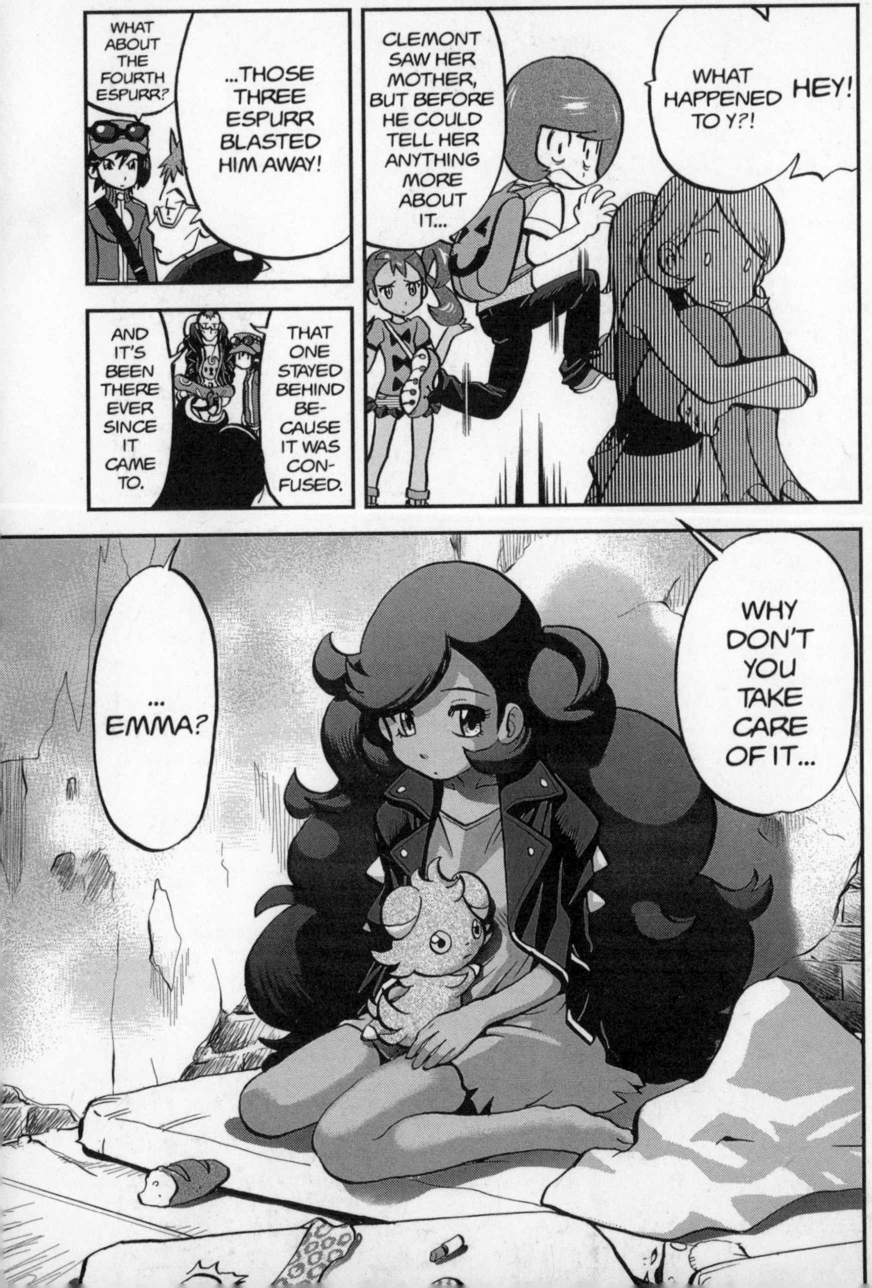
HEY!
WHAT HAPPENED TO Y?!
CLEMONT SAW HER MOTHER, BUT BEFORE HE COULD TELL HER ANYTHING MORE ABOUT IT...
...THOSE THREE ESPURR BLASTED HIM AWAY!
WHAT ABOUT THE FOURTH ESPURR?
THAT ONE STAYED BEHIND BE-CAUSE IT WAS CON-FUSED.
AND IT'S BEEN THERE EVER SINCE IT CAME TO.
WHY DON'T YOU TAKE CARE OF IT...
... EMMA?

Current Location

Parfum Palace

A luxurious palace constructed 300 years ago by a king who wished to display his power to all.

Camphrier Town

This ancient town was once famous for the long-neglected manor home of a noble family.

No.

Date

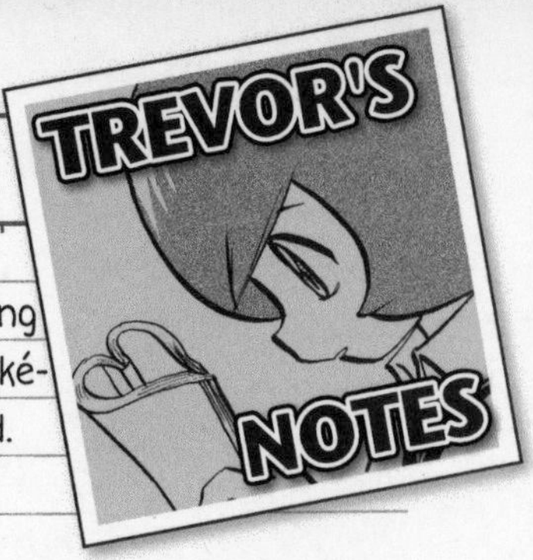
TREVOR'S
NOTES

◆ CURRENT DATA ◆

- I performed an experiment by handing Kanga's Mega Stone to a different Poké-mon (Chespin), but nothing happened.

- Was it because Chespin can't Mega Evolve? Was it because Chespin isn't X's Pokémon? I came up with a lot of theories, but I couldn't find the answer.

- I witnessed another Mega Evolution at the café, involving the actress Diantha's Gardevoir. I suspect a Mega-Evolved Gardevoir is called a Mega Gardevoir. I noticed that Diantha's Key Stone was embedded in the necklace she wore. As I suspected, the form of the Key Stone holder differs from person to person. I also noticed that Gardevoir had the Mega Stone with it. (Come to think of it, its color was different from Kanga's Mega Stone.)

- Then we met a man who said he'd been ordered to collect a Mega Stone on the outskirts of Camphrier Town. That's how we discovered two new pieces of information.

- First, there is more than one kind of Mega Stone. There are as many Mega Stones as there are Pokémon who can Mega Evolve. Mega Stone is a generic term for the stones, and each stone has a unique name.

Kangaskhan's Mega Stone = Kangaskhanite
Manectric's Mega Stone = Manectite

Second, the enemy has a list of Pokémon who can Mega Evolve...!

Pokémon X • Y
Volume 4
Perfect Square Edition

Story by HIDENORI KUSAKA
Art by SATOSHI YAMAMOTO

©2015 Pokémon.
©1995-2015 Nintendo/Creatures Inc./GAME FREAK inc.
TM, ®, and character names are trademarks of Nintendo.
POCKET MONSTERS SPECIAL X•Y Vol. 2
by Hidenori KUSAKA, Satoshi YAMAMOTO
© 2014 Hidenori KUSAKA, Satoshi YAMAMOTO
All rights reserved.
Original Japanese edition published by SHOGAKUKAN.
English translation rights in the United States of America, Canada, the United
Kingdom, Ireland, Australia and New Zealand arranged with SHOGAKUKAN.

English Adaptation—Bryant Turnage
Translation—Tetsuichiro Miyaki
Touch-up & Lettering—Annaliese Christman
Design—Shawn Carrico
Editor—Annette Roman

Printed in the U.S.A.

Published by
VIZ Media, LLC
P.O. Box 77010
San Francisco, CA 94107

10 9 8 7 6 5 4 3 2 1
First printing, September 2015

PARENTAL ADVISORY
POKÉMON ADVENTURES
is rated A and is suitable
for readers of all ages.
ratings.viz.com

www.perfectsquare.com   www.viz.com

Pokémon
BLACK & WHITE
STORY & ART BY SANTA HARUKAZE

YOUR FAVORITE POKÉMON FROM THE UNOVA REGION LIKE YOU'VE NEVER SEEN THEM BEFORE!

Available now!

A pocket-sized book brick jam-packed with four-panel comic strips featuring all the Pokémon Black and White characters, Pokémon vital statistics, trivia, puzzles, and fun quizzes!

www.viz.com

RATED A ALL AGES
ratings.viz.com

<<< READ THIS WAY!

THIS IS THE END OF THIS GRAPHIC NOVEL!

To properly enjoy this VIZ
Media graphic novel, please
turn it around and begin
reading from right to left.

This book has been printed
in the original Japanese
format in order to preserve
the orientation of the original
artwork. Have fun with it!

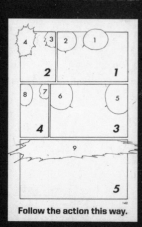

Follow the action this way.